CA___ SPARKS

and the
Crossing to Cambria

RUSTY ANDERSON

ISBN-13: 9781097390533

For Jayne...

who never doubted.

Acknowledgements

It began many years ago. My kids would prolong bedtime by pleading, "Tell us a story about when you were little." I eventually exhausted my supply of childhood tales, but they wanted more. So, I began to make up stories. And I continued throughout the years, sharing made-up tales involving anything imaginable. A big thank you goes out to my kids. Braydon, Morgan, Jaxton, Drew, Beckham, and Maddyn—thank you for always asking for one more story. You have kept my imagination alive. You have helped me become a storyteller.

Braydon Anderson, Morgan Anderson, Jaxton Anderson, Robert King, Brooke King, Amy Bean, Mason Bean, and Stacy Hart—thank you for reading the early versions of *Calvin Sparks*. Your feedback and continued support have been appreciated as I have taken this journey.

Thank you, Lee and Sharon Nelson, for your energy and excitement upon learning that we have a shared passion for writing. Thanks for your interest in *Calvin Sparks*, for taking time to review the manuscript, and for inviting your grandchildren to read it. Thanks for your encouragement and advice, and for seeing potential in the story.

Thanks Mom and Dad, Kevin, Mike, Tim, Ryan, Carly, Christiana, and Kellie. There was never a dull moment growing up. Life was full of adventures. Many of those adventures still live in my head and continue to inspire my writing.

And finally, a huge thanks goes to my beautiful wife, Jayne. When I first shared with you the idea of me writing a book, you supported me immediately. You have been patient and encouraging throughout this journey. You have been a wonderful sounding board for endless ideas. Thank you for connecting with my vision, for supporting me in my dreams, and never doubting that *Calvin Sparks* would become a reality.

Contents

1 • The Crossing

They were getting close. They *had* to be. They had spent every free moment during their summer vacation exploring the tree-covered hills near their home in Wolf Creek. Once again, the thought crept into Calvin's mind that the old, abandoned cottage might be imaginary. But he pushed the feeling aside and pressed on, leading the way through a tight deer trail. Branches brushed against his body as he barreled through the thick foliage, his friends close behind.

"Tell us again," said Anna. "What are we doing out here? We've circled this area a hundred times now."

"A hundred?" Perry jumped in. "I'm pretty sure we're up to a million by now." He rolled his eyes.

Calvin knew the support from his friends was fading fast. Perry and Anna were right. They had been trekking through the same forest day after day. They had found no clues. They had nothing that would bring them closer to the magical cottage.

"Seriously," said Anna. "What exactly did your grandpa say?" She blocked a branch from snapping back into her face.

"Come on," said Perry. "We've heard the story a hundred times now. You think the details are going to change?"

Calvin ignored him. "He said there was a spring that bubbled up from the ground behind the cottage and forked into two streams—"

"Yeah, yeah. They ran around each side of the cottage," said Perry sarcastically, "merging in the front and disappearing—no wait, I believe the word was *vanishing*—beneath the ground."

"You're on one today, Perry," Calvin said.

"Just frustrated. I'm wondering if it's really out there."

"Perry's right, Calvin," said Anna. "We've been looking for this magical place forever now. Maybe it's time we explore somewhere else."

"Come on, guys. I know it's around here," said Calvin. "I

1

can feel it." He followed the trail around a bend. Perry and Anna followed behind.

Calvin and Anna had been best friends for as long as they could remember. They lived on the same street in Wolf Creek—just two houses apart. They had spent countless hours in the woods behind their homes, which they considered their backyard. They had known Perry for a shorter period. Four years, to be exact. On his ninth birthday, Perry's family moved into the home that sat right between Calvin and Anna's. Calvin and Anna took Perry in. They introduced him to the hills. Together they explored, discovered, and conquered anything imaginable.

After another minute of ducking through branches and winding along the scraggy trail, Perry and Anna heard it again, just like they had heard it countless times before: a big sigh of disappointment, followed by, "You're kidding."

"Let me guess," Perry said. "Another dead end?"

"Another dead end," Calvin said softly.

"Can we go now?" Anna asked. "I should probably check in at home." Anna didn't have the best relationship with her parents. They had rules—too many of them—that prevented her from staying out for too long.

"Yeah," Perry said. "Let's go. I'm hungry."

Perry was usually fun to be around. He had a dry sense of humor and sarcasm that he used to overshadow many of his weaknesses, but when he started thinking about food, he got grumpy. He was chubby and, of the three, he was by far the most uncoordinated. Perry liked sports; his favorite was basketball. But unlike Calvin, Perry never made the basketball team. Instead, Perry made the football team every year—not because of his ability, but because of his size.

Calvin quietly stood in the tight spot observing the thick wall of brush in front of them. "I do remember seeing another trail not too far back," he said, beginning to retrace his steps. "Maybe we can see where that one takes us. I have a feeling we're—"

"Oh, brother," said Perry. "You and your feelings. You know where your feelings have taken us? Dead end after dead end."

Anna didn't let Calvin see her expression. But it was one

that told Perry that she partly agreed with him. Nevertheless, she followed Calvin back down the trail.

As Perry turned to join them, he noticed a dark shadow near the ground. He crouched onto his knees, lifted up the low branches, and saw an opening. "Wait a second," he called to the others. "I found something!" He slipped underneath the brush.

Calvin and Anna turned around but couldn't see Perry anywhere. They retraced their steps, looking for any sign of him.

"Perry?" Anna called. "Where are you?"

It was quiet for a moment. Calvin and Anna looked at each other, puzzled and slightly nervous.

"Ahhh!" Anna screamed and jumped back.

"What?" Calvin asked. "What is it?"

Anna pointed toward the ground at a hand that was sticking out from the bushes. It was frantically reaching, as if trying to grab onto something—or someone. They heard Perry laughing. Calvin tried to keep a straight face but couldn't. "Nice one!"

"Did I get her?" Perry's head stuck out from under the brush.

"Look, she's still shaking."

"That was *not* funny." Anna tried to say it sternly, but even she cracked a smile.

Perry held the branches up so Calvin and Anna could crawl through the small opening. Calvin and Anna scooted past him and eventually rose to their feet when the vegetation finally gave way to a small glade.

Perry grunted as he rolled out from under the bushes and pushed himself awkwardly to his knees. "You were so freaked out!" He was still laughing at Anna, overly proud of his prank. "I wish I could have seen your face…Calvin, what did she look like when I—"

"Shhh!" Calvin raised his hand. "I hear something."

A slight breeze swayed the tall pine trees and emitted a low, steady bellowing from high above. Birds chirped a melody that rang throughout the forest, and squirrels chittered, jumping from branch to branch. But it wasn't these noises that caused Calvin to freeze. His ears were fixed on the faint sound of water.

"Do you hear it? It's coming from over there." Calvin took

a few steps through the scrub oak. He stepped over some branches and ducked under a few more, weaving his way through the shrubbery. Anna and Perry stayed close behind, carving their own paths through the thick vegetation, following the sound of water.

After several pokes and scrapes, the three of them finally reached the end of the brush. They anxiously broke through the remaining entangled branches and marveled at the century-old cottage. Calvin circled the structure and saw—just as his grandpa had described—a stream wrapping its two meandering arms around the cottage, merging together in the front, and vanishing into the ground. The exterior was made from stones of various shapes and sizes that fit together perfectly like a puzzle. Windows provided views from each side of the cottage. A crooked, stone chimney scaled up one side of the structure and stretched high above the shingled roof.

"I told you," joked Perry. "I told you we'd find it." Calvin smiled and shook his head at him.

"You were right, Calvin," Anna said, standing in awe. "You were absolutely right. And I'm sorry I doubted you."

Calvin stood gazing, smiling.

"Come on," Anna said, punching Calvin on the arm. She jumped across the stream and approached the front door. It was made of heavy wood and creaked violently when she twisted the knob and pushed it open.

The inside was surprisingly small but was beautifully furnished with items that seemed to be hundreds of years old. An antique leather chair, sofa, and wooden rocker were arranged in a half circle facing the fireplace. The dark-grained wood floor exhibited dents and dings. A large, colorful woven rug covered the majority of the space in the center of the room. The wooden mantle above the fireplace matched the color of the floor, and was decorated with old knickknacks, including a teakettle, candlesticks, and a clay figurine of a gnome.

A large wooden chest sat next to the stone hearth. It was buckled shut. On the wall opposite the fireplace, a bookcase housed hundreds of leather-bound books. An hourglass and some wooden carvings of various magical creatures had been placed on one of the shelves. Calvin also noticed a miniature globe that had countless white specks twirling around as if it were continuously snowing on the tiny village inside.

"No way," said Calvin. "Check this out."

Perry joined Calvin in front of the bookcase. "Did you shake that?" Perry asked, looking at the globe.

"No," said Calvin.

"Anna?" said Perry. "Did you?"

"No."

"Come on," said Perry, sounding concerned. "Are you guys pulling my leg? Which one of you did it?"

Calvin and Anna shook their heads in disbelief as they watched the snow continue to swirl inside.

Perry sighed. "It's probably battery operated. There's a motor in there swirling the water."

"I don't think so," said Calvin, turning to look over the rest of the living room.

The cottage was immaculately maintained. Not a speck of dust was found growing stale or multiplying on the shelves.

Hanging above the fireplace was a tarnished sheet of metal with an etching on it: The Crossing. It was a place where Calvin's dad hung out—and his grandpa before that. As old as it seemed, he wouldn't be surprised if another generation, or two, had also explored there.

"What is this place supposed to be?" Anna asked.

"My grandpa told me it was an old refuge believed to be a safeguard from evil," said Calvin. "He used to explore here when he was a kid. He said my dad and his friends also came here. I think he knows a lot more, but for some reason he always changes the subject when my mom walks into the room."

"Why doesn't your mom want you to know about it?" asked Anna. "This place is neat!" She picked up the hourglass from the bookcase shelf, which appeared to have been recently turned on end. Fine grains of sand flowed through the narrow neck. She flipped it over, but the flow continued in the same direction, traveling from the bottom bulb to the top. She watched the sand flow upward against gravity as she replaced it on the shelf, next to the globe, which still portrayed a violent snowfall.

"This is crazy," said Anna. "Guys, check out this hour-glass."

Calvin and Perry joined Anna once again in front of the bookcase. The sand continued to flow upward.

"That's weird," said Calvin. "How does it do that?"

"There's got to be a trick to it," said Perry. "Probably magnets."

"There aren't any magnets in here," said Calvin, examining the hourglass.

"Then static . . . or something," said Perry.

"I doubt it," said Anna.

"All right," said Perry. "This is freaking me out." He broke away and looked at the titles of some of the books on the shelf.

"It could be magic," said Calvin.

"Magic?" said Perry. "Come on . . . you don't believe in that stuff, do you?"

"I don't know," said Calvin. "I remember my grandpa telling me once that this cottage had magical powers that took him places."

"Maybe it's kind of like us," Perry said. "Remember the club we used to have—The Grand Committee? Half the members in our club were make-believe. This place was probably just a cool hangout for them where they imagined they traveled all over the world."

"Yeah . . . maybe." Calvin didn't sound convinced. He knew this had to be more than just a cool hangout.

"Look at the titles of some of these books." Perry was running his finger across the spines. "This one is called *The Magical Language of the Gnomes.*" He carried the book over to the fireplace, sat down on the stone hearth, and flipped through its pages.

Calvin also pulled a book off the shelf and plopped down on the couch. The title of the book intrigued him—*Portals: The Gateway to Magical Worlds.* As he opened the book, the pages seemed to come alive, turning quickly on their own. Calvin turned to see where the draft had come from, but the windows and the door were closed. The pages had stopped on a high-lighted passage. "Listen to this."

Anna joined him on the couch as he read. " 'Most people

are unaware of the workings of the magical world. There are various portals that connect one world to another. All worlds must work together to conquer evil. One without the others will ultimately end in defeat for all.' "

Calvin felt something. It wasn't a feeling of fright, necessarily, but it was one that left him uneasy. He closed the book and looked around. He wasn't sure whether or not the feeling came from the passage he had just read, or from something else.

"Magical world?" Calvin wondered aloud. "Portals?"

A noise that sounded like heavy footsteps filled the room. Someone was coming! Only it sounded like they were coming from somewhere below.

"Look!" Perry pointed.

All three of them stared at the rug in disbelief.

"Quick! Hide!" Calvin whispered.

The rug began to move and mound up. Calvin and Anna swiftly dove behind the couch. Perry remained on the hearth, frozen. The sound of loud clicks filled the room and the lumpy rug rose up off the floor.

Pressing their cheeks against the wood floor, Calvin and Anna peered from under the couch, hoping to catch a glimpse of what was happening. They could no longer see Perry. Calvin secretly hoped that he had hidden himself somehow. Somewhere.

From under the couch, Calvin saw the rug fold back. He watched as a figure wearing a black dress climbed out. Then the trap door slammed into the floor and the rug was neatly straightened back into place. Calvin saw black shoes smooth the bumps out of the rug and walk over to the front door. The door creaked open and then squealed shut. The room was quiet.

Calvin and Anna popped up from behind the couch. "Perry!" Anna called quietly. "Where are you?"

"In here!" came an echoing reply.

Calvin and Anna looked toward the sound and laughed when they saw two legs standing inside of the fireplace. Perry ducked his way out of the chamber and greeted them with a soot-spotted face. "That was close."

"Who was it?" Anna asked.

Calvin walked to the window and pulled back the heavy

drapes. He paused for a moment. "You're not going to believe it," he said finally.

"Who is it?" echoed Perry.

"Come see for yourselves."

Perry and Anna rushed to the window. Their eyes grew wide. They looked at each other and said simultaneously, in disbelief, "Miss Jasmine?"

Miss Jasmine was their seventh-grade history teacher at Hidden Valley. She was very unpopular among the students—the teacher nobody wanted. But Calvin, Perry, and Anna took a liking to her. She was tall and slender and her long hair was jet black except for a few white streaks. She always wore black, usually a long dress—she must have had a wardrobe full of them—and she was never without her big black bag slung over her shoulder. Her pale skin next to her black hair and clothes made her an easy target for jokes. The school kids called her names like Miss Zebra, Skunk, or Black Widow—usually behind her back, out of earshot.

"What is she doing here?" Anna asked as they watched her skip from one rock to another across the stream toward the concealed passageway from where they had just crawled through.

"Oh, this will be good," Perry said. "I'd like to see her crawl through that while wearing that dress."

Miss Jasmine stopped in front of the forest wall. She swung her large, black bag around in front of her and removed a short stick. She held it out and swished it back and forth twice. A second later, the trees that stood in her way began to sway, open up, and stretch apart. A clear pathway formed and she entered the thick brush untouched. As Miss Jasmine advanced through the forest, the pathway closed behind her, leaving the trees and bushes tied up in gnarly knots once again.

Calvin, Perry, and Anna watched in disbelief.

"Did you see that?" Anna exclaimed.

"That was impossible!" answered Perry.

"No," Calvin said, smiling. "That was magical."

2 · Cambria

Anna walked over to the rug and peeled it back to reveal a wooden hatch that folded flush with the floor. There was a small handle, a ring that folded into a notch carved into the door. Anna reached for the ring.

"No! What are you doing?" said Perry. "We can't go in there!"

"Why not?" asked Calvin.

"You don't know what's down there."

"Sounds like a good enough reason to go in and find out," said Anna.

"But what if there are dead bodies under there?" Perry said.

"Come on." Anna twisted the handle and pulled the hatch open, bending it back so it rested on the wooden floor. "Why would there be bodies in there?"

"But what if there are big snakes in there? You guys hate snakes, right?" Perry continued.

"Hey, if you don't want to come, you don't have to," Calvin said, stepping down the staircase and disappearing from view under the cottage floor.

"Fine. I'll come." Perry followed Anna down the stairs and muttered, "Why do I always have to do what you guys want to do?"

"Pull the hatch closed in case someone comes," Calvin said to Perry.

"Who's gonna come down here?"

"You never know," said Anna. "Obviously we're not the only ones who know about this place."

Reluctantly, Perry smoothed the rug as best he could and pulled the hatch door closed. He quickly descended the staircase to where Calvin and Anna were standing. Lamps were hanging from the wall, creating a dull glow. They found themselves in a small room with three wooden doors. The door on the left was labeled Cambria. It was written elegantly in a font that had a magical feel, each letter shimmering in the low light. The middle door had a triadic symbol carved into it—three circles contained in a larger sphere. The last door, labeled Paragon, had three other words carved into the wood—Pathway to Enlightenment.

"Which one is it going to be?" asked Calvin.

"You really think they'll be unlocked?" asked Perry.

"Good point," Calvin said. "Let's see." He tried to open the door labeled Paragon, but just as Perry had suspected, it was locked. Calvin then tried to enter the middle door. Locked.

Perry's nerves seemed to settle.

Standing in front of the door labeled Cambria, Calvin grasped the handle, turned it, and pushed it open. Perry sighed.

"You can stay if you want," Anna reminded him, as she and Calvin walked through the door. Perry, not wanting to be left behind, quickly slipped through the door and closed it.

Calvin, Perry, and Anna found themselves standing in a cellar that was nearly identical to the one they had just left. It had a similar staircase leading to the upper floor. They could see the outline of a square, hinged door closed flush with the floor above them.

"It's like we didn't go anywhere," said Perry.

"Yeah, except for that," Calvin said, pointing at the wall. There was only one door—the one they had just come through. *The Crossing at Wolf Creek* was beautifully carved on the surface of the door.

"Come on. Let's have a look around," said Calvin as he began climbing the stairs.

"Why am I not surprised?" muttered Perry under his breath.

The cottage was identical to The Crossing, except for a sign above the fireplace that read Cambria. Similar furniture was arranged in the same layout. The fireplace was crafted out of the same type of stone, and the woven rug had a similar colorful pattern.

Calvin strolled over to a window and immediately spotted another difference. "No way . . . Check this out!" They were in the middle of a bustling village. A creature with the legs of a goat, but the upper body of a man, walked past the window.

Another magical creature trotted down the lane carrying a bow. It had the body of a horse, but from the waist up it was a man. Short human-like men and women with pointed ears walked through the town square. They wore bright-colored hooded coats and pants tucked into black pointed boots.

"Is this like some kind of dream?" Perry said. "Those costumes look real."

Humans also walked by, unfazed by the various creatures on the streets. Most of them wore long, hooded cloaks, leather pants, and high-laced boots. Many had daggers strapped around their waists, while others had swords tethered at the hip.

From the window, the trio could see cars—makes and models they were familiar with in Wolf Creek—driving up and down the lane. They spotted three cottages, each identified by a sign: Fountain Green; Yester Year: Ye Olde Books of All Ages; and Herb's Magical Herbs.

Calvin and Anna led the way out of the cottage and walked down the cobblestone street toward Fountain Green, a quaint café with moss-covered walls. A hand-painted sign hanging out front read "Warm Apple Cinnamon Cider Served 'Round the Clock."

"Are you guys crazy?" Perry panicked as he reluctantly followed them into the magical world. "We can't be here. We'll stick out like a sore thumb."

A mother walking along the sidewalk gathered her two children in close to her and rushed quickly by.

Three satyrs, visiting near a lamppost, watched them as they passed.

"See?" Perry said. "We don't belong here. They're looking at us like we're strange."

"It'll be fine," Anna replied.

Calvin pushed the door open to Fountain Green. The loud jingling of a bell hanging from the interior doorknob alerted the hostess that they had entered. Within seconds, a lady came to greet them.

"Good afternoon. My name is Priscilla. Is a booth okay for you?"

Perry looked at his friends, discreetly shaking his head. He shot them an expression as if to say, "Let's get out of here."

"A booth would be great," Anna answered with a smile.

Priscilla was mystical. She stood about five feet tall and had blue eyes and pointed ears that stuck out from under her long blonde hair. She brought them to a table with two decorative, high-backed benches on either side. It butted up against a window that looked out into the town square.

Calvin slid into the booth, taking his seat on one side of the table, while Perry and Anna occupied the other. Between the three of them, they had only a few dollars in their pockets. Would this world accept money from their world? He thought he would feel out the matter. "Umm . . . we're not really from here."

"I know," the waitress interrupted. "I realize this is your first time to Fountain Green—Cambria, for that matter. Please, order what you'd like. For first-timers, we always take care of the tab."

Perry's eyes perked up. He liked food, and he like *free* food even more. "Did you say we could have whatever we want?"

"That's right," said Priscilla.

"And it's all free?"

"If you don't leave here filled up," Priscilla said, "it's your own fault."

"Hey, how did you know we haven't been to Cambria before?" Perry asked.

Priscilla crinkled her brow. "Are you serious? Look, darling. Look at your clothes. Just a bit of advice for you three. If you plan on coming back, I'd try to look the part. Go get yourselves some boots. Some pants. Tie a strap of leather around your waist. Down the street, third door on the right is a shop called Medieval Wear. They sell everything you need to look the part." Priscilla was quiet for a moment, and then asked, "May I ask who you are?"

"I'm Calvin. Calvin Sparks. And this is Anna Jones and Perry Goldwin. We live in a place called Wolf Creek."

"Hmm. The name Sparks I know. But Jones and Goldwin? Not sure I have heard of those surnames. How did you find Cambria?"

Calvin shifted in his seat. He wasn't sure how he would answer the question. He looked at Anna. He could tell that she was also trying to think of what to say. Just as Calvin was about to speak, Perry beat him to it.

"Our schoolteacher showed us the way."

Calvin and Anna looked at Perry, not sure how to react. Was it a good confession? Or was it something they should have kept quiet?

"And who is that?" Priscilla asked.

"Miss Jasmine," Perry said.

"Yes." Priscilla's eyes lit up. "I know her well."

Calvin and Anna nodded in agreement, feeling somewhat relieved.

"She comes through here all the time. A lovely lady, Miss Jasmine is. Well, if Miss Jasmine has shown you the way to Cambria, let me be the second to welcome you three to our world."

"Second?" asked Calvin.

"Well, obviously Miss Jasmine was the first. Let me be the second."

"Oh, yeah," said Calvin. He stuttered a reply, "Th-thanks."

Priscilla removed a wand from her apron and waved it over the table. Various dishes appeared in the air, hovering in front of each of them. "What you see are the chef's recommendations for each of you. You will have different foods displayed in front of you . . . all according to your individual liking."

Calvin saw a chocolate mousse dessert floating in front of him. Three words—Yeti Volcano Pie—were attached to the image. Calvin loved chocolate cream pie and thought that this would be as close as he would get to his favorite dessert. He also saw a chocolate peanut butter cup with a scoop of ice cream and hot fudge piled on top. It just so happened that peanut butter cups were also a favorite.

Perry reached out to grab one of several desserts that were hovering in front of him, but his hand passed right through the image. "These are cool holograms," he said. "So, anything we'd like?" he clarified one more time.

Priscilla patiently smiled and gave a polite nod.

"In that case, I'll have some of your warm apple cinnamon

cider," said Perry. "And I would also like . . . " he quickly glanced over the various dishes hovering over the table, "the Magician's BLT, a bowl of the King's Chowder . . . and maybe a piece of Chocolate-Butter Peril Pie . . . a slice of Chocolate Lava Mud Cake . . . and a Triple Threat Chocolate Sparkle Cookie."

"Cookies come in small or large," Priscilla said.

"Are they really good?" Perry asked.

"Most people's favorite."

"I better go with a large, then."

When Perry had finished, he looked over at Calvin and Anna, waiting for them to order. They were both staring at him. Their jaws had dropped and their eyes were wide in disbelief.

"What?" Perry asked. "Did I do something wrong?"

Priscilla acknowledged his order with a small smile. She then turned to Anna, and asked, "And for you, sweetie?"

"How about some cider, a small Wizard Salad, and a slice of Gnome-made Banana Bread?" replied Anna.

"You got it. Calvin?"

"Well, I guess I better try some warm cider too. And a slice of Pick-Pocket Pizza and a piece of your Yeti Volcano Pie."

"Nice choice." Priscilla removed a wand from her apron and swiped it to erase the menu that hovered over the table. She then swirled the wand over each of their mugs. A steamy, sweet-smelling liquid appeared from the air and filled each of them. After a few more twirls of her wand, they each had their food sitting in front of them. "Please enjoy. Let me know if I can get you anything else."

"How did she do that?" Perry said, eyes wide with amazement.

"Magic," said Calvin.

"No, seriously," said Perry. "How did these desserts just appear here out of nowhere? And the cider flowing from thin air?"

"It's magic," Calvin said again. "We're in a magical world."

"Never mind," said Perry. "This is awesome service!" He blew over his steamy mug of apple cider. "I could get used to this."

Perry suddenly had a serious look on his face. "Do you

think it's okay that I told her Miss Jasmine showed us how to get to Cambria?"

"Well, it is true," said Anna. "We wouldn't have found the cellar door if it weren't for her climbing out of it. I guess the only thing misleading is that Miss Jasmine doesn't know she showed us it."

"It's probably fine," Calvin said.

"How did you think to mention Miss Jasmine, anyway?" Anna asked. "I mean, it turned out great. Not sure that's what I would have said, but it worked."

"When food is on the line, I'm at my best," joked Perry. "When she said everything was on the house, I wasn't about to miss out on free food."

Their conversation was suddenly interrupted by the pitter-patter of footsteps filling the air. Hostesses were scurrying about, whispering under their breath. They wore expressions of nervousness and excitement.

"He's coming!" whispered an elfish hostess. Only seconds later, the door to the café squeaked open. A rugged, handsome man filled the doorway with his large, broad-shouldered frame. He wore a short, tightly trimmed beard. His hair was long, just past the collar. He was tall and lean, dressed in black from head to toe.

Anna gawked at the apparent hero. She was beginning to slip into a daze with the rest of the girls. Calvin slowly waved his hand in front of Anna's face, trying to break her gaze. The hunk strolled coolly over to a seat at a table next to where Calvin, Perry, and Anna were seated. They couldn't see the man directly, but they were close enough to listen. Other customers abandoned their tables and scurried over to gather around him.

A short waitress clumsily hurried over to the man. "Hi, Grayson." She waved her wand and filled his mug with steamy cider. Grayson acknowledged her with a gracious smile, which sent her off to the kitchen blushing, holding a hand to her mouth and giggling.

Perry imitated her by fanning his face with his hand while falling back in his seat, pretending to catch his breath. His small act, however, ended abruptly with Anna thrusting her elbow into his ribs.

"How's everything?" asked Priscilla. "Can I get you anything else?"

Calvin leaned in and asked, "Who's that guy?"

"Oh, that is Grayson Starkweder. He's the town hero—a Bordarian. He comes in every so often sharing his stories. People drool over him all the time. He's a nice guy, but I'd rather keep my dignity and not act like such a sap."

Perry nudged Anna a few times with his elbow, agreeing with Priscilla's opinion.

"What's a Bordarian?" asked Calvin.

"Someone who offers protection to our world. Kind of like a knight. Willing to give his life in the fight against evil."

"Is there much evil in the land?" Calvin asked.

"Unfortunately yes. It's getting worse all the time. Stick around. Listen." Priscilla gestured toward Grayson. "I'm sure you'll learn a bit about it. And let me know if I can get you anything else," she offered. "Stay as long as you'd like. The bill has been taken care of."

The room grew quiet and Calvin, Perry, and Anna listened to Grayson.

"You have never known evil until you've come face-to-face with Galigore," Grayson said. "No adjective can describe his character. Evil. Wicked. Murderous. Insert whatever miserable word you'd like, and multiply it by ten. Then you might catch only a glimpse of what Galigore is like."

"What makes him so powerful?" asked one of the fascinated onlookers.

"His power resides in the staff he carries. It's a long, gnarly, twisted baton made of molten metal. The top of the staff has a carving of bony fingers wrapped tightly around a blue luminescent stone. I have seen Galigore use his staff to levitate objects and hurl them at his attackers. He launched a boulder at me once, but I dodged it right before it smashed into powder on the wall behind me. Galigore's Society is growing daily. His power is mounting up quickly.

"Two weeks ago, Galigore invaded a coastal village in Cambria." Gasps filled the air. "He and several of his servants ransacked homes in rage and set fire to barns and cornfields. Many villagers died that day trying to ward off the evil intruders. Galigore and his people rummaged through a dozen homes before they discovered what they were looking for."

"What was it?" asked a pudgy man who held a mug of cider on his lap, cupped with two hands. "What did they find?"

"When the air cleared," Grayson continued, "the residents took inventory of the damage. No one found anything missing except for one." Grayson paused.

The same man asked, "What was he missing?"

"A villager claimed," said Grayson, "that a small round stone was taken from his home."

The cluster of patrons gasped. "Not another orb?" said the same pudgy man.

Grayson shook his head. "It was an exceptional find, but it was not the orb he thought it was. It was a red diamond, the most rare diamond known to man. But that's all it was. Valuable—for sure. But it was not a stone that would increase anyone's power."

As time ticked by, the number of onlookers had multiplied.

"Just last week," Grayson continued, "I happened upon an elf of unusual character. He was much shorter than the elves we know here in Cambria. This important distinction makes him more powerful than . . ." Grayson made eye contact with Calvin and froze.

"What?" one of the onlookers asked. "What was he more powerful than?"

"Yeah. Tell us the rest," another cried.

"Tell us the story, Grayson. Tell us." Several tried to bring Grayson back to the story.

Grayson's eyes were still affixed on Calvin's. Calvin wondered why he didn't feel awkward staring into a stranger's eyes. The silent interaction seemed comfortable.

Finally, Grayson put his hand up to quiet the commotion and looked over the crowd. "I must go. I need to make a visit . . . in another land."

"But you've been here for merely an hour," complained one of Grayson's admirers.

"My apologies," said Grayson. "I made a promise long ago to visit someone when something occurred. I must go." Grayson stood and took a final swig of his cider. As he threw his coat over his shoulder, he turned toward Calvin, shot him a subtle smile, and then marched out of Fountain Green.

"That was kind of weird," Perry said, leaning back in his seat, trying to stretch himself out to create more breathing room. There wasn't a single crumb left. The meal had filled him up completely, and he was very satisfied.

Calvin sat still, thinking about what had just occurred. He had felt a connection with Grayson—a man he didn't even know.

"Maybe we should go," suggested Perry. "I need to walk off some of these calories." Calvin reluctantly agreed and he and Perry made their way toward the exit of Fountain Green.

"I'll meet you out front," said Anna. "I need to find the restroom."

Calvin and Perry pushed their way out the door.

"It's about time we see you around here," a high-pitched voice came from behind.

Calvin turned around but saw no one.

"Down here."

Calvin looked at the ground and saw a bearded creature standing in front of him. His hands were pudgy and hairy, similar to his bare, thick-soled feet. He appeared to be only a couple of feet tall with his short legs and small torso.

The old creature was hunched over and had a large hump on the center of his back between his shoulders. His forehead was wet from perspiration. He was dressed in a trench coat, worn out and frayed at the seams. Discolored square patches were stitched to the elbows, with the corners peeling off. His skin was pale. Atop his head sat a floppy beanie with the top coming to a point. Thin white strands of hair flowed out from under his hat and lay over his shoulders. He looked old. Decrepit. His breathing was loud and labored.

"Who are you?" asked Perry, feeling a little uncomfortable.

"Don't be frightened," assured the feeble creature as he shot Calvin a wink. "I'm on an errand from the castle. Bordarian work." He shot another wink at Calvin as if he should know what he was talking about.

Several seconds of uncomfortable silence ticked by. "Okay then," said Perry. "Good luck with that." He grabbed Calvin by the arm and began to lead him away.

"Your time is at hand, Calvin. Be strong, my lad. It's a part of you. Believe in yourself." He shot yet another wink. "Always trust your instincts." He turned to Perry and poked him in the knee. "And as for you, laddie, do not succumb to darkness. Do not let jealousy control your actions. You know better." A wink was fired at Perry. "You have a role in this work too, you know."

The words of counsel from the stranger lasted only a moment. "Well, I must be off. Thanks for the break," he said in a playful tone as he shot another wink and began to hobble down the lane. "I have a delivery to make. It was nice to run into a couple of pleasant kids. You behave yourselves, you hear?" He forced a toothless grin and shot them a final wink.

"What did you say your name was?" asked Calvin, the man already several feet past.

"Trixel," he called back. "Trixel Strait."

Calvin and Perry watched Trixel as he tottered down the lane. Trixel, without looking back, raised his hand over his shoulder and snapped his fingers. A small fountain of sparks surrounded his body and he vanished.

"Where'd he go?" Perry said.

"I'm telling you," said Calvin. "This place is magical."

"Haven't you seen those famous magicians on TV?" Perry winked in jest. "It's all illusions."

"How did he know our names?" asked Calvin.

"Oh, brother. Just knowing our names makes him a magician?"

Anna rushed out the door and joined Calvin and Perry out front of Fountain Green. "I better get home," she said. "I'd hate to be grounded after finding this place. Can we come back tomorrow?"

"I think we'll be spending a lot of time here," said Calvin.

The three walked back to the cottage and climbed down the stairs through the trap door. Calvin turned the handle and pushed the door open. Before they knew it, they were back at The Crossing in Wolf Creek.

"Can you believe what we just found?" Calvin said, smoothing out the bumps in the rug.

"No, I can't," said Anna. "Cambria is so cool!"

"Hey, anytime you get free food, it's pretty cool," said Perry.

"Look at the hourglass," Calvin said. "It's still flowing up."

"Yes," said Perry. "Magnets and static can cause crazy things to happen."

"And look at the globe," said Anna. "It's still snowing."

"It's a wonder what a little motor can do, isn't it?" Perry rolled his eyes.

"You don't believe in it, do you?" Calvin said.

"Believe in what?" said Perry.

"Magic."

"I just think there has to be an explanation for all of these illusions."

The three of them walked out of the cottage and crawled underneath the brush.

"What about those stories Grayson told?" said Anna. "About Galigore?"

"Just because I say something doesn't make it true, does it?"

"You think he made the stories up?" said Anna.

"I think he exaggerated," said Perry. "Come on. Didn't you see the way he strutted through that restaurant? How he worked the crowd?"

"I liked him," said Calvin.

"Me too," said Anna.

Perry looked at Anna. "Yeah . . . that was pretty obvious."

"What about Miss Jasmine parting the bushes?" Anna said. "What's your illusional explanation for that?"

"A strong breeze?" Perry said.

Calvin and Anna laughed. "Are you serious?" Anna said.

"Look," said Perry. "A lot has happened today. I've grown up thinking that magic was not real, that it was all illusion, and that there has to be some logical explanation for any magic trick.

This is the first time ever that I'm beginning to doubt myself. Yes, we saw a lot of crazy stuff today, some of which I have no explanation for. And yes, some of that just might be magical. I just need some time to take it all in."

"Okay," said Anna. "Fair enough."

"Hey, what about you two?" said Perry. "Why aren't you guys weirded out by this?"

"I've never seen magic before," said Calvin. "It's all new to me too. But for some reason, I felt comfortable in Cambria. It's hard to explain, but I felt perfectly fine. Like it was normal."

Anna looked at Calvin and smiled. "That's *exactly* how I felt."

"Well, then," said Perry. "Maybe I should just excuse myself so you two can have a moment together—talking about magic and feelings."

"I'm going back tomorrow," said Calvin. "Anyone coming with me?"

"For sure," said Anna. "As long as I'm not grounded. My parents have been impossible lately."

"Perry?" said Calvin. "How about you?"

"Fine. I'll tag along."

3 · A Gift

A few weeks later, Calvin awoke early to find his grandpa sitting in his usual rocker, thumbing through the headlines of *Cambrian Affairs*. "Morning, Cal." For being a grandpa, he was in good shape. His hair was hardly gray and he still had a lot of it.

"Hi, Grandpa," Calvin said, yawning.

"Late night?"

"We're on summer break." Calvin, Perry, and Anna had gotten home late the night before. Since discovering The Crossing and Cambria, they had been spending nearly every day there.

Calvin took a seat across from his grandpa and looked at his newspaper. Until that moment, he assumed it was a paper full of gossip and speculation like many that were sold in the local grocery store—a paper he never saw any value in reading. But now, he was interested in the content of *Cambrian Affairs*.

Calvin leaned toward his grandpa and whispered. "We found it."

His grandpa lowered the paper from his face. "What?"

"We found it," Calvin repeated. "The Crossing."

His grandpa sat up straight in his chair and shot him a curious smile. "That explains why I haven't seen much of you lately."

"Cambria is amazing," said Calvin.

"You've already discovered Cambria?" His eyes opened wide. "It took me years before I found the cellar door. Yes. It's magical, isn't it? I remember when I was your age I spent more time at The Crossing than my own home. I occasionally skipped school to read through the collection of books there. Your father was the same way, you know."

"What about the other doors?" Calvin asked. "Have you been through them? They've been locked every time we've tried."

"I'm afraid Cambria is as far as I have gone. I long for the day that I can see what's behind the other two."

"Are you telling stories again, Ainsley?" Calvin's mother entered the room.

Grandpa shot a quick look at Calvin suggesting they be quiet. He folded the paper he was reading and stuffed it behind his back. "Good morning, Kristal," Grandpa said, quickly picking up his mug of tea and taking a sip. "Just reliving some of my childhood memories with Cal."

Kristal Sparks was a petite woman. Her hair was blonde, with natural highlights, hanging just past her shoulders. Her long-lashed, blue eyes were pretty and engaging.

Calvin glanced over at a cluster of family pictures atop a small end table. The foremost picture was his favorite. It was of him, just days old, being held by his father.

"How did Dad die?" Calvin never knew him. He had died a few months after he was born. Calvin had heard the story numerous times before, but he wanted to hear it again.

"Your father was a brave . . . soldier in the army," his mom began. "He . . . he fought for what he believed was right. And that's how he lived until his . . . last dying breath."

It was a typical answer, given in her typical way. Hesitating a bit, stumbling to find the right words, losing eye contact. Calvin's mom never felt comfortable talking about the details surrounding his dad's death. It had always frustrated Calvin, not knowing, but ever since discovering the world of Cambria, he had a new suspicion.

"You mean he was a Bordarian?" asked Calvin.

Kristal choked on her tea. "Ainsley! You need to stop bringing those tabloids into the home."

"Did Galigore do it?" inquired Calvin.

Kristal glared at Ainsley. "I . . . I . . . Calvin, your father was on a mission," she said. "Whatever he was doing that night . . . was . . . I assure you . . . it was to preserve our freedom."

Calvin listened patiently, but had one question running through his mind: Why was she hiding it?

* * * *

Calvin loaded up his backpack. When he reached the edge of his property, he looked around to see that no one was watching. When he felt it was safe, he slipped into the thick forest through a concealed deer trail. The pathway was narrow and branches stretched across his legs and stomach, snapping back behind him as he barreled his way through the brush. After several minutes of putting up with the annoying limbs grabbing at his ankles, Calvin finally reached a clearing. He stopped and listened for the sound of the stream flowing nearby. He turned in a full circle, checking to see that he was not being followed before crawling on all fours and disappearing into the dense foliage. How did she do it? Miss Jasmine parted the sea of bushes while she walked through unscathed. Could he ever learn to do it?

The forest floor was alive with insects. With each crawl forward, bugs scattered out of the way as if they were trying to avoid getting squashed by a knee or a hand. Calvin hated bugs, but seeing them disperse as he approached made him feel better. At least they were afraid of him too. He continued to slither through the brush.

Calvin kept his head down to avoid the pokes and scrapes across his face. He continued to bulldoze through the brush when he found he was suddenly hovering over a giant spider. His reaction was immediate and automatic, and he couldn't help but quickly slap the spider away from him.

"Ah!" A sharp sting shot up his arm. He immediately clenched his fist. Blood steadily trickled from his grip. In the leaves ahead he heard some rustling and saw the giant tarantula-like spider quickly scurry away. Its body was the size of a baseball. Its legs were long, thick, and hairy. Returning his attention to his hand, he slowly opened it. The flow of blood continued to spurt from his palm through two distinct puncture marks. Calvin swung his pack around and pulled out his first-aid kit. He always brought it when he explored the forest. He knew it might come in handy sometime, although he never imagined dealing with a spider like that. He dressed his wound with snakebite ointment and pulled a long wrap from the bag, winding it firmly around his injured hand. He hoped the pressure would stop the bleeding. The pain in his hand was intense, but he was able to crawl still, using his elbow for support. Worried thoughts raced through his mind. Where did that spider come from? Was it poisonous? Was the venom spreading throughout his body? Would the pain in his hand end soon? Will the swelling stop? Will the throbbing go away?

As soon as the brush allowed, Calvin anxiously stood to his feet and marveled at the cottage he had discovered with his friends just weeks before. His excitement at finding The Crossing hadn't worn off yet. He never thought it would. As he admired the cottage, he was surprised to notice something by the front door. Sitting on the ground was a package wrapped in burlap, held together with twine. There was an envelope fastened to the bundle with a single word written on it that made his heart skip a beat: *Calvin.*

Calvin peered around the corners of the cottage, looking for signs of someone. He circled the cottage. He saw nothing.

"Hello?" he called.

No answer.

Calvin unfastened the envelope and slipped it into his pocket. Using his knife, he hacked through the twine and gently unwrapped the burlap. Inside, he found an old wooden chest—the size of a small shoebox—weathered and worn. The lid was secure—tightly latched with two rusty buckles.

Looking over his shoulder to make sure he was still alone, he curiously loosened the buckles and cracked open the lid.

"Your time is at hand," came a hushed voice. He heard the words clearly. They sounded so real, as if someone standing next to him had whispered them. He quickly scanned the surroundings but still saw no one. Calvin buckled the chest closed and slid it into his backpack. He no longer had the desire to go inside the cottage and read books. He wanted to get to a place where he knew he would be alone—somewhere private. He quickly headed for home with questions racing through his mind. Who could the chest be from? What was written inside the envelope? What was inside the chest?

Calvin carefully slid the antique chest underneath his bed as soon as he arrived home. He removed the envelope from his pocket and stared at his name written decoratively in black ink on the front. Calvin peeled the flap open and removed the piece of paper tucked inside. He carefully unfolded it and read:

Calvin,

I have been waiting for you. The contents of this chest are not to leave your possession. In the wrong hands, these items will bring destruction to Cambria and eventually all other worlds. As you are learning, we are at war against evil. If used properly, the artifacts in this chest will help you unlock the powers of virtue and eliminate the influence of evil. Do not succumb to temptation. You are now endowed with a power and a responsibility that must not be taken lightly. Many things needed to fall into place before I could entrust you with these heirlooms. The time is now, Calvin. Be assured, there are many that are counting on you. Don't take this responsibility lightly.

P.S. It would be wise to burn this letter after you have read and understood its contents.

Regards,

O.I.

Calvin read the letter one line at a time. He stared at it until the entire message was etched permanently into his mind. Who was O.I.? How did he know him? Calvin struck a match and lit a corner of the paper, which quickly caught fire. He watched as the words curled before turning into black dust that crumbled to the wooden floor. In a matter of seconds, the entire letter was consumed, and the flame disappeared into a stream of smoke.

"Calvin?"

Calvin jerked suddenly when he heard his mom's voice from the other side of his locked bedroom door. His aerosol deodorant was within reach. He grabbed it from his dresser and sprayed two quick spurts to help disguise the smell of smoke.

"It's time for dinner."

* * * *

"What have you been up to today?" Grandpa asked while they sat at the dinner table. Calvin occasionally got the impression that his grandpa wanted to be involved in his explorations.

"I was just out messing around in the woods," said Calvin.

"Is that when you hurt your hand?" Grandpa pointed at the wrap.

Calvin gingerly held his bandaged hand up and nodded. He knew his mom didn't like talking about Bordarians or Galigore, so he felt it better to keep the spider bite concealed. "Yeah. Something bit me. It hurts, but it should be fine." He tried to convince himself that his hand was okay—even though it still throbbed painfully. The swelling hadn't stopped since he received the bite, and some of his fingers tingled and were now twice their normal size. Just before coming to dinner, he had re-wrapped his hand in a way that would conceal the puffiness. He feared that he was in trouble.

Calvin was the first to finish his meal, but he politely sat and visited. Although he was talking, his mind was not in the conversation. He was thinking about the letter. The chest. Cambria. His hand.

"What else are you going to do over summer break?" Grandpa asked.

Calvin sat in silence for several seconds, in a daze, and finally muttered, "Unlock the powers of virtue."

"Wow," Grandpa said stifling his laughter. "Very noble of you."

"Are you okay, Calvin?" asked his mom.

"Uh . . . yeah," Calvin shook his head and rattled himself from the trance. "I mean . . . I'm going to . . . " He rubbed his face. "Sorry, I must be tired."

"Why don't you go lie down, Calvin," his mom offered. "We'll handle the dishes tonight."

Calvin nodded and cleared his plate, along with a few other things he could manage on his way to the kitchen. On his way back through, he gave his mom a kiss on the cheek. "Good night, Mom."

"See you in the morning, Cal," said Grandpa.

Sleep was the last thing on his mind. Calvin entered his dark room and clicked on a lamp sitting on the bedside table. The glow was dull, illuminating very little, but his eyes grew accustomed to the ambiance.

Calvin reached under his bed and pulled the chest toward him. He unlatched the buckles and raised the lid. "Your time is at hand," came the same hushed voice. Calvin quickly looked up and glanced around his room. There was nothing. He turned to the window and saw a face staring back at him. He blinked and narrowed his eyes to focus on the shape, but it was gone. It happened so fast that he wondered if he was just imagining it. Focusing his eyes intently upon the window once more, he decided no one was there, but looked again, just to be safe. Calvin found himself glancing at the window frequently—nervous that someone would be watching him.

Returning his attention to the chest, Calvin reached in and pulled out a leather pouch cinched tightly with a sturdy cord. The leather was soft and worn. On the outside was a symbol—made up of three parts—branded into the leather, which Calvin recognized from the middle door at The Crossing. He wrapped both of his hands around the pouch and gauged the article inside to be hard and round.

Calvin's injured hand distracted him momentarily. He was curious to see what it now looked like and if he could force any movement down through his fingers. He unwrapped the bandage and discovered that his fingers still looked the same—huge and tightly swollen. He could barely make a fist, but was relieved he at least had some movement in his fingers. Proving to himself that his hand may not be as bad as it seemed, he used it to help stretch open the top of the pouch and loosen the leather tie.

Calvin carefully dumped the contents onto his bed. A smooth, milky-colored orb rolled out. He went to pick it up, but as soon as he made contact, a familiar sharp pain pierced his injured hand and shot up his arm. Seconds later, the pain was gone.

Calvin looked at his injured palm. The sting had faded. There was no trace of puncture marks from the spider bite. The swelling was reduced to normal. The numbness had ended. His hand was completely healed. He sat in amazement, staring at his hand, turning it from front to back. Clenching it tightly and re-opening it again, Calvin extended his fingers. He repeated the movements several times. He sat incredulously staring at his pain-free hand.

Mustering up his courage, he again reached for the orb. He wondered if he would feel the jolt of pain run up his arm again.

He took hold of the round object. There was no flash of light. There was no jolt.

Calvin held the golf ball–sized stone up to the lamp. It was translucent and heavier than expected. After carefully examining the stone, Calvin returned it to the pouch, pulled the strings together to cinch the opening tight, and placed it on the floor next to him. He again examined his hand and saw no trace of the wound. He couldn't believe what had happened and wondered about all the magical powers the orb must possess.

Situated in the bottom of the chest, along the backside, was a tightly rolled piece of parchment, tethered with a leather cord. Calvin reached in and pulled it out. Slipping the tie off one end, he unrolled the old, wrinkled piece of leather onto his lap. The edges were jagged and burnt. Calvin examined the marks. It was a map—but of what?

He moved the parchment closer to the lamp and studied it further. A very faint hashed line connected three islands: Doom, Volcan, and Shadow Gorge. Inside the triangle of islands was situated another island labeled Misery. Decorative ink strokes, forming fanciful words, marked more lands unfamiliar to him: Crater of Bitterness, Desolation, Peril Cove, Dragon Lookout, Raven Point, and Labyrinth.

Focusing his eyes on the southeast corner, Calvin saw another land bleeding off the edge. The letters C-A-M were visible before the others faded into the charred, black edge. It took only a moment's consideration before he imagined the missing letters: B-R-I-A.

Calvin had never traveled beyond the town square in Cambria. Seeing the various lands and islands of the sea on the map, he wondered where on the map all of Grayson's adventures had taken place. He wondered where Grayson was now. Was he off on another adventure? That day in Fountain Green was the only time he had seen him.

Calvin carefully rolled up the parchment, affixed the cord, and set it aside the leather pouch. There was one final item inside the chest. It was a shallow, hardwood box about six inches long and three inches wide. Calvin unfastened the clasp, lifted the lid, and found a heavy, discolored, bronze key. Pulling it out of the box and raising it for a closer look, he examined the intricately decorated handle. A long, thin metal chain, matching the color of the key, was strung through a loop on the end of the handle.

Calvin's imagination took him to a land far away, where he saw himself admiring heaps of treasure. He placed the chain around his neck—the key dangling just above his waist. In his mind, he reviewed the endless possibilities of what the key might open. Could it belong to a castle treasury? Treasure chests lying on the ocean floor? Could it unlock an entrance to a secret passage? Perhaps it would grant access to a dragon's lair? Or maybe even a dungeon cell?

Thoughts crawled in and out of Calvin's mind as he drifted off to sleep.

4 · Life's Calling

Fountain Green was unusually crowded, but Calvin, Perry, and Anna still managed to secure their typical spot: the cozy, somewhat private booth in the corner of the café with two high-back benches that faced each other.

The three of them were becoming more comfortable with the magical world and were even visiting it on their own when they couldn't all make it together. Priscilla had taught them how money worked. The coins were called jingles, and it was all based off of honesty. One could borrow any amount of money as long as he agreed to pay it back in a timely manner, with a little extra for good measure. The pay-me-back-when-you-can system had worked for years. It was much easier to put the responsibility on the shoulders of the citizens than to create laws and appoint officers to enforce it. The payback rate was nearly 100 percent.

Many establishments, Fountain Green being one of them, had no price tags on its items. The customer just paid a fair amount—whatever he felt the meal was worth. Once Perry saw a man pay 50 jingles for a large cookie. It made him feel a little embarrassed when he filled out a pay-me-back-when-you-can certificate for 10 jingles for the same cookie. A bank was located on the main street in the town square where Calvin, Perry, and Anna could convert their currency. One dollar was equal to two jingles. Perry figured five bucks was plenty for the large cookie—the same cookie he saw a man pay 25 dollars for.

Calvin, Perry, and Anna mostly planned short trips to Cambria so their parents wouldn't worry about them being gone all day. Usually, after their morning chores were finished, they would go to Cambria for a couple of hours. About midday, they would return home for lunch, make sure their moms saw them, and then return back to Cambria for a few hours in the afternoon.

They had spent countless hours in the café over the past few weeks. Often they would dream up imaginary quests. From that corner booth, they had defeated every beast and escaped every trap imaginable. They would often strategize against the wicked Galigore. In fact, in their minds, they had already defeated him several times.

"Suppose you found a chest," Calvin began. He had no concern that Perry or Anna would raise an eyebrow at the random thought. They each had a history of throwing out hypothetical scenarios. "And inside," Calvin continued, "was a secret map. Would you follow it?"

"Of course," Perry answered, sounding brave, even though he was the most cautious of the bunch.

"But what if it led you deep into the forest . . . into enchanted woods, where ferocious beasts live?" asked Calvin.

"I would look at alternative routes," Anna suggested. "Perhaps the map would lead through perilous lands only to weed out the weak. But the smart ones," she sat tall in her seat, "would avoid the danger altogether."

"Go on," urged Calvin.

"We would travel by horse along the edge of the woods in the general direction," continued Anna, "and would pick up the trail just past the dangerous parts."

"Can you do that?" interrupted Perry. "Outsmart a treasure map and take a detour?"

"Let's say it involves traveling across the sea, how would you do it?" probed Calvin.

"The seas are full of dangerous monsters," Perry reminded them. "We would have to find a dragon that would carry us across the water. Hopefully the map would be leading us to a chest of valuable treasure."

"Right!" Calvin affirmed. "And what do you think we would need to unlock such a chest?"

"A key?" asked Perry.

"Yes!" Calvin exclaimed. "And where do you suppose we can find this dragon and key?"

Perry and Anna looked at each other, brows raised. "Calvin?" asked Anna.

Calvin smiled and stared at her.

"Calvin?" she said again. "Are you feeling okay?"

"Listen," Calvin said seriously, leaning toward the center of the table and speaking in a hushed voice. "I'm going farther. Beyond the borders of Cambria."

"What are you talking about?" asked Anna, worried.

"There are other lands out there that I need to visit," said Calvin. "These lands must have some clues that will help bring down Galigore."

"Come on, Calvin. You can't just go off on your own looking for Galigore," said Perry.

Calvin sipped his cider and continued. "Ever since discovering The Crossing and coming to Cambria and listening to Grayson's stories and learning about the evil growing throughout the land, I have felt that my purpose in life is to play a part in this battle. I asked my mom if Galigore killed my dad. She seemed uncomfortable when I mentioned Galigore's name, but all she would say was that my dad was killed trying to fight against evil."

"You think your dad fought against Galigore?" said Anna.

"Yes, I do."

"You think Galigore killed your dad?"

Calvin nodded. "Look. I'm sure my dad was a Bordarian. I would bet my grandpa was too. It's a part of me. It's in my blood. I'm not sure what my part will be, but I do know it's time I start figuring it out."

"Oh, I see what this is about," said Perry. "It's a part of you? That's what Trixel told you! That guy was weird. You can't listen to him."

"Who's Trixel?" asked Anna.

"Some guy we met on the road a while ago," said Perry.

"But it doesn't have anything to do with Trixel," said Calvin. "I had forgotten about him."

Anna leaned in, with a worried look, and asked, "What is it, Calvin? What's happening?"

Calvin motioned with his head, suggesting that Perry and Anna follow him. He flung his heavy pack over his shoulder and led them out of Fountain Green. Calvin walked quickly ahead while Perry and Anna tried to keep up. No one said a word. Perry and Anna gave each other a wondering look.

Perry finally broke the silence. "Where are you taking us?"

"The Crossing."

"Do you feel like we're being watched?" Anna asked in a whisper.

"You feel it too?" Calvin said.

"Yeah . . . It feels creepy."

"I don't feel anything," offered Perry.

The three managed their way into the cottage and disappeared underneath the floor. They quickly passed through the door labeled The Crossing.

"How do you feel now?" asked Calvin.

"Better," Anna said.

"Me too." said Calvin.

Calvin pushed his way through the door in the floor and held it open for Anna and Perry to pass. Perry flung himself over the chair, and Calvin and Anna sat together on the sofa.

"When I came to The Crossing yesterday," Calvin explained as he swung his pack around to his lap, "I found a package on the ground right outside the door."

Perry and Anna continued to sit quietly, listening to Calvin.

"The package had my name on it." Calvin pulled the wooden chest from his pack and opened it.

"Inside the chest was this pouch." He removed the orb from the leather pouch, held it up, and explained how it had healed the spider bite on his hand.

"Oh, and you know those circles on the middle door downstairs?" Calvin continued. "That same symbol is branded on the outside of this pouch." He turned the pouch so they could see it.

Perry and Anna remained silent and watched Calvin as he removed a second item from the chest. "There was also this map. Cambria is on it. So are a bunch of other places I've never heard of. There are three islands that form a triangle. And each island is marked with a symbol: a sword, a staff, and a bow."

Calvin removed a third item. "There was one more thing inside the chest. This key with a chain looped around it. I think all of these things have something to do with Galigore. The orb. The map. The key. Maybe they'll unlock some of the secrets behind Galigore's power."

"Yeah . . . ," said Perry. "Or maybe not." Perry looked at Anna anticipating a reaction. She didn't give one.

"So what now, Calvin?" asked Anna.

"I need to learn all I can about Galigore. Who is he? What powers does he possess? What is his weakness?" Calvin sat quietly, thinking.

"How are you going to do that?" Perry wondered. "Yester Year doesn't have any books about him…We've looked."

"Grayson," Calvin whispered. "I need to see Grayson."

"You know I'm coming with you," interrupted Anna.

"I guess that means that I am too," replied Perry, walking over to the window and peering outside. "Wow, check this out!"

Calvin and Anna quickly walked over to the window and gazed out into the woods toward the sound of snapping twigs. A graceful creature walked daintily into the clearing.

"It's beautiful!" breathed Anna.

"Awesome!" added Calvin.

"Where did it come from?" asked Anna.

"I don't know," Calvin said. "We are on the edge of Cambria. Maybe some of the magical creatures there have crept into this world. Kind of like the spider that bit me. It was huge and hairy. I've never seen one so big. It couldn't have been from here."

"Well, I have never seen one of these in real life," said Anna, still gazing out the window. "It's magnificent."

"What are you talking about?" asked Perry. "We see these all the time in the woods. Maybe not as *big* as this one."

Calvin and Anna looked at Perry, confused. "What do you see, Perry?" asked Calvin.

"A buck. Granted . . . it's a *big* buck."

Calvin and Anna took another glimpse out the window.

"That's not what I see," said Calvin.

Perry looked over at Anna. She shook her head.

"What do you see then?" Perry asked.

After a long pause, Anna answered, "A unicorn."

5 • Grayson Starkweder

Grayson Starkweder lived in Bear Valley, a neighboring village situated on the opposite side of Cambria's town square. Down the tree-covered lane where Grayson lived, cottages were spread out far and wide. His was the last one on the lane. An iron fence with a gate in the center lined the front of the property. Calvin opened the gate and the three entered.

"Wow," said Anna. "I *like* this." Meticulously trimmed hedges, about waist high, neatly lined the walkway up to the front porch. It was a small cottage. The exterior was made of gray, weathered stones held together with light-colored mortar. "Grayson has good taste."

Smoke billowed from the chimney, filling the air with the aroma of a campfire. Three steps led to a spacious porch. "And look!" continued Anna. "Two rocking chairs for . . . rocking."

"Uh, yeah," said Perry. "That's what rocking chairs do." Perry rolled his eyes. "Look. I know Grayson is, like, this super hunk and all, but my goodness, let's try to keep it together."

Calvin smiled at Perry. Anna just kept walking toward the house.

A torch hung on the porch wall, giving off a flickering yellow glow. The top of the wooden door was rounded. A metal door knock was intricately designed with the head of a dragon.

Calvin grasped the dragon head and firmly struck it against the metal plate a few times. The footsteps inside the door became more distinct as they drew closer. Calvin watched as the knob turned and the door cracked open. A chain inside the door stopped it from opening any further. A man, unrecognizable in the dark shadows, peered through the opening and spoke. "Can I help you?"

"We're looking for Grayson," said Calvin, in a voice that was deeper than normal.

"I'm quite sure Grayson isn't expecting you."

"We have some questions we want to ask him . . . about

Galigore," said Calvin.

"He is of no concern to you. You're only children."

"What about the Island of Misery?" Calvin asked desperately.

The door quickly slammed shut. Chains rattled from the inside and the door opened wide. Grayson narrowed his eyes and scanned the front yard left, then right, before ushering Calvin, Perry, and Anna inside.

The inside of the cottage was dark, lit only by flickering flames dancing in the fireplace. Steam swirled from a cup resting on a square table in the center of the room. Also on the table was an old, leather-bound book titled, *Mystical Creatures of the Unknown.* Calvin caught a glimpse of the spine of another book that was open, resting face down on one of the arms of a leather chair: *Advanced Incantations for the Intuitive.*

Grayson motioned for Calvin, Perry, and Anna to sit down. It was a tight fit, but they managed to squeeze together on a small sofa. Grayson left the room. Perry seemed a bit uneasy being in a stranger's home, but Calvin and Anna were comfortable. Since listening to Grayson at Fountain Green the one time, Calvin had wondered about him. The connection he felt when their eyes made contact left him feeling curious. Even though he had never spoken to him before, he felt like he knew him. Anna, on the other hand, thought Grayson was brave, but it was his strikingly good looks that charmed her most.

Leaning forward, Calvin reached for the mystical creatures book and cracked it open in the middle. He saw drawings of several unfamiliar creatures as he skimmed through its worn pages. He didn't take time to read it but merely browsed the pictures.

Grayson entered the room carrying three cups of elderberry tea. He placed one in front of each of them on the square table and motioned for them to drink. Grayson took his seat in the armchair. Calvin quickly closed the book as discreetly as he could and replaced it on the table in front of him.

The four sipped their tea. Grayson broke the silence. "How do you know about Misery?"

"Just some old folklore we read about at Yester Year,"

replied Calvin.

"You will find nothing written about Misery in Yester Year," said Grayson.

Calvin began to feel hot. "I . . . I know I saw it somewhere. Does it exist?"

"Listen, Calvin. The dark world is a real one," answered Grayson. "Galigore has dedicated his life to obtaining power and wealth. He coerces others to follow him, promising them treasures beyond their imagination. High-minded people have succumbed to his temptation, joining the dark world. Galigore is relentless. He is deceptive, sly, and malicious. He has been known to turn even the most saintly beings into villainous monsters."

"Grayson?" asked Calvin.

"Yes?"

"How did you know my name?"

"Calvin, I've known your family all my life. Your father and I have a strong past. We served together as Bordarians."

"I knew it," breathed Calvin.

"I don't believe I know who you are." Grayson looked at Perry and Anna.

"My name is Perry Goldwin." Perry looked over at Anna.

"Oh!" Anna ran her fingers through her hair. "My name is Anna . . . Anna Jones. I . . . live . . . I live next to . . . to these guys." Calvin never knew Anna to be tongue-tied. She stuttered. She blushed. A subtle elbow to the side from Perry seemed to wake her up.

Grayson acknowledged Perry and Anna with a slight smile. He then stood and took a step toward the mantel above the fireplace. He reached for a photograph, handed it to Calvin, and returned to his seat. "There were four of us who were very close. Pictured there from the left are Stone Stryder, myself, your father, and Elgar van Galigore. We were a close bunch. Your father was a great influence on us. He made us laugh. He made us believe—believe that we could do anything. We accomplished a lot, the four of us. We were the perfect team of Bordarians."

"Galigore was a Bordarian?" asked Anna, shocked.

"Yes," said Grayson. "Galigore was a Bordarian."

"What made him turn evil?" Perry wondered.

"First, you must understand that the problems we face today are not entirely credited to Galigore. He has certainly moved the evil work forward, and at a rapid pace. But he is only the latest of a long line of wicked lords that date back many generations. Today, we are at war with Galigore. Before Galigore, it was Tyrus . . . before Tyrus, Sidon. Karzon was one of the earliest rulers we have record of. It was Karzon who formed the evil Society of powerful servants. There are thousands of Zarkon assisting the evil warlock with his work. As one lord would fall, another would rise. The mantle usually falls on the one with the most influence."

"Zarkon?" said Anna.

"Remember I said even the most saintly people could become the most villainous monsters? Those are the Zarkon. Just one look at the most corrupt Zarkon is enough to make your stomach turn. The darker they become, the deeper their souls are lost. Their appearance becomes frail. Their skin turns pale. And their flesh seems to wither away. Their bodies become skeletal and their skin translucent."

Grayson pointed at the picture Calvin had in his hands. "One day the four of us discovered a magical orb while on a mission to a remote island in the sea. It was believed to be one of the three lost magical stones that can endow certain people with supernatural powers. We each handled the stone and admired its beauty. For the three of us, that's all it was—a beautiful, rare stone. But for Elgar, it was more.

"He insisted that he carry the orb back to the castle. We noticed that just in the short trip home, his countenance changed. He was overcome by feelings of greed. He felt strong and invincible. When he was asked for the stone, he did not want to give it up. He offered to protect it and keep it safe. He finally did relinquish the orb, but that was the last time we knew Elgar as the good person we knew and loved.

"He lost his self-control. He longed to hold the jewel in his hand again. He hungered for power. He spent the next several weeks secretly devising a plan to break into the treasury to steal the orb. He was successful. He joined forces with Tyrus and he quickly became his right-hand man."

"Are there other orbs that have been found?" asked Calvin.

"I know of one other," replied Grayson.

"Where is it?" asked Calvin.

"Recently, there was an unusual amount of Zarkon activity on the island of Volcan, a dreadfully hot place with pools of bubbling lava. The captain of the Bordarian Army sent Stone to the island to see if he could figure out what the Zarkon were up to. While prowling around some ancient ruins, an ogre attacked him from behind. It was the last time that beast would swing a club." Grayson clearly warmed to the tale, sitting forward in the armchair as he described the ensuing battle.

"Stone easily slew the ogre." Grayson jabbed his hand forward as if holding a sword in his hand. "But not before it yelped, sending out a warning. A Zarkon came rushing to find his ogre slain and Stone holding his bloodstained sword. The Zarkon charged Stone, drawing his sword from his sheath. They smashed their steel together in a heated battle." Grayson cut his pretend sword back and forth in the air out in front of him as if he were reliving the battle. "In the end, Stone finally backed the Zarkon against a wall. With one last mighty swing, the Zarkon lunged toward Stone, but Stone was ready for the desperate attack." Grayson ducked his way out of what seemed to be a sword swinging in his direction. "He disarmed the fiend and hurled his body to the ground.

"Stone finished the deed and thrust his sword deep into the Zarkon's back. He searched the place and left with two curious artifacts. In the inside pocket of the Zarkon's cloak, Stone removed a rolled parchment. It was a map. And tied around the Zarkon's waist was a leather pouch that contained a magical stone."

"If Stone has one . . . and Galigore has one . . . where's the third orb?" asked Perry.

Grayson gave Calvin a long stare that began to make him feel uncomfortable. He felt like Grayson could see right through him. The quiet seconds felt like minutes.

"It seemed like a promising breakthrough . . . to have recovered one of the three orbs," said Grayson. "But the night he found the map and orb, he had them stolen from his cottage. We're not sure where they are today."

"Grayson?" Calvin asked. "Did Galigore kill my dad?"

Grayson paused. "You don't know the story?"

Calvin shrugged. "My mom never talks about Galigore. She's never said anything of Cambria. Doesn't talk about magic. She gets upset when I bring those things up."

"Kristal was devastated by the loss of Miles and she couldn't stand the thought of losing you too. She vowed to never mention the name Galigore, believing that if she did, it would pique your curiosity. So, she took you away from us and moved from Cambria—to Wolf Creek—hoping that good would prevail. Troubling as it is, evil seems to be prevailing now. Kristal has always been overly cautious of you. You're the best memory she has of Miles. You look just like him, you know."

"You know my mom pretty well, then?" Calvin asked.

Grayson took a deep breath, and then continued. "We were very close growing up . . . used to do everything together. I know her better than you can imagine."

"You still have strong feelings for her?"

"I love your mother very much, Calvin."

"But not as much as my dad," said Calvin, feeling slightly defensive.

"Oh . . ." Grayson laughed. "It was a much different kind of love."

"I don't get it," said Calvin.

"She's going to kill me," Grayson said under his breath. "Look, Calvin. What is your mom's full name?"

"Kristal."

"Kristal . . . what?"

"Kristal Sparks," Calvin answered.

"Does she have a middle name?"

"She uses an initial."

"Which letter?"

"It's Kristal S. Sparks," said Calvin.

"Has she ever told you what the letter S stands for?" Grayson asked.

"No."

41

"Might be a good question for her. Could explain a lot."

"Why don't you tell me?" asked Calvin.

"I promised that I wouldn't reveal it."

Calvin had so many questions filtering through his mind. Some relative to the topic at hand, while others seemed completely random. "What happened at Fountain Green when we saw you there?" asked Calvin. "Why did you stop in the middle of one of your stories? You froze exactly when we made eye contact."

"You're a curious one, Calvin." Grayson said. "I promised Kristal that I would tell her if I ever saw you in Cambria. Your mother knows you know about this place. She's just not yet ready to open up. She's having a hard time accepting that another loved one might have a desire to become involved with the conflict of evil. She knew you would discover it eventually, and she wanted me to notify her as soon as you did. It was a family vow I took long ago."

Calvin nodded and paused, and then asked again. "So, did he?"

"Did who what?" Grayson asked.

"Did Galigore kill my father?"

"Stone and I were with your father the night he was killed. The three of us were battling against Galigore and the Zarkon. Stone and I got separated from Miles. Two Zarkon followed us, and Galigore chased after your father. I saw Galigore back him into a cave. Stone and I finally took care of the Zarkon, but we were each so badly wounded, we were forced to conceal ourselves in the trees outside the cave and wait. Just as we feared, Galigore exited the cave . . . alone. We searched for your father's body, but we never did find him. We lost a great man that night."

Calvin had never heard it told to him straight before. He was grateful to hear it. Somehow it brought closure to the mystery surrounding his dad's death.

Calvin, Perry, and Anna sat silently on the sofa, trying to digest everything they had heard. They felt it was no longer a question of *if* they would be fighting against the dark world, but *when*. Holding his empty cup of tea in his hands, Calvin wondered silently if he should divulge his findings to Grayson, but his thought was interrupted.

"Look, it's getting late," Grayson said. "I probably told you too much tonight. Your mom would kill me if she knew what we've been talking about."

Calvin, Perry, and Anna rose from the sofa and thanked Grayson for the visit. Calvin felt Grayson's hand on his shoulder as he approached the door. He stopped and turned around as Grayson handed him *Mystical Creatures of the Unknown*.

"This is for you, Calvin. The woods are enchanted. Filled with dangerous creatures. It would be wise to know them inside and out. Know their strengths. Know their weaknesses." Calvin took the leather-bound book and tucked it snugly under his arm.

The three of them left Grayson's cottage and walked toward the town square. Lamps illuminated the cobblestone streets. Most of the shops were closed. Fountain Green was still bustling with people, but the three of them just walked on by. They were making their way to the portal within the cottage that would take them home.

"Do you think you have the same map and orb that Stone had?" asked Perry, once they were back in the woods, outside The Crossing.

"I don't know." Calvin replied.

"I don't know, either," said Anna. "I mean . . . Grayson said nothing about Stone having a key."

"You know, we really need to figure out how to move these bushes out of our way," said Perry as they crawled through the underbrush, making their way to the clearing.

They were finally able to stand up and walk through the narrow, twisty trail. They made their way mostly in silence, thinking about the developments of the night. The trail was dark. The only glimpse of light came from the moon, which shone faintly through the trees.

They passed a huge willow tree right as a soft breeze rattled its leaves. The sound of small animals scurrying through the nearby bushes caught their attention. An owl, perched atop a tree branch, uttered a hoot. Every sound alarmed them, though none of them would admit it. The thick trail seemed extra spooky that night.

"Calvin?" asked Anna, walking close by his side, her arm clamped around his.

"Yeah?"

"Are you scared?"

"No . . . I've been on this trail lots of times . . . even on darker nights."

"That's not what I meant. Are you scared about Galigore?"

"I don't know. Yeah . . . a little, I guess. But I kind of feel excited too."

"Are you going to tell Grayson about the chest?" asked Perry.

"Probably. But I don't know when."

"He seems like a nice guy," Anna said.

"Yeah . . . but it's a little creepy how well he seems to know your mom," said Perry.

Before long they stopped in front of Anna's door. "What do you say we meet at Yester Year tomorrow afternoon?" asked Calvin.

"Good idea," agreed Anna. "We have a bit of studying to do, don't we?"

* * * *

Calvin sat up in his bed and opened the cover of *Mystical Creatures of the Unknown*. In the inside cover written in faded ink he could barely make out the letters of a name: Miles Sparks. This book had belonged to his dad? He continued to flip through the pages. Next to many creatures, notes were scribbled in the margins. Some of the creatures Calvin was already familiar with: pegasus, ogre, cyclops, griffin, phoenix, troll, minotaur, centaur. He kept flipping through the pages and saw a unicorn, satyr, mermaid, manticore, chimera, pixie, fairy, and yeti.

A few pages deeper into the book, he saw a picture of the type of spider that bit him while crawling through the brush on his way to The Crossing. Calvin was relieved to find out that he wouldn't have died, but had the wound gone untreated, it would have deadened his hand. It would have turned an ugly dark brown and then gone limp.

He turned to the name of a beast that he had never heard of: feldinari. Calvin looked at the picture. It was a vicious beast with a powerful, well-defined, muscular body, protected by scales. It sported two enormous heads, of the canine family, with scrunched faces and jowls drooping below its jawbones. Razor-sharp teeth protruded from the perimeter of its mouth. The nose was flat and the eyes intimidating. It had large paws with sharp claws. Wings extended from its sides. Its long tail was thick and scaly and curled back over its body. The end tapered a little, transforming into a snake's head with green, glowing eyes and two sharp fangs. It looked like the feldinari's back bowed just enough to form a natural saddle for a rider.

"Feldinari are very loyal creatures," Calvin read aloud in a whisper. "They live in packs. By instinct, the feldinari is a protector and will defend its rider to the death. Throughout history only a few men have been able to capture and tame a feldinari—although possible, it is an improbable task."

Next to the picture of the feldinari, Calvin saw Stone's name written on the page and circled. There were also his dad's hand-scribbled notes:

Venomous bite is fatal within minutes. Antidote: immediate application of moon rose sap. Use the Tiempo Parar charm to help slow the effects of venom. Weakness: inject the beast with its own venom.

"*Tiempo Parar* charm?" Calvin wondered aloud. Excitement rushed through his body as he imagined his dad being able to perform magic, perhaps like Miss Jasmine.

6 · History of Cambria

Calvin was the first to arrive at Yester Year. He sat down at a small, round table that had four chairs surrounding it. He draped his light coat over the back of one of the chairs, and then walked down an aisle, reading the titles of the books. One particular title caught his eye—*The History of Cambria*. He pulled it from the shelf and carried it back to the table. It was a newer publication, printed only a few years earlier.

Calvin thumbed through its pages and found it was divided into sections. The section entitled "Bordarians" contained a record of every Bordarian who had served in Cambria, arranged in alphabetical order. He found the name Sparks and saw a picture of his dad. He looked to be in his early twenties. He had neatly trimmed brown hair, blue eyes, a thick neck, and broad shoulders. He seemed to have a look of confidence that radiated from the photo. Under his picture, Calvin read the following entry:

SPARKS, Miles. Miles Sparks served honorably as a Bordarian for five years. One of the youngest to be appointed Bordarian, at age eighteen, Sparks received high marks in archery, swordsmanship, dexterity, and intuition. While on a mission commissioned by the Captain, Sparks was killed by Elgar van Galigore. At the time of his death, Miles and his wife, Kristal, lived in Cambria with their infant son, Calvin.

Calvin sat there, expressionless, his eyes fixed on his father's obituary. He missed his father, even though he never knew him.

Calvin flipped the page back. Just as he had suspected, his grandpa was a Bordarian. He read the bio:

SPARKS, Ainsley. Ainsley Sparks, a decorated Bordarian, continues to be a valiant supporter in the fight against evil. Ainsley has been a member of the Bordarian Army for more than thirty-five years. His son, Miles (also a Bordarian), was killed in battle while on a mission. Ainsley has presently taken on a new role in the Bordarian Army as a recruiter, where he looks for young talent with wizardry potential.

Calvin closed the book but kept his place with his thumb.

He sat back and thought for a minute. It made sense to him now—why his grandpa told him about the old cottage in the woods. He was supposed to find it, eventually. He was one of his grandpa's recruits. His grandpa had it all planned out.

After a moment, Calvin flipped forward a couple of pages. He recognized another name.

STARKWEDER, Grayson. Grayson Starkweder became the youngest Bordarian in history at seventeen years and five months. His natural abilities have made him one of the most skilled all-around fighters. Grayson holds high marks in swordsmanship and archery.

Calvin turned the pages, casually, looking at the pictures of Bordarians. His eyes rested upon a photo of a man who had a familiar face. His eyes were brown. His hair was jet black, shoulder length. He was a large, broad man, with a muscular build. He read on.

STRYDER, Stone. Stone Stryder continues to serve nobly as one of the most skilled Bordarians in Cambria. He was appointed Bordarian when he was just eighteen years of age. He is the all-time record holder for highest marks in swordsmanship and dexterity.

"What are you reading?" asked Perry as he and Anna took a seat near Calvin.

"This book has the history of every Bordarian in Cambria," replied Calvin.

"Hey, I wonder if Trixel Strait is in there," said Perry.

"Good idea," agreed Calvin.

Calvin flipped again to the surnames ending in S. "Not in here."

"Doesn't surprise me," said Perry. "I thought there was something fishy about that guy."

Calvin walked over to another aisle and scanned the books on a shelf at eye level. None of the titles caught his interest. He browsed another aisle. A few rows later, he finally pulled a book from the shelf. It was old and worn. *Mythology of Cambria.* Calvin carried the book back to Perry and Anna and sat down. Fingering through the pages, he eventually landed on one that had a picture of an orb, slightly blue.

"Listen to this," said Calvin. "According to folklore, during the eighteenth century, Osgar Ivins, a magical gnome of

Emerald Pass, Paragon, forged three small stones out of one large moon stone. A charm was placed over the stones, each one infused with magical power."

Calvin lowered the book. "You know what? The letter that was written to me was signed by someone with the initials O.I."

"Osgar Ivins?" said Anna.

"Probably."

"Keep going," said Anna.

"It is known that a staff, sword, and bow were constructed to encase each of these stones. Power is not granted to the possessor of the stone alone. But if a person of certain distinction brings the artifact and stone together, his power becomes great. Bring together two and two, and increase in power ten fold. Bring together three and three, and the possessor becomes immortal. As the story is told, Osgar, the possessor of all three, found himself in a most frightening predicament. His character, which once was noble, began to deteriorate. Fearing that he would not be able to control his desire for more power, he removed the stones from their housings and hid them all away, each one buried in a separate distant land."

Calvin looked up at Perry and Anna. "The map had markings on a few of the islands," he recalled. "One was marked with a bow. Another with what could have been a staff. I know I saw a sword and a key and some other strange symbols."

"If Osgar hid the stones away in separate lands, the map is telling us where they are," said Anna. "That map you have is not just a treasure map, but a map to infinite power. We can't let it get into the wrong hands."

"Grayson told us last night that Stone had the map stolen from him," said Calvin. "So obviously, people are aware that these things exist. Others are searching for them. The question is how far have they gotten on their search."

"And who else knows about the map?" asked Perry.

"And what other relics have been recovered . . . and who has them?" added Anna.

"If any relics have been recovered, you can bet Galigore would have them," said Calvin. "Remember what Grayson told us about Galigore's staff?"

"Yeah. Grayson said it gave Galigore unnatural powers," said Anna.

"Right," said Calvin. "But what about Osgar Ivins? What more can we find out about him?"

"Remember what you just read?" said Anna. "Osgar is from Emerald Pass, Paragon."

"Paragon?" Calvin said. "Paragon is one of the inscriptions written on a cellar door."

"Looks like we need to figure out how to get through that door," said Anna, "if we're going to learn a thing or two about Osgar."

Calvin nodded in agreement. Perry just rolled his eyes.

"I'm sorry, guys," Calvin said abruptly, "but I need to get going. My mom wanted me home early." He started packing up his things.

"Yeah, I need to get going too," said Perry.

"Great," said Anna. "One of the few nights I can actually stay out late and *both* of you have to go." She fastened her backpack.

The three of them straightened their chairs and headed back to the portal.

As Calvin and Perry were about to exit the cottage at The Crossing, Anna paused and glanced over at the numerous books sitting on the shelves.

"I think I'm going to stay here for a bit and read some more," she said as she smoothed the last few bumps out of the rug on The Crossing floor.

"You'll be all right?" Calvin asked.

"I'm fine," Anna said. "I'll see you tomorrow."

Calvin and Perry closed the door behind them, making their way back to Wolf Creek.

* * * *

Calvin was surprised to see four places set at the table when he walked into the dining room. His grandpa was already sitting at the table, waiting.

"Are we having someone over tonight?" Calvin asked.

"A dear family friend is coming for dinner," said his mom.

"Who is it?"

49

"Oh, someone you will find very interesting," Grandpa replied.

"Yes, Calvin. I'm sure you'll be surprised. Why don't you wash up? He'll be here shortly."

"Sure, Mom."

Calvin was in the bathroom when he heard the knock at the door. He heard his mother open the door and invite the guest in. He finished washing up and went to join them.

"Calvin," his mom said as she got up from her chair. "Say hello to my best friend, Grayson Starkweder."

Calvin froze.

Grayson extended a hand toward Calvin. "Nice to see you . . . again."

Calvin didn't know what to say. He stuttered a reply. "Uh . . . you too."

"Well, shall we eat?" suggested Grandpa.

The aroma of roasted turkey filled the air. Calvin scooped himself some mashed potatoes, then passed them to his mom. Grayson handed him a dish of corn. The silence was awkward.

"Calvin, I knew you'd learn about the magical world sooner or later. I have been trying to protect you from it," Kristal said. "I . . . I just always hoped it would be later. Much later." Kristal shot a glance at Calvin's grandpa. He replied with a guilty smile and a shrug of his shoulders.

"I moved us out of Cambria when your dad was killed. Grayson and I knew that you would one day discover the magical world. And when you did, we agreed that he would come and let me know. So, now that we have this all out in the open, I think you can make your own choice whether or not you want to pursue the magical arts. You need to discover for yourself if you want to live your life aspiring to become a Bordarian and fighting against evil, or if you would rather stay here in Wolf Creek away from the dangers of Cambria.

"Of course, I would rather have you decide the latter, but that would be selfish of me. You must decide for yourself." Kristal reached for a warm roll and spread butter on it. "Once you get involved with Cambria's plight of ridding evil from its land, you immediately assume great responsibility, Calvin. And if you never get involved in the first place . . . what a freeing feeling it must be. If you choose to be involved in the magical world," she continued, "Grayson will teach you a few things. Just an introduction, though." Kristal gave Grayson a look with her eyes, as if to say, "Don't go too far."

"Yes, Calvin. You would be my apprentice," confirmed Grayson.

"I do want to be part of Cambria," said Calvin. "It feels so good, so right, when I'm there."

"Well, then," Kristal said. "As difficult as this is for me . . . I will allow Grayson to begin mentoring you. It's better to have someone experienced teach you the correct ways than to have you off trying to learn on your own. You can get into trouble that way."

Calvin smiled. "When can we start?"

"I believe we'd be better off training in Cambria," Grayson said. "We don't want to be seen in Wolf Creek swinging swords and casting spells. The people here are unaware of Cambria . . . or magic, for that matter. But I suppose if evil continues to pollute Cambria, it will creep into this land."

"Did you say casting spells?" Calvin said in awe.

"Nothing advanced," his mom assured. "Only elementary charms for now. Your body wouldn't handle anything beyond a beginner's dose of magic."

"How about I pick up Calvin on Thursday morning?" Grayson suggested. "We'll spend the weekend at Stone's place. He lives on secluded acreage—ideal for training."

"Yes," said Grandpa. "I heard Stone is off on Bordarian affairs. He wouldn't mind you crashing at his place for a few days."

"That would be acceptable," said Kristal. "Just promise me—"

"Kristal," Grayson interrupted, "I'll take care of him. He'll be fine."

"Can Perry and Anna come with us?" Calvin asked.

"Oh, I don't think so, Calvin," his mom answered. "Their families know nothing of the magical world."

"True," agreed Calvin. "But they've been practically living

there lately. They love it."

"It wouldn't be a hinder, now would it?" Grandpa said. "In fact, it may prove beneficial to have more students with Calvin, learning together . . . having someone of equal ability to combat with."

Grayson nodded in approval.

"Well, I suppose that would be up to their parents," said Kristal. "I'll speak with their mothers."

"Yes!" Calvin said under his breath. His excitement was obvious.

Grandpa smiled.

"I should probably explain," Kristal said just as Calvin said, "Mom? What does—"

"Sorry," he said. "Go ahead."

"No, you first."

"Well, I was going to say, now that we have this out in the open, can I ask you a question?"

Kristal answered Calvin's request with a simple nod.

"What does the initial S stand for in your name?"

Kristal looked at Grayson and then she glanced back at Calvin. "Funny," she said. "That's exactly the thing I was going to tell you." She reached out and held Calvin's hand. "The S stands for Starkweder. I'm a Starkweder, Calvin. Kristal Starkweder Sparks."

Calvin didn't speak a word. He was hastily putting the pieces together in his mind.

"You guys were married?" asked Calvin.

Kristal laughed. "We weren't married, Calvin. Grayson and I are siblings."

Calvin let out a big sigh. That explained the connection he felt with Grayson. The reason was simple. He was blood-related. He was family. He was Uncle Grayson.

7 • Herbal Creations

Anna wasn't much of a reader. She never had been. She could count the number of chapter books she had read during her life on one hand. She just couldn't get into them like others could. Perhaps it was because she became bored too easily. She didn't earn her smarts from reading. She listened well. She asked a lot of questions. It didn't matter if the setting was at home with her parents or in a classroom at school. She retained information easily. That all changed, however, since discovering Cambria. The magical world intrigued her. She devoured books.

Anna walked over to a bookcase, pulled some books from the shelves, and stacked them upon the coffee table. She had kicked her feet up on the couch and leaned back resting against the side. She was comfortable. The book she held in hand, *Herbal Creations*, was worn and well highlighted.

A clicking noise came from the front door. Anna froze. It happened so suddenly that she had no time to hide.

"Anna?" said Miss Jasmine. "What are you doing here?" Miss Jasmine entered through the door in her familiar black garb with her usual large, floppy black bag slung over her shoulder.

Anna smiled awkwardly. "Um . . . just reading." She held up the potions book.

"Anna Jones reading?" said Miss Jasmine with a smile. "I'm not sure I've ever seen that before."

"You're right," Anna said. "But ever since discovering this place, I can't seem to put the books down."

"Oh, I know exactly what you mean," said Miss Jasmine. "I wanted to learn as much as I could about magic after I discovered The Crossing." Miss Jasmine walked to the couch. Anna spun around and put her feet on the floor in front of her. Miss Jasmine took a seat next to Anna.

"Potions, huh?" Miss Jasmine asked, recognizing the title of the book in Anna's hand. "It will do you well to become familiar with the earth's resources. There is a solution to almost every problem, if you can find the right combination of ingredients."

"Are you a potion master?" Anna asked.

"Not a master. But it's good to know how to benefit from the earth's gifts."

"There are some pretty cool potions in here." Anna looked at the book. "Do they work?"

"They sure do," said Miss Jasmine. "But you must follow the recipes with exactness, or you'll end up with something you didn't expect. There's not a lot of forgiveness for substituting ingredients."

"Where do you find the ingredients for these potions?" Anna asked.

"There is a nice shop in the town square—" Miss Jasmine stopped and gasped. It was obvious to Anna she had started saying something she thought she shouldn't have. "I mean," Miss Jasmine said, trying to disguise her own words, but the outcome was a bit clumsy. "You can find these ingredients at various herbal shops around . . . certain towns . . . here and . . . there . . . and elsewhere."

"When you said town square, you wouldn't be talking about the town square in Cambria, would you?"

"Anna! How do you know about Cambria?"

"Well . . . " Anna hesitated a bit. "You are the one who showed us."

"I . . . I never showed you."

"Not on purpose, anyway."

"What do you mean?" Miss Jasmine asked.

"One day Calvin, Perry, and I were exploring the forest when we came upon this cottage. As we were looking around and flipping through books, we saw a door open from underneath this rug. Calvin and I hid behind the couch and Perry hid inside the fireplace. We saw you crawl out of the cellar door."

"Well, I guess I did show you then." Miss Jasmine thought for a second. "I'm sorry I'm the one who got you into this mess."

"This mess?"

"Yes," said Miss Jasmine. "This is a dangerous world to be

associated with."

"I know. But there's something about this place that seems so right . . . for me. It's hard to explain, but I feel like Cambria is where I belong."

"I think I understand," said Miss Jasmine. "The minute I discovered The Crossing, that's all I thought about."

Anna nodded. She then glanced down at the book in her lap. "So, which potions have you used?"

"I have a handful that I carry with me. You never know when you're going to need one."

"Like what?" Anna asked.

"Well . . . " Miss Jasmine paused. "Since you're so interested, and you know much more about Cambria than I presumed, I'll show you a few." She pulled her bag to her lap and spread the top open. She reached in and removed a small glass vial that she held in her fingertips. "This potion is for age acceleration. One dose of this will make me many years older. Turns me into a little old lady."

"Why would you ever want that?" asked Anna.

"It comes in handy from time to time when I need a disguise," Miss Jasmine explained. "Once I was being chased by some people who were up to no good. I ran into a crowded place and quickly sipped a dose of age acceleration. I transformed into a much older and fragile version of me. The men passed me several times, staring me right in the eyes, but didn't suspect a thing."

"Wow. That's pretty cool."

Miss Jasmine nodded.

"What other potions do you have?"

Miss Jasmine rummaged through her bag and removed three more glass vials and laid them in her lap. She held up one of them. "This is similar to the other, but transforms me into an animal. Depending on which ingredients you've used to make the concoction, you can turn into that class of animal. For instance, this fauna metamorphosis contains hair from a feline. I can transform into any type of cat I desire. This particular potion has been helpful to me when I have needed to travel somewhere quickly. I have turned into a cheetah lots of times and have

55

outrun many enemies."

"Does it hurt to have your body turn into things?"

"No, it doesn't hurt," said Miss Jasmine. "It's a little uncomfortable for sure. Your body squeezes and squishes here and there. You definitely feel it."

Anna smiled with amazement.

"Well . . . I must be off," said Miss Jasmine. "I didn't think I was going to be able to pass through the cellar door with you here. But since you seem to know a lot about Cambria already, I will continue with my journey." Miss Jasmine folded the rug back and opened the door. She smiled and pointed to the book. "Keep up the reading. There's a lot of good stuff to know about potion making in there."

"So Herb's Magical Herbs will have everything I need?"

"Herb will have a lot of the common ingredients you'll need. Leaves, feathers, seeds, hair. He'll even have a nice selection of the more hard-to-find items. And you'll pay a hefty price for them. Some of the more complicated potions, however, will require ingredients from the wild. Herb will have a lot, but others you'll need to find and gather yourself."

Anna acknowledged her advice with a smile.

"Sorry I need to leave you, but I do have some pressing things I need to take care of."

"That's okay," said Anna. "I understand."

"You know where I live in Wolf Creek, Anna. Stop by anytime."

"Thank you."

"And I'm sure the chances of us seeing each other here at The Crossing or in Cambria are pretty good." Miss Jasmine took several steps down the staircase until the floor was about even with her shoulders. "Do you mind closing the door for me and smoothing the rug?"

"Not a problem," Anna said.

"Thank you, dear."

Miss Jasmine disappeared under the floor. Anna closed the door and smoothed the bumps from the rug. She sat back down on the couch and her eyes immediately fixed on a small glass vial wedged between two cushions—a potion Miss Jasmine failed to stow away in her black bag. She picked it up and held it in her fingers, turning it upside down and right side up again. The silvery liquid inside sparkled as it sloshed from one end of the bottle to the other. She unstopped the vial and smelled the heavy liquid inside. "Yuck," she said moving her nose away. "Smells like canned dog food."

Anna was disappointed that she didn't pay closer attention to be able to distinguish one potion from another. All the jars were identical. Which one was this? Was this the aging potion? Or could this be the one to turn her into a cat of her choice? But what intrigued her even more was that it could be an entirely different potion—one that Miss Jasmine hadn't told her about.

With the vial still unstopped, Anna plugged her nose, brought the rim of the vial to her lips, and forced its contents down her throat. Then she waited for something to happen.

Anna began to grow nervous waiting for the transformation to take place, but it didn't take long. She felt her face squish together. Her mouth became long, stretching from one side of her face to the other. Her nose deflated and left behind two small holes for nostrils. Her eyes began to bulge from her head. Her shoulders twitched uncontrollably as two large sets of wings emerged from her shoulder blades. Her legs mutated and became one long pointed tail. Skin from her stomach pulled and stretched, forming extra legs coming out of her sides. She looked down at her body and watched her skin become thick, and then rigid. She was encased in an exoskeleton, which would offer her protection. The metamorphosis happened painlessly. She felt like she had shrunk. Her surroundings appeared gigantic. The fireplace looked as a tall as a house. The bookcases seemed to tower above her like skyscrapers. The ceiling was as high as the heavens.

Not sure exactly what the potion had turned her into, Anna moved toward the window to see her reflection. As she began to move, her wings thrummed, and she was carried through the air in the direction she intended. She flew close to the window and focused on the flying insect looking back at her—a beautiful dragonfly. Her body was made up of shades of pink and purple. Her wings were thin and see-through, and were defined by fluorescent pink veins. Anna couldn't get over the vibrant coloring in her new form.

She flew quickly, zipping through the air, from one place to another, directing her movements with exactness. She felt so light and so free.

Anna hovered in one place, high in the room. A clicking sound came from far below, and the rug, which appeared to be the size of a large lake, began to mound up. Anna quickly flew to the top of the bookcase and landed. She watched as a large figure, with a black handbag slung over her shoulder, climbed out of the staircase. Miss Jasmine looked around the room. She noticed the stack of books still piled on the table. Then she spotted the empty vial. She picked it up, replaced the lid, and put the container in her bag.

Anna began to feel guilty. Had Miss Jasmine noticed that she was missing a potion? Did she come back specifically to find it? Anna watched Miss Jasmine scan the room high and low.

Anna began to feel hot. Beads of sweat formed on her forehead. She became uncomfortable when their eyes seemed to have met. Could it be possible that Miss Jasmine saw her—a little dragonfly—from across the room?

"Anna?" Miss Jasmine said, still looking directly into Anna's eyes. "Be careful up there. It's a long way down."

That confirmed it. She had been caught. No hiding now. But how did their eyes lock so easily? Wasn't she just a tiny insect among the large room?

"Anna? Are you feeling okay?"

Still hot, with beads of sweat clinging to her brow from the transformation, Anna began to move off of the bookcase. She felt a little shaky and sluggish.

"Careful, Anna!"

It was then that Anna realized how silly she must have looked—curled up in a ball on the top of the bookcase. The potion she had consumed just minutes before had completely lost its power.

8 • Wishing Well

Calvin, Perry, and Anna trekked through the muddy terrain. The rain had slowed to a drizzle by the time they reached The Crossing. The melodious pitter-patter on the roof was pleasant. But it didn't last long. The rain stopped completely and the air grew still.

They took their usual places in The Crossing—Calvin and Anna on the sofa and Perry on the fireplace hearth.

"I saw Grayson last night," Calvin said.

"You did?" Perry said. "Without us? How could you?"

"My mom had him over for dinner."

"He came to your house?" asked Anna.

"Yeah . . . it turns out my mom *does* know him really well."

"Were they boyfriend and girlfriend or something?" asked Anna. "The way Grayson was talking about your mom was a little uncomfortable."

"You sound a little jealous," Perry said, smiling at Anna.

"Grayson is my mom's older brother."

Anna was astonished. "Are you kidding?"

Calvin shook his head. "I'm serious. The S in my mom's name stands for Starkweder."

"Uncle Grayson," Perry said in a whisper. "That's so cool. You're so lucky!"

Calvin agreed. "Yeah. Pretty crazy, huh?"

"So I guess your mom knows about you knowing about Cambria?" Anna asked.

"Oh, yeah. She asked if I wanted Grayson to teach me . . . take me in as his apprentice."

"That's so cool," Perry said again. "You're so lucky!"

Calvin stood up and walked over to the window. Out of the corner of his eye, he saw a blur streak by, disappearing into the woods.

"What was that?" he said.

"What?" Anna rushed to his side.

"I saw someone run by."

Calvin walked outside and looked around. Whatever he saw seemed to be long gone. "Do you hear that?" he said.

"No," answered Perry. "What?"

"I hear it," Anna said. "Music." They walked around to the back of the cottage.

"It's coming from over there." Calvin pointed deep into the woods beyond The Crossing.

"You don't really want to go in there, do you?" complained Perry.

"We won't go far," Calvin promised.

"Yeah, let's go check it out," Anna added.

"You're not serious, are you?" Perry protested.

Calvin and Anna ignored him. Calvin grabbed some branches and moved them aside while Anna entered the thick forest.

"Are you coming?" Calvin asked Perry, smiling.

Perry didn't say a word but reluctantly wedged his way through the prickly opening.

Even in the rain, the ground was dry underneath the canopy of entangled branches high above them. The air was darkened by heavy shadows. Anna quickly spotted a trail that appeared well traveled. Calvin pointed out deer tracks and a set of boot prints.

"What are you doing?" asked Calvin as he watched Perry build a tower of four rocks piled on top of each other.

"It's a cairn," replied Perry.

"A cairn?" asked Calvin. "What's a cairn?"

"It's a marker for us so we know where to turn to find our way back. I saw it on TV once."

"Sounds like a good idea," said Anna, rolling her eyes.

"Come on, let's go." Calvin led the way along the trail in the direction of the music. After a few minutes, the tune faded and finally disappeared completely.

"Should we turn back?" asked Perry.

"No way," Anna said. "I say we keep going. What do you think, Perry? You're okay, aren't you?"

Perry stopped, frustrated. "Does it really matter what I

think?"

"Good point," Anna joked.

Calvin smiled at the two and hiked on.

They walked along the narrow path single file. The woods remained dense with trees and the trail narrowed. Branches scraped against their legs. It was uncomfortable, especially in the dark shadows. The brush formed a tall wall on each side of the trail that reminded Calvin of walking through a cornfield maze. He kept telling himself, and the others, that they should keep going, "Just a few more minutes."

The trail wound back and forth. Their vision up ahead was limited.

"What do you say, Calvin?" said Perry. "Maybe we should go back now. This is getting a little spooky."

Anna bent down, picked up a rock, and piled it on top of another. "Just wait right here by this cairn," said Anna. "That way we'll know where to find you on our way back."

"Funny," Perry fired back.

"Let's go just one more minute," said Calvin. "I have a feeling we are getting close to something."

"Yeah, maybe a three-headed, man-eating wolf." Perry looked at his watch. "Okay. I'll hold you to it. One more minute."

The time ticked along and Perry rarely took his eyes off the second hand. "Thirty seconds."

Calvin picked up his pace.

"Twenty."

Calvin continued onward as Anna and Perry stayed close behind.

"Ten . . . nine . . . eight . . . " Perry began to count down, his voice growing louder with every second.

"Shhh!" Calvin interrupted with a whisper. "Look."

Calvin pointed up ahead through the woods. The trees gave way to a small clearing where an old shack resided.

"That must be a hundred years old," whispered Anna.

Most of the glass windows were broken. The door hung in place but was crooked. The paint had peeled off the door almost entirely, exposing the weather-beaten, raw wood underneath.

Patches of wooden shingles clung in their place on top of the roof and extended down the walls of the structure.

"Let's go check it out." Calvin motioned for Perry and Anna to follow him.

Perry groaned and rolled his eyes. "I wish we could just get out of here."

Calvin peeked through a nearby window, but it was too dark to see anything. He quietly made his way around the corner to the front door. The doorknob turned easily and Calvin nudged it forward. The hinges were tight and let out a shrill sound that pierced the silent air. Calvin hesitated and then gave one steady push.

Inside the shack, the floor was dirt and the room was vacant except for a well situated in the middle of it. A low, stony ring surrounded the well, with a wooden roof covering the top. Calvin went to the edge of the stone wall and peered inside. Hanging at eye level, underneath the wooden canopy, was a metal dowel with a rope wrapped around it. The end of the rope was attached to a bucket that was suspended in the air. Extending from underneath the roof was a handle used to lower and raise the bucket up and down the deep, narrow, dark hole. The bottom of the hole was not visible in the dark shadows.

"Maybe there's magical water down there," said Perry. "Calvin, take a drink and see what happens."

Calvin looked at him like he was crazy.

"Hey, look at this," said Anna. The outside door was still open and permitted enough light into the shack for her to make out the words etched faintly into the stone.

"What does it say?" asked Perry.

"It says 'Wishing Well'," replied Anna.

"Cool. Let me try," said Perry.

"No. I'm not finished," warned Anna. " 'Wishing Well. Beware of dreadful consequences.' "

"Sounds like we better study up on this before we go wishing for anything," said Calvin.

"I don't know," said Perry, smiling. "Why don't you give it a try?"

Calvin ignored him. He picked up a small rock and dropped

it into the well. Three seconds passed. Then five. And seven. They heard nothing. Not a single splash.

"That's a deep well," said Anna.

"Yeah," said Calvin. "I'm not sure anything is down there."

"Okay, have you guys had enough fun?" said Perry. "Can we please get out of here?"

"Why are you in such a hurry" Anna asked.

"It's just creepy," said Perry. "Let's head back to The Crossing."

"All right, Perry," said Calvin. "Find those cairns and get us back to The Crossing."

9 • Lucero

The next day, Calvin was relieved to hear that Perry had been given permission to go with him and Grayson on their journey. But he was more excited when he found out that Anna was also able to come. Calvin always thought there was something special about Anna. They related very well to each other and oftentimes even had the same thoughts. They both had intuitive dreams on a regular basis, and they would spend many afternoons at The Crossing trying to interpret them.

One afternoon, they were discussing a recent, reoccurring dream she had where she saw two figures, a man and a woman, casting spells into the dark sky, repelling an eerie green glow that seemed to be swallowing them up. The scene would inevitably flash to a room, where two infants lay together, alone in a crib, crying. Nobody else seemed to be in the room—only the two sad newborn babies. Was it her birth parents fighting off an evil presence? If so, were they familiar with the magical world? Was she one of the babies? Was this why she seemed to have a disposition toward magic? Could this be why she related so well to life in Cambria?

Over the next couple of days the three spent every free moment they had at Yester Year, rummaging through the collection of books scattered throughout the shop.

The bookstore owner, Glenburn, was an old friend of the Sparks family and permitted Calvin and his friends into the shop after hours. That night Glenburn had left for the evening and entrusted his store to the youth, asking that they lock up on their way out. The only light in Yester Year came from a glowing lantern, its light barely sufficient for reading.

"Check this out," said Calvin as he stopped on a page in a book entitled *Beginning Spells for the Instinctive*. Calvin began to read aloud. "The art of wizardry is best acquired by the highly intuitive mind. Those who possess the ability to recognize their sixth sense will likely gravitate toward sorcery and excel in the technique of spell casting. To determine one's level of intuition and affinity for magic, practice the following elementary charm for illumination. Note, however, that the more advanced the spell, the more energy it will drain from the magician. Although one can build up a tolerance to perform more advanced spells, some require so much energy that the inexperienced magician may black out before seeing the effect of the spell."

Calvin placed a finger in the book to save his place and looked up at Perry. "Here you go. Try this."

He continued to read. "Extend arms out in front of the body. Place the heels of the hands together, palms rounded, fingers slightly opened and curled, as if holding a rounded object." As Calvin read, Perry followed the instructions. His hands were rounded, his fingers wrapped around an empty sphere, and his fingertips pressed together.

Calvin continued. "Do not allow fingertips to touch each other." Perry flushed slightly and quickly pulled his fingers apart.

With a smirk, Calvin began again. "Close eyes and concentrate on the rounded open space held within the hands. When the mind is completely focused on creating light, say aloud the following word: *Lucero*."

"*Lucero!*" cried Perry, his eyes closed and arms extended in front of his body. "*Lucero!*" he repeated again. Each time he said the word, he opened his eyes. "*Lucero!*" he said again, checking to see if there was even the faintest flicker of light appearing between his hands. He closed his eyes again and concentrated hard. His eyes were squeezed tightly shut, his brow wrinkled.

Calvin continued to read. "The mind is powerful. Once the mind's thoughts are mastered, one may not need to close his eyes. Furthermore, he may not need to verbally speak the spell at all. The more relaxed one can be, the more easily he can control his thoughts, and the more readily he can access the earth's energy. Aspiring wizards who can't make the spells work may be required to use a wand. But don't fret—the majority of magicians use one. See *Wands* under the *Tools* heading."

Perry's face was red now, strained from attempting his first spell. Calvin and Anna burst out laughing.

"Well, you try it," challenged Perry, feeling a bit

embarrassed.

"Fine. I'll give it a try," said Anna. "Quiet down."

Anna slowly closed her eyes. She took a deep breath, and as she exhaled, her body seemed to sink heavily into the chair. After a few more slow breaths, Anna slowly raised her hands and extended them out in front of her body. Her eyes remained shut as the heels of her hands connected. Her fingers were rounded, slightly spread apart as if she were holding a weightless ball between her palms. She looked completely relaxed. After one more deep, slow breath, she spoke the word. "*Lucero.*" Her eyes remained closed.

Calvin and Perry quietly looked at each other and then back at Anna's hands. The space between her hands exhibited a small ball of light that lit up the room.

"Anna," Calvin whispered, breaking the silence. "Anna, you're doing it. Open your eyes and see."

After a few seconds, she became conscious of her surroundings and slowly opened her eyes. As she did, she caught a glimpse of the hovering light just before it extinguished.

"Did you see that?" cried Perry softly. "How did you do that?"

"I don't know," Anna said. "I just tried to concentrate, I guess."

"That was awesome!" Perry said.

"You try," Anna told Calvin. "Take a deep breath."

Calvin closed his eyes and took a few deep breaths. He felt his body becoming more and more relaxed. His thoughts took him away from Yester Year and brought him to an unfamiliar place. Although his vision was slightly foggy, he recognized his mom there. Another figure was standing next to her. It was a man that he imagined to be his dad. Calvin saw him walk across the room, kneel on the floor, and pick up a baby. After a long, gentle squeeze, his dad kissed the baby on the cheek and laid him on a blanket.

Calvin saw a tear collect in the corner of his dad's eye. His mom's emotions were more obvious. Tears streamed down her cheeks as she threw her arms around her husband and held him tight. When Calvin's dad opened the door to leave, Calvin saw a large creature outside. There was a mark on the beast's left hind leg in the shape of a crescent moon. Unsure of what the animal was, Calvin imagined it to be a dragon. His dad mounted the creature and flew off into the night. His mom stood there with the door open, tears still rolling down her face, and watched until the airborne silhouette had vanished in the moonlit night.

Calvin wondered if that was the last time his mom and dad saw each other. He felt sad for his mom as he watched her finally close the door. Calvin now had a memory of his dad. He didn't know if this was a dream or not, but it didn't matter. He felt a connection to his father he had never felt before.

Calvin noticed someone gently shake his arm. "Calvin . . . look," came the whisper from Anna. "It's amazing. Open your eyes."

Calvin forgot what he was doing, but as soon as he opened his eyes, he instantly remembered. His arms were outstretched with both of his palms together side by side, facing up. Levitating just a couple inches above his hands was a brightly lit globe the size of his fist. It didn't seem to surprise Calvin, but Perry and Anna looked on with amazement.

"Calvin?" asked Anna. "Do you realize that you said nothing when this light appeared?"

"Really?" Calvin wasn't sure what to do now. He wondered if he could make the light bigger. He placed his hands around the globe and spread them apart. The globe grew and filled the gap. Calvin brought his hands closer together and reduced the globe to the size of his fist.

"Are you seeing this, Perry?" said Anna.

Perry nodded, his mouth wide open. "Throw it in the air."

Calvin tossed it up in front of him and it floated about eye level. He raised his palm up and guided the globe to the left, and then gently guided it back to the right. He held the ball of light up and clapped his hands together, smashing it into thousands of smaller bulbs that filled the room. The bulbs illuminated for only a moment before burning out.

"What's that all about? Why did it work for you guys?" asked Perry.

"It's . . . just beginner's luck. That's all," said Calvin.

67

"Well, try some more," demanded Perry. "Let's see what you got."

Calvin looked through the pages of the book and found more entry-level charms.

"Ah, here's one." Calvin read aloud. "The charm for slumber is *Sedativo*. When successfully cast, *Sedativo* will cause creatures to become drowsy and fall asleep. The smaller the creature, the quicker the fall and the longer they remain dormant. Very large creatures will be slowed by this charm, but it will most likely not cause them to slumber."

Calvin spotted a mouse making its way across the wood floor, scurrying from place to place scavenging for food. It finally found a crumb to nibble on near Perry's feet. Calvin closed his eyes and relaxed his mind, disposing of all distracting thoughts. When his mind was clear, he stretched forth his hand in the direction of the mouse, opened his eyes, and said, "*Sedativo.*"

He felt a jolt of energy shoot out of his palm, heading for the mouse. Immediately the rodent fell over motionless. Calvin went closer and examined it. He could see it was still alive—still breathing. He wondered how long it would remain dormant. Several minutes? Hours?

Calvin couldn't believe it. He had grown up reading stories about magic, but never thought they could be real. He had always assumed that the stories were mostly make-believe. But now he knew magic was real. And he was doing it!

A loud thud and a snort echoed throughout the room. Calvin and Anna looked up and saw Perry's face resting on the table. The two couldn't help but laugh.

"It'll be a while until I perfect these spells, I suppose," said Calvin. He grabbed Perry's hair and lifted his head. A string of drool stretched from Perry's lip to the table. Calvin cringed slightly in disgust.

"Calvin?" asked Anna. "When you were doing the *Lucero* charm, what were you thinking about?"

"I just relaxed my mind," answered Calvin.

"But where did your mind wander?"

Calvin felt very transparent all of a sudden. He wondered

how she would have known his mind had taken him anywhere.

"You had tears in your eyes, Calvin."

"My mind took me to a time in my life that I can't remember. But it seemed so real . . . so familiar to me. I was just a baby. My dad was saying good-bye. I think it was the last time my mom and I saw him alive. He picked me up and held me. He kissed me. And then he turned to my mom. They hugged and he left. My mom was crying. My dad was crying. I imagine I was too. I felt a connection to my father that I have never felt before. I guess I've gotten used to the fact that he died so long ago. I never knew him. I never thought I really could. Stories are nice, but . . . but they seem so . . . out there. This memory I had tonight, though, seemed so close . . . and so real."

Calvin thought quietly for a moment. "How can someone be so evil?"

A loud groan filled the air. They looked over at Perry, who blinked his eyes wide and stretched his arms above his head. Calvin and Anna smiled at each other while Perry rubbed his tired eyes with the heels of his hands.

"What happened?" asked Perry in a dazed voice.

"You decided to take a nap," explained Anna. "Couldn't keep your eyes open."

"What time is it?"

"It's time for bed," said Calvin. "Come on. Let's get home."

10 · Fiddler Forest

The next morning, Calvin removed the mysterious key from the box, hung it around his neck, and tucked it inside his shirt. The key was completely concealed. He then reached for the leather pouch that held the orb. He firmly pulled the leather straps, tightly closing the bag, and then tied it to a belt loop on his pants. His jacket hung below his waist and hid it well. Lastly, he took the map and tucked it away in a pocket of his jacket and zipped it shut.

Calvin heard a quiet knock at the front door and the sound of his mom's footsteps.

"Good morning." Calvin recognized Grayson's voice.

"Hello. Please come in. Would you like some breakfast?"

"No, thanks. We're on a tight schedule. Is Calvin ready?"

"He's in his room, gathering his things."

Calvin scanned his room for anything else that might catch his eye. Over on his dresser he saw his father's old dagger resting in the corner. His mom had given him his dad's dagger earlier that year on his thirteenth birthday. But ever since discovering The Crossing, the dagger became even more special to him. He imagined his dad using it to fight against the Zarkon, or even Galigore himself. It was intricately decorated with a carving of a serpent spewing flames. Red, white, and green stones were embedded in the scabbard and sparkled in the light. Calvin unsheathed the dagger and raised it out in front of him. He held it up and twisted the blade. The dagger was pointed and had two razor-sharp edges. After slicing the blade through the air a few times, he slid the weapon back into its sheath, and stored it inside his small suitcase.

Calvin noticed his backpack hanging in the closet. Assuming it would be a good idea to bring it with him he placed it inside his suitcase next to the dagger. It took all of his body weight to smash the lid of the suitcase with his knees while he zipped it closed. After one last glance around the room, checking for any last-minute items he might need, he was ready to go.

"Hi, Grayson," Calvin said as he entered the front room, pulling his suitcase behind him.

"Good morning, Calvin. You all set to go?"

"I think so."

"Well, give your mother a kiss, and we'll be off."

Calvin stepped over to his mom and kissed her on the cheek. She held him tight. "Be safe, Calvin."

He could see a tear in his mom's eye. "I'll be fine, Mom," Calvin said. He tried to sound brave.

As soon as the hug ended, Calvin stepped outside and cut across the lawn to where Grayson had parked a black jeep. Calvin threw his suitcase in the back and glanced at his mom, who was still watching from the porch. He climbed into the front seat, rolled down the window, and gave his mom one last wave as Grayson drove toward Perry's home.

Calvin had hardly begun to knock when Perry opened the front door to greet them. "Hey, guys," he said, dragging his baggage out the door. Perry looked back at his mom who was now standing in the doorway.

"Bye, Mom!" Perry called to her as he continued down the walkway toward Grayson's jeep.

"You be good, now," she called to him. "Mind your manners, Perry?"

Perry looked back and blew her a kiss. Then he turned to Calvin and called, "Shotgun!"

Calvin made a face as if he wished that he had called it first. But inside, he was glad to be sitting in the back seat. In just a couple of minutes Anna would be keeping him company.

When they pulled in front of Anna's home, they saw the drapes from the front window fall back into place. Anna had been watching for them from inside the den. The front door opened and Anna came out dragging her luggage behind her.

"I've got this," said Calvin as he jumped out of the vehicle and rushed toward Anna.

"Here, let me help you," Calvin said, reaching for the handle.

"Thanks." Anna smiled.

"I still can't believe you're coming with us," said Calvin.

"No kidding." Anna looked over her shoulder. "Never in a million years would I have thought my mom would let me come. Let's get out of here before she changes her mind." Anna's relationship with her parents was always unpredictable. She was adopted when she was only days old. She was an only child, which was probably why her parents were overly protective of her.

Grayson steered his jeep toward the mountains. The steep gravel road was a familiar one. Calvin had spent many hours on his mountain bike exploring the trails that branched off the main road.

"Okay." said Grayson. "This is it." He took a sharp right turn into a grassy meadow. They carved their way through the tall grass dotted with wild flowers. In the distance, Calvin saw a wall of thick trees.

"Where are we going?" asked Perry.

"You'll see," replied Grayson. "You'll like this."

Grayson pressed on the gas pedal and accelerated.

"What are you doing?" asked Perry, nervously.

Grayson sped up more. The trees were getting closer as the car rattled its way through the meadow. Calvin looked through the window behind them and saw the trail they had blazed in the grass disappear, hiding the evidence of their passage.

"Are you crazy?" said Perry as they barreled toward the trees. "We're going to crash!"

"We'll be fine. Trust me," said Grayson. He calmly looked at Perry, smiled, and continued onward.

"What are you talking about?" said Perry. "Slow down!"

"If you concentrate, you'll see it," said Grayson.

Calvin quietly assessed the situation. The jeep was approaching sixty miles an hour. The terrain was bumpy. It frequently jolted the four of them up out of their seats. Calvin tried to be open to Grayson's suggestion, but even he was beginning to get a little nervous. He looked at Anna, who also appeared tense.

Calvin turned to stare out the windshield at the trees ahead.

He wanted to see what Grayson was talking about.

Calvin's vision turned blurry, and when he refocused, he saw it. The opening in the trees became clear.

"Stop!" yelled Perry. "We're going to die!"

Calvin, his eyes still affixed on the open path ahead, put a hand on Perry's shoulder to comfort him. "Don't worry," he said in a calm voice.

The vehicle continued to accelerate. Perry brought his feet up and braced himself against the dashboard. He screamed as he closed his eyes and held his head back, pressing it firmly against the headrest. He tried to prepare himself for the huge collision with the impenetrable trees.

Calvin and Anna remained calm.

The passage through the bosky barrier was fast, but to Calvin it seemed like it happened in slow motion. Everything seemed to liquefy, distorting his vision a little. A flash of light took him out of his tranquil state and in an instant, he found himself seeing clearly, in present time.

"Am I alive?" asked Perry, hunched over in a ball on the front seat. He slowly opened his eyes and discovered that they were traveling on a smooth road. "What the heck was that?"

"We have just traveled through a portal. We are now in Cambria," answered Grayson.

"What was that all about?" said Perry. "Why did you speed through the portal so quickly?"

"You can access the portal at whatever speed you choose," said Grayson. "But the faster you go, the quicker the transformation happens. Believe me, you wouldn't have wanted to pass through any slower. It puts you in a weird state of dizziness."

It was beginning to make sense to him now. Calvin had wondered how Cambria had some of the same cars as Wolf Creek. Jeeps, trucks, small cars, big cars, motorcycles—vehicles of all kinds—were driven up and down the streets of Cambria. At the town square, cars were always parked along the sides of the streets. Now Calvin knew how the cars got there. They used portals.

The road came to a fork, and Grayson slowed the car to a stop. "That way will take you to the town square in Cambria.

There you will find Fountain Green, Yester Year, and all the shops you have recently discovered." Grayson pressed on the gas and steered the jeep to the left. "And this is the way to Fiddler Forest."

The road to Fiddler Forest was long, narrow, and twisty. They traveled for several miles on a byway that had various exits heading toward what were probably different villages in Cambria. The cutoff to Fiddler Forest was one that could easily be missed. There was one small, weathered wooden plank near the turn-off with two lines of faded words painted on it: Fiddler Forest and Yeti Mountain. The plank was nailed to a short post that was mostly concealed by overgrown, tangled bushes and trees. "This is our road," said Grayson. He turned sharply to the right, steering his jeep through a small, dark opening in the trees.

The jeep squeezed through the thick forest. The dirt road was barely wide enough for the vehicle. Tall grass covered the trail entirely except for two shallow ruts along which they traveled. Calvin felt the undergrowth scrape along the bottom of the jeep as they continued to crawl up the forsaken road.

"I don't like this," said Perry. "How can you even see where you're going through all of this tall grass?"

"I've traveled this road countless times. Yes, there are a few risky parts along the route. Some parts are better than others."

"What do you mean risky?" inquired Perry.

"Well, naturally there are all kinds of beasts in these woods. This route passes through the fringes of some dangerous parts."

"What would be the worst beast you could encounter in this forest?" asked Perry.

"We are sure to see snakes—large ones," said Grayson. "But if we're lucky, we won't encounter the colossal Komodo dragon."

Perry looked back at Calvin and Anna, eyes wide with horror.

"It'll be fine." Anna patted him on the shoulder.

Grayson was quiet for a moment and then shared a thought. "Come to think of it, the worst thing we would encounter in this forest would be a yeti."

Calvin was familiar with the yeti. He had read about them

in a book. One had nearly defeated a fire-breathing dragon.

"What exactly is a yeti?" asked Perry.

"Think of it as a bear. A very large, tall, hairy bear that walks on its hind legs as humans do," Grayson answered. "They typically live at higher elevations where the snow falls, but they have been spotted here in the forest, probably in search of food. The yeti is territorial and can be provoked easily. If you even look at them wrong, you're in for some trouble. The good news is the yeti is nocturnal. So we probably won't run into any."

Perry slowly turned around and shot Calvin and Anna another look that they recognized instantly. What were they doing?

Grayson brought the jeep to a stop and pushed a button, engaging the four-wheel drive. He proceeded to slowly advance the vehicle up the steep climb.

Calvin had an uncomfortable feeling in the pit of his stomach. He wasn't sure why, but he was immediately prompted to look behind him. He saw nothing out of the ordinary—just grass swooshing back into place after the jeep brushed through it. He turned and faced front.

"What is it?" asked Perry.

"I don't know," said Calvin. "I just felt like something was back there."

Perry turned to look back. About ten feet behind he saw the grass moving and thought perhaps it was a small animal scurrying about. But with the sun's glare, he wasn't sure.

Only seconds later, Calvin quickly turned back again. "I could have sworn something was back there," he whispered to Anna.

"Don't worry," Grayson said. "You'll be fine."

"How long has it been since you've traveled this road?" Anna asked.

"A few weeks," Grayson replied.

Grayson continued to climb up the steep grade. The wheels slipped a little but maintained their traction.

"It will be nice to get out of this nasty grass," said Calvin. "I just don't like it."

They continued the climb. It was getting steeper. Their pace slowed even more.

"Hang in there. We're almost to the top," said Grayson.

Calvin still felt uneasy as Grayson steered the jeep over what seemed like large roots that crawled along the ground. The terrain became more slick and the tires began to slip further.

Only a few feet from the top, a loud cracking sound came from underneath the jeep. The road leveled off and Grayson came to a stop.

"That didn't sound so good," Grayson said. "We better check it out."

Grayson climbed out of the jeep. Calvin, Perry, and Anna reluctantly did the same. Anna slid out the same door as Calvin—on the same side as Grayson. Perry walked around the back of the jeep to meet them.

The grass was still thick and reached just above their knees. As Grayson crawled under the jeep, Calvin saw him remove a thin stick—about fourteen inches long—from his inside coat pocket.

"Is anything wrong?" asked Calvin, walking toward Grayson.

"Looks like there's a branch stuck in the wheel. It's in there pretty tight." Grayson pulled hard on the branch to try and dislodge it. It shifted. Barely. "Let me work at it for a minute. I think I can get it out."

"C-C-Calvin! Help!" Perry screamed.

Calvin turned around. Just beyond the jeep Perry was on the ground scuffling with something in the tall grass. Calvin couldn't tell what it was, but immediately ran toward him. As he approached, he saw a large snake, about six inches wide at the thickest part, wrapped around Perry's leg.

Pushing with his hands, Perry tried to slide his leg free from the coiled serpent. It would not budge. The snake's large, square head rose above Perry. Its mouth was open. Its fangs were long and sharp.

Without hesitation, Calvin instinctively threw his hands out toward the towering snake. *Sedativo!* He desperately yelled the word in his mind.

He felt a jolt of energy shoot from his palms and blitz the serpent. The snake's head swung from side to side, then stopped and held still, before falling unconscious to the ground. The tight hold around Perry's leg softened as the snake's body went limp.

Calvin fell to the ground and rolled to his back. The world above him was spinning, making him feel dizzy. It felt like the sky was spinning one way, but the ground he was firmly against was spinning the opposite way. He was breathing hard. Sweat beaded up on his forehead. He lay on the grassy bed, exhausted.

Anna ran to his side. "Calvin! Are you okay? Can you hear me? Calvin?"

The world slowly stopped moving, and he pushed himself up to a sitting position.

"Are you okay?" Anna tried again.

"Yeah. Just give me a minute."

When he regained his strength, Anna helped him to his feet. They walked over to Perry to help him free his leg from the grips of the sleeping snake. The trio looked back at Grayson, who was running over to help. He looked perplexed.

Calvin helped Perry to his feet and brushed him off.

"Are you okay?" asked Calvin.

"I think so. It scared me more than it hurt. Did you see that . . . that . . . that head staring at me? Now that bite would have hurt."

"Well done, Calvin," Grayson said, wearing a proud smile. "I had a hunch. Well done."

The four of them climbed back into the jeep and continued making their way through Fiddler Forest. Grayson was particularly quiet. It was apparent that he was in deep thought—probably contemplating what had happened a few miles back. "We'll stop in a few minutes for some lunch," Grayson suggested, pointing to a portion of the trail up ahead where it seemed to widen even more. "There is a nice spot up here by a spring. It's a beautiful setting."

"Beautiful?" Perry said. "In this forest? I'm not sure I believe you."

The deeper into the mountains they traveled, the denser the forest became with trees. The trickling water from the spring ahead turned the trail slippery with mud, but it was nothing the jeep couldn't handle.

Grayson turned at a fork in the road and followed it back a couple of turns. "Now, I have to warn you . . . I haven't been to this exact clearing for a number of years. It used to be a nice spot for a picnic."

Grayson maneuvered the vehicle around one last bend. "Ah . . . here we are." The four of them climbed out.

The clearing was hardly clear. The thick, overgrown trees and shrubs crowded the place that was once spacious. On one side of the road, a large bench-like boulder had tall weeds crawling up its edges. Calvin jumped on top of it.

"Yes," said Grayson, walking over to Calvin. "This brings back memories. We used to come up here all the time. You wouldn't think it by the looks of it, but that rock you're standing on is one of the most comfortable chairs you'll ever sit on. And it faces one of the prettiest canyons in these mountains."

Calvin sat down. As soon as his bottom and back joggled into the right position, he agreed with Grayson that it was very relaxing.

It was a tight squeeze, but Perry sat down next to Calvin and wriggled to find the perfect spot. "Wow!" said Perry. "This *is* comfortable."

The two sat for a minute looking out toward the canyon. The web of entangled plants and trees blocked most of the view, but Calvin could imagine that it was a beautiful vista at one point in time. The water from the spring trickled down the hill behind them, adding a nice, soothing tone to the ambiance.

"Grayson?" asked Anna. "It seems like this setting is special to you. Why did you come up here so often?"

"This place was perfect for watching the sunset. In the summertime, the sun would go down right over there." Grayson pointed over at a ridge in the distance. "That bench you guys are sitting on was the coveted spot for couples. Sunsets were magically romantic. I had my first kiss right there where you're sitting."

Alarmed, and feeling embarrassed, Calvin and Perry sat up quickly and looked at each other with disgusted faces. They scooted their bodies off the rock, away from each other.

Anna laughed.

"It's not the same anymore," said Grayson. "I'm sure you would have appreciated it, though."

It was the first time Calvin remembered hearing Grayson talk of romance, but he had never heard him speak of a wife or kids. "Grayson?" asked Calvin. "Do you have a family?"

Grayson hesitated and then stammered a reply. "Wh-what do you mean?"

"Were you ever married?" Calvin asked. "Do you have kids?"

"No . . . I don't have any kids," answered Grayson.

"A wife?" continued Calvin.

"No. No wife." Grayson swallowed and then his eyes rolled upward, staring off into the distance. It was apparent that Grayson was digging up old memories in his mind.

"Who was it then?" probed Calvin.

After a long pause, Grayson replied, "Alyssa Moon."

Calvin remained quiet, waiting to see if Grayson would continue.

"We were best friends . . . we did everything together," he recalled. "She was beautiful. Bright. Brave. We had a date set to be married. But just days before our wedding, she disappeared."

Confused, Calvin asked, "Where did she go?"

"Not sure. My best guess is a Zarkon got her."

Calvin was unsure how to console Grayson. He felt like he needed to say something, but couldn't think. This was way too grown-up for him. He was only thirteen years old.

He was relieved when Grayson continued: "My heart was broken. I invested so much in that relationship, and to have it all taken away like that . . . just killed me. I decided that I could never love again. It hurt too much."

"I'm sorry," Calvin said.

"Thanks, Calvin. I still dream about the day I'll see her again. For some reason, I keep holding onto a thin thread of hope that she's out there . . . somewhere."

Perry wiped his eyes, trying to conceal his tears, but a few continual sniffles gave him away. Calvin and Anna turned to him.

"What?" Perry asked.

"Are you okay?" said Anna.

"Yeah, my allergies are getting to me, that's all."

"That's funny. I don't remember you having allergies," said Anna.

Perry rolled his eyes at Anna and wandered away.

Calvin walked to the other side of the road where wild flowers were being swallowed up by weeds. Large spider webs spanned from branch to branch.

"Do you hear that?" Calvin called back to the others.

"Hear what?" replied Perry.

"Something's up there. I hear a whining sound."

"The forest is full of insects," Perry said. "Maybe it's a cricket?"

"No, not a cricket. It's like a humming sound."

Calvin looked up the trail and saw a dark cloud hovering in the air, quickly moving toward them.

"There," Calvin shouted, pointing ahead. "It's coming from that!"

Long-legged, bloodthirsty insects dive-bombed toward their exposed skin. Perry waved his arms, swatting the mosquitoes away from him. It made little difference.

"They're huge!" cried Perry, trying to cover his face with his jacket. He swatted one away that had a body as large as his thumb.

Anna pulled her hoodie over her head and screamed.

Calvin felt a painful sting on the top of his hand and immediately clapped the gigantic insect with his other. It made a sticky mess. Blood and slime oozed from between his hands. It was that mosquito's last meal.

"*Incendario!*" Calvin heard a cry. The air immediately flashed bright and hot. Calvin shielded his face from the heat with his arm and looked to the source of the light. A huge fireball was suspended above him. Brilliant white sparks flashed each time the fire consumed a mosquito. The flickering was continual as millions of mosquitoes disintegrated in the searing flame. Heaps of mosquitoes fell to the ground from exposure to the blazing heat.

Calvin noticed a stream of fire connected to the infernal ball. He traced the stream to the tip of a stick that Grayson held in his hand. The flashing of dying mosquitoes slowly whittled to a halt. Grayson twirled his wand and muttered, "*Minimo.*" The size of the fireball decreased until it diminished into Grayson's wand.

"I didn't know you could cast spells!" Calvin was excited. "In all the stories you've told, I've never heard you talk about it."

"Well, I guess that makes two of us," replied Grayson, raising a single eyebrow at Calvin. "What I find curious, Calvin, is that you cast a spell without speaking a word. There aren't too many left that possess such a gift."

Calvin knew he had some explaining to do.

"I'm curious. How long have you been developing your wizardry skills?" marveled Grayson.

"Since last night," replied Calvin.

Grayson laughed. "No, seriously," he said. "How long?"

"Last night at Yester Year I was reading in a book about beginning spells. It had directions for an illumination spell—*Lucero.* I tried it . . . and it worked. So, I tried another one, and that one worked too. It kind of wore me out, though."

"Yes, I remember trying those same spells hoping that somehow I would have that gift," said Grayson. "After countless attempts, I resorted to a wand. A first-timer like yourself, Calvin . . . what you can do already. It's remarkable."

"What about Anna?" asked Perry. "Without a wand, she at least made a flicker. What does that say about her?"

"Even a flicker proves tremendous talent," said Grayson, turning to Anna. "You obviously have deep roots in the world of magic. I presume you'll have a place in this work too. We know that a younger generation will be instrumental in this battle. It doesn't necessarily say it will be one person, or two. It could be several."

Calvin stared at the ground. He contemplated whether or not he should tell Grayson about the chest. He knew he was going to—at some point—and figured this would be as good a time as any. After going back and forth a few times in his mind, he took a deep breath. "Grayson?"

"Yes?"

"I need to tell you something."

"What is it?" asked Grayson.

"I discovered a few things the other day while exploring the woods near my home. Have you ever heard of Peril Cove, Shadow Gorge, or Labyrinth?"

Calvin could tell that he immediately had Grayson's full attention. Grayson's eyes were intently focused on Calvin. With a look of utter surprise, he asked, "Calvin . . . where did you hear about those places?"

"A chest was left for me in front of The Crossing the other day. It had a note on it that was addressed to me. I opened the chest and inside was an old map. Those were the names of the islands off the coast of Cambria."

"I have heard Stone speak of such a map. He had one stolen from his home," said Grayson. "Do you have the map with you?"

Calvin softly patted his coat over his left breast. "I have it right here."

"Keep it safe," urged Grayson. "And I wouldn't tell anyone about it."

Calvin unzipped his coat and reached in the neck of his shirt. "Also inside the chest was this key." Calvin pulled out the antiqued key and showed it to Grayson. "I'm not sure what this key goes to . . . other than there is a sketching of the same key on the map at Peril Cove."

Grayson looked astonished.

"There's one more thing," admitted Calvin. "Probably the most important of them all." He opened his coat and held up a small leather pouch that was securely fastened to his waist. "Inside this pouch is a magical orb."

Grayson's eyes grew wider. "Do you realize, Calvin, that there are only three of those in existence?"

"Yes," affirmed Calvin. "And if all three of them get into the wrong hands, we're doomed."

Grayson nodded. "Keep those items safe, Calvin. Do not let them out of your possession."

11 • Wizards & Wizlums

The road began to improve drastically. The lane widened and the trees and shrubbery clung to its edges.

"Whoa! Do you see that?" Perry pointed up ahead as a large animal crossed their path and disappeared into the trees. "That elk was huge!"

Calvin's heart skipped a beat as he ducked behind the seat. Anna also cowered away.

"Yes, Perry," said Grayson, seeming a bit frazzled. He checked his rearview mirror and looked over his shoulder nervously. "The forest is full of wildlife, among other things. Let's feel lucky that it was only an elk this time." He continued checking back over his shoulder as if he was afraid something or someone was following.

An elk? Calvin wondered. *Is that what they saw?* An elk was nothing compared to the creature he had seen. Calvin looked at Anna. Anna was crouched down to the floor with a similar horrified look.

Perry looked back at Calvin and Anna to see if they appreciated seeing the animal as much as he did.

"What's wrong with you two?" Perry asked. "You look terrified!"

Calvin tried to catch his breath. Amid her heavy breathing, Anna sat up again in her seat.

"You guys didn't see it, did you?" inquired Perry. "You saw something different."

Calvin remained quiet but gave a nod.

"What are you talking about?" asked Grayson.

"Calvin sees things," said Perry, his voice agitated. "So does Anna. They always see things that I don't. The other day we were out in the woods and I saw a big buck pass by. Calvin and Anna saw the animal too, but they saw it as a unicorn."

"It's not always like that," Calvin responded.

"It happens more than you think," Perry said.

"The reason you didn't see the unicorn," said Grayson, "is because you have not yet tapped into your magical potential. Until you awaken your magical abilities, you may not see things as they surely are. You are fortunate you didn't see the creature that we saw back there. It was enough to make you sick. Luckily it was scrambling away from us. If we were traveling in the dark, we surely would have been in trouble."

"How do I go about 'awakening my magical abilities'? By getting a wand?" Perry asked.

"Yes. There's a wand shop back at the town square called The Wanderer. They sell decent ones," said Grayson. "Or . . . I know of some gnomes who have a history of making quality wands. I still have my first wand, which might work well for you. I brought it with me, anticipating that one of you might have use for it."

"Cool," replied Perry.

"Who taught you how to do magic?" asked Calvin.

"I had a mentor," said Grayson. "He taught me everything I know. But I am still learning the art of wizardry. I'm not sure anyone can ever master it. But he who is most prepared will certainly have the advantage. I intend to teach you a few things on this trip. Not everything comes down to using spells, you know. You must learn to develop your skills in other areas, like archery and swordsmanship.

"I knew a man once who was an excellent wizard. He knew more spells than you could ever imagine. However, one day he was caught off guard, without his wand. He was useless. He tried with all his might to defend himself with the sword, but failed.

"Another acquaintance of mine had the makings of an excellent wizard, but he did not build up enough tolerance to withstand the energy needed to perform some of the more complex spells. He conjured a spell and fired it at his attacker. It was a direct hit. Did a lot of damage. But it knocked him to the ground as well, and left him in a daze. When you do magic, it uses the energy in your body to connect with the elements of the earth. The more convoluted the spell, the more it takes it out of you. You must build up a tolerance."

It was quiet for a moment, except for the sound of four

tires milling over sticks and stones.

"Tell me, Calvin. Have you often had feelings that something was about to happen . . . and it did?"

"What do you mean?" asked Calvin.

"Take today, for example. You felt like something was behind you in the grass, and moments later, a snake found Perry's leg. Or you felt you heard something when the rest of us heard nothing. And of course, a minute later we were swarmed by monstrous mosquitoes."

Calvin thought about it for a second. Until then, he hadn't realized that it happened as routinely as it did. In fact, it happened all the time.

"I guess it does happen to me a lot," admitted Calvin.

"I've never known anyone as intuitive as you seem to be at such a young age. Your father had a tremendous gift of intuition also. You see, everyone can receive impressions. Some are more in tune with them than others—they recognize them more readily. Intuition comes in many forms—dreams, thoughts, feelings—you must learn to trust those premonitions, and act upon them."

It was quiet again, but only for a moment. Calvin wanted to take advantage of the time he had with Grayson.

"Grayson, by chance . . . did my father ride a dragon?"

"Yes, he did. How did you know?"

"I had a dream where I saw my father mounting what seemed to be a dragon. It appeared to have the mark of a crescent moon on its left hind leg."

"You're exactly right, Calvin," said Grayson. "Your father's dragon was named Amalga. They made a great team."

"Where is Amalga now?" asked Calvin.

"When a rider has fallen, the dragon returns to the Cliffs of Tarnin. There it remains on the cliffs with the other dragons until a new rider comes and invites it to be his companion. Once the rider has selected the dragon, and the dragon accepts the call, an immediate, unbreakable bond is created. The dragon will not fly for anyone else. The bond is only severed when the rider has fallen."

"How do you get yourself a dragon?" asked Perry.

"Dragons are presented only to the very gifted," Grayson said. "They are for wizlums."

"Wizlums?" asked Perry. If Perry hadn't asked, Calvin would have. It was a word they had never heard before.

"In the world of magic, there are two types of magicians: wizards and wizlums. Wizards can learn the art of magic through earnest practice and the aid of a wand. With the right amount of will power and dedication, one can learn to become a wizard. One doesn't become a wizard until he acquires a wand and performs his first spell. Many of Galigore's followers are wizards. They have formed a secret Society—made up of Zarkon—that seems to be growing in numbers, day by day.

"The wizlum . . . now that's a special kind. Wizlums have a sixth sense. They have keen intuition. They are predisposed to magic. The power of their mind is impeccable. Wizlums can perform magic without a wand. And the skilled wizlum . . . " Grayson turned to Calvin. "The skilled wizlum can perform wizardry without speaking. But these are few and far between."

"How do you become a wizlum?" said Anna.

"Wizlums are linked through generations. One can only be a wizlum if his mother and father are both wizlums. But not all offspring of wizlum parents become wizlums. Only those children endowed with the innate gifts of enchantment can become wizlums."

"Hmm . . . ," said Perry. "Not sure I follow you. Can you dumb it down a little?"

"Wait a second," said Calvin, "I think I got it. Since I am a wizlum, my parents are wizlums. And if my mom is a wizlum, that means her parents are wizlums. You and her are brother and sister, but you are not a wizlum."

"That's what I'm talking about," said Perry. "I get it now."

"That's exactly right, Calvin. I just wasn't born with it. But that's the way it goes."

"This is all fine and dandy," said Perry, "but can you get us back to the dragon part . . . please?" said Perry.

Calvin reached into his pocket and removed a candy bar. He brought a stash with him for times like this. "Here." He hit the bar against Perry's shoulder.

"Thanks," said Perry. "You read my mind." He immediately tore open the wrapper.

"Because of the wizlum's acute mind," Grayson looked at Perry, "he is able to decipher the thoughts of dragons, allowing him to communicate with the beasts. Only wizlums are given the opportunity to form a connection with a dragon. Wizards are unable to communicate with them well enough to develop a strong bond of loyalty. Wizlums, on the other hand, can learn to speak to dragons in their minds as clearly as we are communicating right now. To be given the opportunity to receive a dragon, the wizlum must travel, by foot, to the Cliffs of Tarnin and speak with the dragon keeper. It takes only a couple of days to get there."

"That's it?" Perry said.

"It's harder than it sounds," said Grayson. "The keeper assesses your abilities, as the hopeful rider. He may test your strength—although the journey to the cliffs will inevitably do that. Or he may test your wits. If you pass his appraisal, he will present a few dragons to you."

"How do you know which dragon is right for you?" asked Calvin.

"You will know, Calvin. You will know."

* * * *

Traveling to Stone's cottage took most of the day. Calvin felt a little discouraged that another full day would be required to get back to Wolf Creek, which left him just two days of training with Grayson. He didn't express his disappointment, though. He was still very grateful and excited for the opportunity.

The jeep finally emerged from the thick brush. There were only a few cottages in view, spread far and wide throughout the green, rolling hills. Stone's was a quaint, two-story home with three chimneys jutting from the roof. The exterior was made of various shades of brown stone. The yard was quite shaggy with overgrown rose bushes running the length of the house. An occasional board was missing from the weathered picket fence. The white paint was blistered and peeling. The lawn was brown with prickly, broadleaf weeds scattered about trying to overtake it.

Grayson pulled in front of the house. "Doesn't look too promising." he said, pointing to the apparently vacant cottage.

"My grandpa said he thought Stone was out on Bordarian work."

"That's true," said Grayson. "Last night I received confirmation of that from the castle. Whatever he is doing has to do with the attacks from a few nights ago."

"Attacks?" said Perry. "What attacks?"

"A Bordarian spotted Zarkon in your world."

"In Wolf Creek?" Perry said.

Grayson nodded. "We have several Bordarians living in Wolf Creek. You already know Miss Jasmine. It appears that Galigore has stooped so low as to exercise his power in other worlds—worlds where the masses know nothing about magic or our conflict of evil. In your land, a Bordarian was found dead inside of his burning home."

Perry gave an audible gulp.

"I don't want to scare you," said Grayson. "Sadly, events like this happen routinely. It's just another reminder that we are at war."

Perry nodded.

"Come on. Let's go."

Grayson gave a few taps on the door and waited. Calvin assumed that Grayson had knocked to show a little courtesy just in case—by some chance—Stone happened to be there. Reaching for the knob, Grayson tried to turn it. It was locked. He waved his wand over the handle and muttered an incantation. The door handle clicked and chains unraveled on the inside. In a few seconds, the clanking ended. "Very well," said Grayson. "Follow me."

Grayson pushed the heavy, wooden door open. The cottage was dark and cold. The curtains were drawn. The front room, just beyond the entry, was typical. A sofa and armchair faced the empty stone fireplace. Stone had pictures of his ancestry hanging on the walls. A nearby bookcase was overflowing with books. Calvin scanned the titles. Some were about spell casting and wizardry, others about defense, and a few more about potions.

An end table separated the armchair and sofa. On top of the table was a thick, well-used candle that had waxy, bumpy drizzles running down its sides. The base of the candlestick had collected a thick ring of wax near the bottom. Next to the candle was a small stack of blank paper and a collection of pens kept in a mug.

Calvin and Anna sat together on the sofa. Perry claimed the armchair. Grayson sat on the fireplace hearth. He pulled a sheet of newsprint from a stack of outdated issues of *Cambrian Affairs*, crumpled it up, and placed it in the fireplace. He leaned thin pieces of kindling against the wad of paper. Gradually, he added thicker pieces of wood to the teepee-shaped kindling.

"Come over here, Calvin," Grayson said. "I want you to try something."

Calvin knelt next to Grayson and leaned his elbows on the hearth.

"I want you to wave your hands over the wood and then flick your fingers toward the sticks. As you flick, say the word *Fuegero*."

Calvin took a deep breath and then raised his hands over the wood. He closed his eyes and concentrated. When his mind was focused, he opened his eyes, flicked his fingers toward the sticks, and whispered, "*Fuegero*."

A small flame shot from his fingers and immediately ignited the paper.

"Nicely done," said Grayson.

Calvin returned to his spot next to Anna on the sofa. As he sat, Anna rose to her feet. She knelt next to the end table and closed her eyes. Calvin, Perry, and Grayson quietly watched. Seconds later, she opened her eyes again, flicked her fingers, and softly spoke. "*Fuegero*." A small flame shot from her fingertips and ignited the candlewick. She looked back at the others. Calvin and Grayson smiled. Perry sat with his arms folded, expressionless.

Calvin leaned back, sinking deep into the sofa. He held the chain around his neck with each hand—the key hanging in the middle. He flung the chain forward in a circular motion and then pulled the chain tight. The key made several full revolutions around the chain and then dangled in front of him as it slowed to a stop. He repeated the movement, watching the key whip around the chain and then, once again, slowing to a dangle.

"If these are the same relics Stone once had, why would someone steal them only to give them to me?" asked Calvin.

"We all realized many years ago, even when you were much younger, that you had special gifts, Calvin. And I think you proved us right today in the forest. You're catching on much faster than anyone would have guessed. Wizlums are very uncommon these days. Perhaps you are part of the chosen generation that has been prophesied to take down Galigore. The orb did not respond to Stone. He felt nothing when he touched it."

"Because he is not a wizlum?" asked Calvin.

"That's correct. The orb responded to you—another indication that you are a key player in dethroning Galigore. Stone is not a wizlum. He ultimately knew that he would not be the one appointed to use its powers. Rather, he planned on keeping it for the one who could use it. He knew that in the wrong hands, the orb could be used to empower evil. So he tried to keep it safe. Obviously, someone else had their eye on the orb and discovered its hiding place. Stone has no idea who the thief was. But it's assuring to know that if these are the same relics that Stone once discovered, they are back in honest hands."

12 · Training

Calvin and Perry, who had spent the night in the front room, awoke to the smell of breakfast. The aroma wafted all the way upstairs into the spare bedroom where Anna stayed. At the table, each plate had a stack of three enormous pancakes with melted butter and warm syrup smothered between the layers. A stack of six more sat on a fourth plate in the middle of the table. A tall glass of fresh milk was next to each setting.

"Good morning," Grayson greeted them as they entered the dining room.

"Good morning."

"Everything is set. Shall we?" Grayson said, motioning them to take a seat at the table.

"Now before we get started with this meal, I have a gift for you, Perry." Grayson grabbed a narrow box from a nearby table and handed it to Perry. "Go ahead and open it."

Perry peeled off the wrappings and lifted the lid. "Seriously?" Perry asked excitedly.

Grayson nodded with a smile. "Use it well."

Perry reached in carefully and pulled out a round, straight stick. He held it in his hand carefully while twisting it, admiring its fine detail. The body of the wand was sanded smooth and tapered toward the tip. The bottom end was a bit thicker and had a carving of a coiled snake wrapped around the handle.

"Give it a try," encouraged Grayson. "Point the wand toward the chandelier and say *Incendario*."

Perry grasped the wand and concentrated. He wondered for a second if he could make it work, but then quickly changed his attitude. Confidence radiated from his face and eyes. With a slight flick of his wrist, Perry pointed his wand at the unlit chandelier hanging from the ceiling and said, "*Incendario*."

Nothing happened. "*Incendario*!" Still nothing.

"Focus," encouraged Grayson. "Concentrate."

Perry closed his eyes and thought about what it was he was

trying to accomplish. He tried to eliminate all other thoughts. Calmly, slowly, and with meaning, he whispered, "*Incendario.*" Perry eagerly opened his eyes to see the effects of his spell. But nothing had happened.

"Don't be discouraged," said Grayson. "It may take some time, but you'll get it. Let's try later."

"Good idea," said Perry. "Sitting at the table with a bunch of food in front of me probably isn't the ideal setting for becoming a wizard. It's kind of a distraction, really."

* * * *

When breakfast was finished, Grayson introduced the trio to a few spells. Calvin, Perry, and Anna stood side by side, facing him in the open area between the dining area and front room.

"Now, everything I teach you," said Grayson, "can be developed and perfected over time so that one day you might be able to stand up against Galigore and his army. We'll start with a defensive spell," suggested Grayson. "The key to this spell's effectiveness is to be in tune with your instincts. You may not always see an attack coming, but you can learn to feel when one is coming. Trust your feelings and act upon them."

Grayson took out his wand and held it ready, in front of his body. His stance was open, one foot slightly more forward than the other. His knees were bent just a little, his back straight, and head held tall. "There are various stances in wizardry. . . . This is mine. From here I can attack in an instant, and I am ready to defend. Now, find a comfortable stance."

Calvin, Perry, and Anna copied Grayson's stance, then made minor adjustments that were more comfortable and natural for them. Calvin stood in an athletic stance, ready with his hands out, as if he were guarding someone on the basketball court. Perry held his wand out in front of his body with his right hand. His left hand was raised with his palm out. His legs were spread about shoulder-width apart. Most of his weight was on his right leg. His left heel was raised with his toe digging into the floor.

"Not bad," affirmed Grayson, looking at Perry. "Not great, either. It will become more natural with practice. You need to work on your weight distribution, Perry." Calvin looked over at

Perry and smiled.

Grayson looked at Anna's stance. "That looks good, Anna," Grayson said. "Now, the spell we will use first is a basic one that will repel many attacks thrown your way, including fire, electricity, wind, water, or hurled objects. The incantation used is *Repallo*. I will throw something your way, Calvin, and I want you to use *Repallo* to defend it."

Calvin nodded. He was focused and ready. He watched intently as Grayson swirled his wand and muttered, "*Culaybra.*" From the tip of Grayson's wand, a thick cloud of mist was emitted. Two glowing eyes slowly emerged out of the cloud and approached Calvin. A colossal snake, with a broad head and stout body, rose from its coils. Its head was suspended about waist high. The viper's sharp, curled fangs protruded downward out the sides of its mouth. Without warning, the snake hissed, opened its mouth and lunged forward.

"*Repallo!*" Calvin yelled, thrusting his hands in the direction of the serpent. Calvin felt the invisible force leave his hands and shoot forward toward the snake. The snake fell on its side, paralyzed.

"Good work, Calvin," complimented Grayson. He waved his wand at the fallen snake. "*Minimo.*" The snake rose from the ground, swirled in the air, and dissipated.

"Perry? Are you ready to give it a try?" asked Grayson.

Perry looked a bit uneasy but nodded in agreement. He hadn't cast a spell yet and thought that this exercise might be a little too intense for him. He stood with his wand ready. He watched closely as Grayson raised his wand and drew a circle in the air. He then flicked his wand toward him. "*Escorpio!*"

From the cloud of mist pouring out of Grayson's wand, Perry saw a huge body take shape on the floor in front of him. He tried to remain calm, but he started to breathe hard. A set of clamping pincers, about a foot in length, extended toward Perry. Perry's eyes were fixed on the scorpion's enormous stinger. His heart was pounding in his chest. Just as the tail swung around and whipped toward him, Perry pointed his wand at the beast and bravely yelled, "*Repallo!*" A wave of energy shot out of Perry's wand and struck the scorpion on top of its head. It halted immediately and fell over onto its side. Perry also fell to the floor.

"You did it!" Grayson said. With a look of relief, Perry forced a smile and tried to slow his breathing. Feeling exhausted, he needed a break. Sweat formed on his brow. The room was spinning as he lay on the floor.

"*Minimo*," said Grayson. The scorpion turned to smoke and disappeared.

"Are you okay, Perry?" asked Grayson.

"I'll be fine. Just give me a minute. I . . . I just feel exhausted . . . weak," said Perry.

"Yes. You have reached your threshold," replied Grayson. "Now listen carefully: with every spell you conjure, energy from the earth and energy from your body are required. The more intricate the magic, the more energy is sucked from your body. The fatigue will dissipate momentarily; then your body will regain its strength. I'm guessing, Perry, because of the level of that charm, you'll be back on your feet in just a few minutes. Calvin, your threshold is higher. Everyone's tolerance is different. With practice, you will each be able to extend your tolerance. Every wizard and wizlum must know where that line is so he can preserve his energy. That's why it's imperative that you develop your skills in other areas."

Perry sat up and took a few deep breaths. "That was pretty intense."

"Why couldn't Perry do a simple *Incendario* spell, but was able to do *Repallo*?" asked Anna.

"Sometimes wizards work their best magic when they are in a life-or-death situation. That is when you must rely on instinct. With that scorpion coming toward Perry, he was focused on one thing and one thing only. Survival. His mind was present. He was in the moment. Focused."

"What if he hadn't been successful?" asked Calvin. "Would the scorpion have stung him?"

"I conjured up a dummy scorpion without venom," explained Grayson. "His stinger looked real, but it was like rubber. Perry would have felt a violent thump on his chest, but no sting."

Perry pushed himself to his feet.

"Good," said Grayson. "You're feeling better already. With your first spell under your belt, you are now officially a wizard."

Perry looked over at Calvin and Anna, uncertain. Calvin and Anna grinned and nodded encouragingly.

"Let's try another one," suggested Grayson. "This next one is a most basic, but effective charm. You will use this under a similar attack. Its purpose is to shield you for a brief moment from anything coming your way. But once the object strikes the shield, the spell becomes disarmed and you must cast the spell again. *Escudo* is the word to remember. Anna . . . would you like to give it a go?"

Anna readied herself and gave Grayson a nod. Grayson held his wand up in front of him and said, "*Relampago!*"

A bright, white ball of electricity sizzled as it floated in the air, still connected to the tip of Grayson's wand. Grayson gave a quick flick in Anna's direction and a bolt of lightning shot toward her.

"*Escudo!*" Anna shouted. A blue shield formed immediately around her body. Anna, still holding her hands out, saw the bolt of lightning launch toward her. The collision made a tremendous flash of light, but then dissipated, and the shield disappeared. Grayson, with the ball of electricity still streaming from his wand, flicked another jolt in Anna's direction.

"*Escudo!*" cried Anna, and again a blue shield formed around her body just before the bolt crashed into her. Anna fell to her back out of breath.

"Good. Very good! Take a break, Anna. Now . . . Calvin you try." Grayson gave a flick in Calvin's direction. Caught a bit off guard, Calvin quickly raised his arms and thrust his hands forward saying, "*Escudo!*" A blue shield formed around his body and repelled the streaking bolt.

"Excellent! Let's keep going!" cried Grayson. "Get ready now, Calvin. Here comes another one!" Grayson extinguished the lightning ball and twirled his wand in a circle. "*Demonio!*"

A skeletal figure, clothed in rags, materialized in front of Calvin. The creature had frail, white, bony fingers. Its nails were long and pointed, its skin translucent. The monster's face was hidden in the shadows, but two glowing eyes peered from within the darkness. The evil fiend raised its hand and pointed a finger at Calvin.

"Say it, Calvin! *Escudo*, Calvin!" commanded Grayson. The worry on Grayson's face was evident.

A stream of fire shot out of the monster's finger toward Calvin. As the fire grew closer, it became larger and more intense.

Anna quickly brought her hand to her mouth and gasped.

"*Reflecto!*" Calvin shouted throwing his hands up at the fire streaking his way. In an instant, the fire bounced back and shot toward the attacker. A bright flash engulfed the frail body. The fiend vanished and the room became calm.

Grayson looked over at Calvin, who was on the ground wincing in pain. Breathing hard, Calvin felt his heart pounding in his chest. The pain was paralyzing but lasted only a few seconds. Calvin sat up. Still catching his breath, he had his fingers interlocked, his elbows around his knees.

"Calvin!" Grayson said incredulously. "Where did you learn that spell?"

"I . . . I don't know. I intended to use *Escudo* . . . but at the last second, *Reflecto* entered my mind," Calvin explained, still breathing hard. "I had no idea what it meant, but I used it."

"That is the difference between a good wizard or wizlum and a great one," said Grayson. "He who can listen to his feelings, and trust them, will be far better off than the one who merely goes by the book, so to speak. Calvin," Grayson said with a proud, fatherly smile, "you're beginning to get a sense for where your threshold is. With practice you'll be able to tolerate more."

Grayson stretched a hand toward Calvin and pulled him to his feet.

"What was that thing?" Perry asked.

"That gives you an idea of what Galigore and his people look like," said Grayson.

"It didn't look human, though," said Perry.

"No, it didn't," Grayson said. "Not exactly. But it is human. Believe it or not, I have known people who have looked perfectly fine—like you and me. But after Galigore pulled them away from that which was good and enticed them to despair, their bodies began to change. The twinkle in their eyes became dim. Their bodies became frail. Their skin lost its color and turned pale. Their eyes yellowed. So did their teeth and fingernails. You could see life being sucked out of them. Happiness left them. And before they knew it, they were stuck. I'd imagine when someone has slipped so far into corruption, it may be easier for him to admit defeat and give up all hope and desire than it would be to take control of his life again."

"What does Galigore really want?" said Calvin.

"Ultimate power. He wants to rule the world. Ever since feeling the power of the orb, his eyes have been fixed on finding all three of them. If one orb almost makes you feel invincible, imagine how two, or even three, orbs would make you feel. Galigore knows that the key to infinite power and immortality resides in a collection of three powerful orbs. And for those orbs he has been searching far and wide. Naturally, he can cover more territory if he has more people on his side to scavenge the land. He makes promises to his followers—promises of wealth and fame. He gets violent when something gets in his way of finding a clue that might lead him closer to an orb. He is unpredictable and his temper is short. He has killed countless Bordarians, including your father."

As Calvin listened to Grayson's words, his expression turned serious. He felt an even stronger urge to destroy Galigore.

"Come on now." Grayson said, breaking the silence. "Rest up a bit. Get your strength back. Then I'll show you a thing or two about how wizards do yard work." Grayson smiled. "It might even help make doing your chores at home more tolerable."

13 • An Unexpected Death

Standing amid the shaggy landscape, Grayson turned to Perry and said, "Wave your wand at the front lawn and say the word *Restoro*."

Perry held his wand up. "*Restoro.*" The messy, overgrown edge of the lawn running along the walkway dwindled into a perfectly straight line. Perry smiled. He was obviously proud. The weeds, however, grew and spread rapidly throughout the flower beds. The patchy, brown lawn filled in, and within seconds it transformed into a stiff, prickly brown carpet of dead grass. Perry's smile quickly faded into despair.

Calvin and Anna tried to muffle their laughter. Perry gave them a scowl.

"Not exactly how it should have gone," said Grayson. "But you'll get it. Now you try," Grayson urged Calvin.

"What should I say?"

"Follow your instincts. Why don't you clean up the flower beds," suggested Grayson.

Calvin looked at the weed-filled beds. The bushes and flowers were hardly visible through the tall, deep-rooted, unwanted plants. Calvin concentrated, focusing on eliminating the ugly and making the bushes and flowers come to life. Holding out his hands and pointing them toward the bed, Calvin suddenly had a word come into his mind. *Segregario*, he thought. Instantly the weeds melted away. The tall, prickly vines withered, while the dry-leaved bushes turned a healthy green. Droopy flowers sprung skyward filling the empty spaces with colorful blossoms. The dried leaves covering the soil vanished and the dirt became rich and black.

"You've got a gift, my boy," Grayson remarked. "Tell me . . . was it *Vibrante* you used?"

"*Segregario*," said Calvin.

"Oh yeah . . . that's what I thought," cracked Perry. "That's what I would have used."

"Anna?" said Grayson. "What can you do about this lawn?"

Anna concentrated and flicked her fingers toward the grass. "*Restoro*." Instantly, the dead grass began to transform into bright green blades. The once-stiff lawn now fluttered in the gentle breeze.

"Show-off," Perry said as he watched Anna restore the mess he had made just minutes before.

The rest of the work went quickly. The trees were trimmed, walkways were swept, missing shingles from the roof were replaced, the shutters were straightened, and the rain gutters were cleared. Calvin marveled at his discovery of magic, thinking how life would be different back home.

When the house and yard looked immaculate, Grayson, Calvin, Perry, and Anna went back into Stone's cottage and sat down in the front room.

"Well, we did a week's worth of work out there in a matter of minutes," said Grayson. "Now, I don't mind you using magic at home, but be smart about it. Don't do it in the open. Obviously, most people where you live haven't seen magic. You must always remember—with this power comes great privileges, but also great temptations. Promise me that you will use what you know for good. Too many people have succumbed to temptation, abusing their magic to gain worldly power. Pride and jealousy set in. And before they know it, their power is not enough. They want more and more. Soon they are so obsessed with wanting more power, they get caught in a vicious cycle that's nearly impossible to break."

"If my mom is a wizlum," Calvin said, "why have I never seen her do any magic?"

"Your mother was so devastated by the loss of your father that she tried to hide the magical world from you. She knew you would be exposed to it sooner or later. She just hoped it would be later. She couldn't stand the thought of you fighting against Galigore. You are all she has. Do me a favor, Calvin…Don't get hurt. I talked her into letting me take you in and teach you a few things. Perry and Anna—that goes for you, too. I couldn't imagine having to tell your parents something happened to you, especially if magic was involved."

Calvin, Perry, and Anna nodded.

* * * *

Grayson and the trio sat around the dining table the next evening. "You are all coming along nicely," he said. "Perry, keep your determination. Being able to cast a few spells after only a couple of days is impressive, even if the outcomes are a little off. Anna, you know you have deep roots. You're a wizlum. Your adoptive parents may not know a thing about magic, but you can bet your real parents did. You may have a bigger role in this battle than you think. Calvin, your instincts are very advanced. And your intuition is incredible. You're much further along than I ever thought."

Perry nodded. "So when does Calvin get a dragon?"

"You must know something about wizlums and dragons. Not all wizlums get a dragon."

"Huh?" Perry looked confused.

"Some wizlums just aren't meant to have one. I know wizlums who have tried countless times, but for one reason or another, they haven't been able to get one."

"What do you mean?" said Perry. "Why not?"

"They may not have passed the physical challenge of Yeti Mountain. Or perhaps they failed the mental challenge. But those tests are all passable in time. The most devastating reason would be they just didn't bond with a dragon. If a wizlum doesn't make that connection with a dragon, a bond is never formed. You can't make a dragon go with a rider. So you just keep trying."

Grayson thought for a moment. "Like I said . . . you're well on your way, Calvin. You should go when you feel comfortable. Remember, I can't go with you."

"You're feeling good, aren't you, Calvin? You've got this magic thing down, don't you?" Perry asked, knocking Calvin in the arm.

"The journey is a rough one," Grayson directed his words to Calvin. "Experienced wizards or wizlums cannot accompany you. It's part of the test. But based on how training has gone these couple of days, you may be ready sooner than you think."

Grayson sat back for a second. "It's actually recommended that wizlums seek their dragon as early as they can. Obviously, the longer the dragon and its rider are together, the stronger the bond is."

Perry smiled and looked over at Calvin, curious to read his expression.

"So . . . ," Calvin said. "Perry and Anna can go with me?"

"I suppose that will be up to them," said Grayson.

Calvin turned to Perry. "Would you even want to go?"

Perry shook his head. "Even if I did, I couldn't."

"Huh?" Calvin said, looking distraught.

"Like Grayson said . . . experienced wizards cannot accompany you," joked Perry.

Calvin breathed a sigh of relief. "I guess that's a yes, then."

* * * *

Calvin lay on the front room sofa, staring up at the ceiling. His muscles were tired, and soreness had already begun to set in. He must have clashed swords with Perry and Anna a thousand times that day. Grayson had taught them some basic swordplay. Most of the skills were defensive, but he managed to throw in a few attacks as well. At first, the sword didn't seem so hefty, but as the day wore on, the heaviness of the steel became apparent. It wore him out entirely.

Calvin thought about Perry. He glanced over at him—lying on the floor—snoring. Perry had come a long way using his wand. He was pretty proud to be called a wizard.

Calvin's thoughts turned to Anna, who was sleeping in a spare bedroom upstairs. He couldn't imagine going through this training without her. They had learned so much. He still wondered how she got permission to come. He knew how impossible her parents were. Anna was usually able to get away from home for a few hours at a time, but it was always somewhat difficult. Her parents were lucky to have her as their only child.

Lately, her parents seemed bothered by the fact that Anna spent the bulk of her days roaming the forest behind the house—with two boys. They wished that she had more friends that were girls. They wanted her to be more involved with activities, like cheerleading—she definitely looked the part. Anna had to be creative when telling her parents where she'd be and what time she would be home. Oftentimes, she would need to check in at home during lunchtime before heading back out to explore the woods. Calvin recalled one conversation she had with her mom. It happened right in front of him and not long ago:

"And where do you think you're heading off to, young lady?" Anna's mom asked, annoyed.

"To the woods. With Calvin and Perry."

"I don't think so. Weren't you just there? Yesterday? And the day before that?"

"You know I love going to the woods," Anna said.

"Yes, but do you have to go to the woods every day?"

"If you'll let me," replied Anna.

"No, Anna. No! You don't get it, do you? I can understand Calvin and Perry messing around out there . . . but you? You're better than that."

"Better than what?" Anna asked.

"Than wasting your time . . . climbing trees, chasing bugs, skipping rocks, squishing ants, and . . . and whatever other nonsensical behavior boys do."

"But I like going to the woods," Anna said.

"Yes. But I don't!"

"You're not the one going. I am."

"Oh, you're an interesting one. Nothing like your father . . . or me."

"You want me to be like you?"

Her mom nodded. "I want you to be just a normal girl!"

"I'm perfectly fine with who I am."

"You're impossible!"

Calvin and Perry got along very well. And it helped that their moms were close friends. They tried to befriend Anna's mom, but she would never open up enough to develop a good relationship. Kristal, however, thought the world of Anna and welcomed her in her home anytime.

Calvin was startled from his thoughts when Perry coughed violently for a few seconds and then rolled from his back to his side. He fell back asleep instantly. The new position muted his snore.

* * * *

It was late in the afternoon when Grayson pulled the jeep

102

to a stop in front of Anna's home. Calvin helped her carry her things to the front porch. Anna waved and thanked everyone for the experience before closing the door behind her.

Grayson and Calvin walked Perry up to his front door. Perry grabbed the doorknob and gave it a turn, but it would not move.

"It's locked."

He rang the bell twice. No one came to the door. He peered inside the window. The house was dark.

"Well, that is a nice welcome home party," said Perry. "I guess they really missed me."

"You can stay over at my house," Calvin offered.

The three turned and left the front porch.

As they approached Calvin's front steps, Kristal opened the door to let them in.

"Oh, nice…That really makes me feel good now," Perry said. "I guess you have a mom that loves you."

"How was your trip?" Kristal asked.

"Awesome!" Calvin replied as he walked through the door. His mom leaned over and gave him a kiss on the cheek as he passed by. Perry and Grayson followed Calvin into the house.

Calvin's grandpa entered the room. "You're back? How did it go?"

"These two are well on their way," Grayson said.

Grandpa smiled.

"Perry needs to stay here for a bit," Calvin said. "He's locked out of his house."

"Oh, yes," said Kristal. "It's going to be a little longer than a bit."

Calvin and Perry turned toward Kristal, waiting for her to continue.

"Perry, your parents had to leave suddenly last night. Your uncle is in the hospital and is not doing well."

"Oh. I knew he was having some health problems," Perry said.

"So I have a key to your house in case you need anything from there," Kristal explained. "I would think they'd be gone for at least a week . . . maybe two. They will likely have to help out with funeral arrangements." The mood in the room turned solemn.

"It's that bad?" Perry asked.

Kristal nodded. "I'm sorry, Perry. He's dying."

"Thanks, Mrs. Sparks, for letting me stay here while they're gone."

"You're welcome here anytime."

"Hey, why don't you grab that cot out of the den," said Grandpa, "and take it up to your room for Perry to use."

Calvin started down the hall and then turned back to his mom. "Don't you have a trip coming up?"

"Yes," said Kristal. "I'll be going away for a few days. It's my yearly trip to the cabin with my friends. But Grandpa will be here with you." Kristal looked at Ainsley. "He'll be watching you." She then turned to Calvin and Perry. "And you two . . . don't get into any trouble while I'm gone."

"Sure, Mom," said Calvin. "Come on." He helped Perry with his bag. "Let's go set up your bed."

Calvin led Perry into his bedroom. "Sorry about your uncle. Do you know him very well?"

"Not really. But it's still sad to think that he's dying."

"Are you going to be okay?"

"I'll be fine." Perry appeared to be deep in thought. "Death is such a weird thing, isn't it? I mean . . . one minute you're here, and the next . . . you're totally gone—poof—somewhere else. I guess we all have to go through it. There's no escaping it. No matter what you do, you can't change that fate. You're going to die. I'm going to die. Someday. Only time will—"

"Hey," Calvin interrupted. "Why don't we keep busy over this next week or two? I think that will help you cope."

"Good idea." Perry sat quietly for a second and then perked up. "Hey, does your mom have any food? That might help."

14 • Herb's Magical Herbs

Calvin, Perry, and Anna sat together in The Crossing.

Anna was reading a thin hardback book.

"You're liking those potions books, aren't you?" Perry asked.

"There's a lot to know about herbs," Anna said. "Did you know that you can do just about anything with ingredients from the earth?"

"What do you mean?" Perry asked.

"I read about a potion you can make that will slow time down or speed it up."

"How can you do that?" asked Calvin.

"I found the recipe in this potion book and then went to Herb's Magical Herbs to find the ingredients," said Anna. "I rang up quite the tab, though. All these pay-me-back-when-you-can certificates are adding up." Anna pulled a certificate from her pocket and showed them. "This one is for one thousand jingles."

"A thousand jingles?" Perry marveled. "That's like five hundred bucks!"

"Yes, it is." Anna concurred. "Calvin, I'm banking on that key of yours to lead us to some treasure. I've got lots of other certificates . . . with larger amounts."

"Where are they from?" Perry asked.

"Mostly from Roland's Linens, a clothing store near the town square. They have nice stuff over there."

"So did you make it?" Calvin steered the conversation back on topic.

"What?" asked Anna.

"The potion. Did you make it?"

"Yes. I made a batch and placed it in this vial." Anna held up a small glass vial that housed a brown liquid inside. "The description said that it only makes time move forward. With this potion you can't go backwards. The more you drink, the faster time goes. Common uses are for getting through pain and traveling places. I guess time kind of flies by without you feeling it."

"Boy, we could have used a few bottles of this last weekend," said Perry. "That was one long drive with Grayson."

"As amazing as that sounds," Anna said, "this one sounds so much better." She pulled another vial from her pocket.

"What does that one do?" Calvin asked.

"Teleportation."

"Tele . . . what?" Perry said.

"This will allow one to teleport, or travel, from one place to another . . . instantly," Anna said. "You disappear from here and then reappear somewhere else."

"Are you serious?" Perry asked. "Does it work?"

"I haven't tried it."

"Let's give it a go," said Perry. "Calvin, your mom left for a couple of days. Let's go somewhere far away, where the food is good," said Perry. "Can it take us to Italy?"

"Where did your mom go?" Anna asked.

"She went with some friends to stay in a cabin, somewhere up in the mountains," said Calvin. "It's a trip they take every year."

"How long will she be gone?" Anna asked.

"A few more days."

"She's leaving both of you alone?" Anna asked.

"My grandpa will be home."

"So, you're pretty much home alone then." Anna knew that Calvin's grandpa was very lenient—even more so since they had discovered the magical world of Cambria. He secretly encouraged them to spend as much time as they wanted at The Crossing and Cambria.

"Well," said Perry. "Can we go to Italy on this stuff?"

"The potion's description says that the distance is limited," Anna said. "The further you want to go, the more you have to drink."

"Does it give any indication for how much equates to how far?" Calvin asked.

"If you drink this entire vial, you would be able to travel about 500 miles, give or take," explained Anna.

"How does it know where you want to go?" Calvin asked.

"Thoughts," said Anna. "It all goes by our thoughts."

"So, you just think of the place where you want to travel to and then drink?" Perry asked.

"That's how it's supposed to work," said Anna.

"How much did that vial cost?" Perry wondered.

"A lot."

"How much?" Perry insisted.

Anna removed a handful of crinkled certificates from her pocket.

"Are you kidding me?" Perry said. "Are all of those pay-me-back-when-you-can certificates?"

Anna nodded.

"Boy," said Perry, looking at Calvin. "She's high maintenance."

Anna pulled a certificate from the stack and unraveled it. She looked at it, nodded, and then handed it to Perry.

Perry's eyes widened. His mouth dropped.

"What's it say?" Calvin asked.

"Ten thousand jingles?" said Perry. "Do you know how many dollars that is?" Perry had to say it. "That's five thousand dollars!"

"Like I said," Anna answered. "Let's hope that key of yours unlocks a lot of gold."

"It's pretty easy, isn't it?" Perry looked at Anna.

"What?"

"Spending money you don't have."

"I'll pay it back!" Anna contested.

"Do they even question you when you make a huge purchase like that?" Perry asked.

"No."

Perry reached for the potion book and flipped through the pages. An idea came to him. "Hey, I'm hungry. You guys up for some Fountain Green goodness? Now that's a tab I don't mind running up."

"No, I'm good," said Calvin.

Anna agreed. "I'll stay with Calvin."

"Okay," Perry said, patting his stomach. "Your loss, my

107

gain!"

Perry opened up the door in the floor. When Calvin and Anna weren't looking, he quickly slipped the potion book into his coat and then disappeared from view, down the cellar stairs.

15 · Grazlum

Calvin awoke just before sunrise. He had spent the night tossing and turning, suffering through Perry's snore. Perry had spent the night in a sleeping bag on a cot in Calvin's room. The orange light of dawn glowed through the curtains.

Calvin glanced over at his nightstand. He noticed something on the table that wasn't there when he had gone to bed the night before. A piece of paper was leaned up against his lamp, and two glass vials stood next to it. Calvin picked up the paper and read:

Calvin,

I know Grayson feels you are ready for a dragon. And acquiring a dragon is a crucial step toward defeating Galigore. I am here to help you get one. Please find two doses of a transportation potion—one for you and one for Perry. This should be enough to get you to the base of Yeti Mountain, where your quest will begin. The journey is a challenging one. I'm cheering you on, every step of the way.

P.S. I hope you're keeping the contents of the chest safe. I'm counting on you and your two friends.

Calvin placed the two vials in his pocket. He then quickly grabbed two backpacks and a sleeping bag from the camping bin in the garage. He had been backpacking many times with his grandpa and had learned how to pack a tight pack. Calvin rummaged the pantry, grabbing anything he thought they might like to eat—water, beef jerky, trail mix, crackers, cookies, and candy bars—and loaded both packs. Then he went back to his room and packed his and Perry's clothes.

"Perry," Calvin whispered. "Perry, are you awake?"

Perry didn't answer.

"Perry. Wake up." Calvin shook his shoulder.

Perry finally rubbed his eyes. "What?"

"We have to go."

"What are you talking about?"

"Here." Calvin threw him a nylon bag to stuff his sleeping bag into. "You'll need to bring your sleeping bag."

"Bring it where?"

"I've got us some food and water for a couple of days," said Calvin. "I think that's all we'll need."

Perry was still dazed. "Slow down, Calvin. What are we doing? Where are we going?"

"I'll explain on the way. Come on."

Perry threw on his jeans and jacket, and then laced up his shoes. Calvin stuffed the sleeping bag Perry was using into Perry's pack.

When they were ready to go, they slipped out the back door.

The morning air was crisp and cool. Vegetation along the forest floor was wet with dew, soaking the outsides of their shoes.

"Where are you taking me?" Perry asked as they slipped away deeper into the forest.

Calvin reached into his pocket and pulled out two glass vials. "We're off to Yeti Mountain, to get me a dragon. And this is going to take us there. One for me . . . and one for you." Calvin handed Perry a vial.

"A teleportation potion?" Perry asked.

"Yes."

"Where did you get it?" asked Perry.

"They were left for me on my nightstand. There was a note that told me what to do with them. It said one was for me and one was for you."

"Wait a second," Perry said. "How did you know one was for me?"

"Because it had your name on it."

"You mean, my name was written in this letter that was left for you?"

"That's right," said Calvin.

"Wow," said Perry. "Maybe I am finally beginning to become someone. . . . Who was it from?"

"It didn't say."

"Whoa . . . wait a minute," said Perry. "You're not going to drink that. What if it's a trick? What if it's poison?"

"Come on, Perry. Somebody is trying to help us."

"What about your grandpa?"

"We'll be fine. We'll just be in Cambria. He knows we're always there."

"Do you think the potion will work?" Perry asked.

"It's got to work. The note said that there should be enough to get us to the base of Yeti Mountain," explained Calvin. "I think if we both concentrate on the same thing, we should arrive at the same place."

"Makes sense," said Perry. "Should we concentrate on going to Stone's house? He lives near the base of the mountain. We're familiar with the area already."

Calvin and Perry shook the vials and then opened them. "Hey," said Perry. "This is pretty cool, huh? You know, just you and me—nobody else—going on an adventure together. Thanks for inviting me along."

"Sure," said Calvin.

"Well, bottoms up!" said Perry, nervously. He clanked his bottle against Calvin's, and then downed the entire potion in one big swig. Calvin quickly followed suit.

Bright lights filled the area immediately around them and their bodies began to feel weightless. Wind blew through their hair as if they were moving quickly through space. The lights flickered one by one, blackening the atmosphere. A sudden flash ignited and they found themselves standing still in a field at the base of Yeti Mountain. They could barely see Stone's cottage a couple of miles away.

"I don't think that could have worked any better," Calvin said.

"Yeah," agreed Perry. "Unless it took us directly to Dragon Lookout."

"Let's get started," Calvin suggested.

Calvin and Perry had their sights set on Yeti Mountain. The very thought of the mountain's name made Perry uneasy about the kinds of creatures there could be lurking in its rocky crevices.

They anticipated the journey to last through the night, and

into the late morning hours the next day.

There wasn't much of a marked trail. Occasionally, there were clearings that spanned some several hundred feet followed by heavily wooded sections that were dark and shady. Looking ahead, they did their best to map out the general direction they should go.

A few hours into their trek, the temperature began to warm up and the air began to thicken with humidity. Calvin and Perry were pleased with the progress they were making. They rested every now and again, for a few minutes at a time, giving their burning calves a break from the steep incline. The thick, damp air made it impossible to stay dry. Their faces dripped with sweat.

"How do you suppose you will be tested?" asked Perry, climbing and jumping from boulder to boulder.

"I'm afraid there are lots of ways to be tested in these mountains. I'm not looking forward to tonight when it gets dark."

Soon they were walking amid tall trees. A steady breeze blew through the treetops and rattled the leaves. Several evergreens with needle-like leaves were scattered about. Large pinecones lay sprinkled across the forest floor. Clouds were strewn across the sky, frequently passing in front of the sun, casting shadows over the already darkened forest.

"What was that?" asked Perry.

"I didn't hear anything," replied Calvin.

"I saw something pass through the trees up there."

"I didn't see it," said Calvin.

"Wait a second," said Perry. "Before we go any farther, let's remember this day."

"What?" asked Calvin.

"The day that I actually saw something before you." Perry walked ahead quietly. He quickened his pace while keeping an eye out for the large beast.

Up ahead, Calvin and Perry heard twigs snapping. They continued to walk as quietly as they could. Through the thick trees, Calvin and Perry could see something large and brown.

"I'm not sure we want to know what that is," whispered

Perry.

"Yeah . . . let's wait here a second for it to go away," suggested Calvin.

The beast continued to make its way through the forest. The sound of snapping wood faded and then disappeared. Calvin and Perry determined it safe to proceed, and they pressed on.

When they approached the area where they had seen the beast pass, they noticed some very large footprints that resembled human prints.

Calvin felt a sudden urge to turn around. As he did so, he barely caught a glimpse of another dark figure passing through the trees.

"What is it?" asked Perry.

"I'm not sure. Come on. . . . Let's keep moving."

"You know . . . it's going to be much better when we are able to travel by dragon," said Perry.

"You mean *if* we're able to travel by dragon."

"Oh, come on . . . Grayson says you've got skills. You won't be turned away. Plus, whoever wrote you that note and left you the potions has confidence in you."

Calvin and Perry made their way uphill through the thick, shadowy forest. Throughout most of the day, they continued to hear various noises nearby, but didn't encounter anything too intimidating. Squirrels seemed to be everywhere, scurrying about, causing most of the startling noises. An occasional deer passed near them. It didn't seem to matter the size of the critter; whether big or small, Calvin and Perry were on their guard.

"More intruders in Grazlum's forest?" bellowed a voice. Calvin and Perry stopped immediately and looked around to see who spoke. They could see no one.

"More dragon rider hopefuls, I presume?" came the voice again. Still they saw no one but knew the voice was coming from just a few feet away.

Perry pointed at the base of the bushes at some large, dried wings, a couple of hollowed out beetle shells, some half-chewed legs that once belonged to a giant insect, and random bones that came from large animals or humans.

"We're just passing through...We mean no harm," said Calvin.

"Oh, how I ever like the company," said the hidden voice. "As you can see, I invited the last passerby to dinner. A very tasty meal, indeed."

Calvin and Perry looked at each other, not sure how they were going to get out of this one.

"Why are you hiding?" Perry asked.

"I'm not hiding. I'm here with you. You just don't see me." The creature took a step toward Calvin and Perry. When he moved, his body came into view. A giant praying mantis that had been camouflaged took shape. His head towered over them. And his big, round eyes bulged from the sides of his triangular head. Each eye was smooth and green with a small black pupil in the center. Grazlum's jaws were large and tapered to a point. When he spoke, his mouth opened and closed from side to side. His legs were long and stick-like, and spikes ran down the back side. He had wings that folded tightly up into his sides. His thin arms were held out in front of his body, bent at the elbows, and claws brought together. In a matter of a few seconds, Grazlum became hard to see again as he stopped moving and blended in anew with the shrubs behind him.

"Who are you?" Calvin asked.

"I am Grazlum. And this is my forest."

"Well, why don't we just leave your forest," said Perry. "Like, right now."

"It doesn't work that way."

"Can't we make it work?" asked Perry. "Please?"

"You see," said Grazlum, "you really don't stand a chance against me."

"We're not looking for a fight," said Perry. "Just go back to minding your business."

"You are my business. You see . . . I spend the length of my days hunting. And I do believe you will make a fine meal tonight." Grazlum chomped his mouth open and closed, exposing his powerful jaws. He slowly took a step closer, coming into view a little clearer.

"Certainly you can't eat both of us," suggested Perry. "It's too big of a meal."

"Not to worry," said Grazlum. "I will consume the more delectable parts. I'm sure I will leave a few limbs behind."

Calvin knew he wasn't joking. He looked at the pile of bones on the ground left from previous meals. They easily could have been from one person, or two.

"I'll tell you what," said Grazlum. "Since I am in a negotiable mood, if one of you will join me for dinner, I'll let the other have a brief head start before I hunt him down."

"That's a tempting offer," said Calvin. "And what if we politely decline?"

"I'd encourage you to take what you can get," said Grazlum. "Declining my offer will only result in twice the meal for me." He smiled a nasty smirk, drool dripping off the corners of his mouth.

"You don't make it hard for one to decide, do you?" said Perry. "Okay. Let us discuss which one of us will be your dinner and who will be given a chance to survive."

Calvin and Perry didn't wait for a response. They huddled together quickly to devise a plan.

"You have your wand ready?" said Calvin.

"I can draw it and have it out in a second."

"Good . . . you'll need it."

"I forgot to tell you one thing," said Grazlum, speaking loudly so as to interrupt their conversation. "You have five seconds to decide." He stepped closer to Calvin and Perry.

"We've made our decision," said Calvin.

"Who's it going to be?" asked Grazlum.

"I have volunteered myself to be your guest for dinner," said Calvin.

Grazlum wasted no time and quickly moved in on Calvin. He was within striking distance. Perry took the opportunity to move away. He didn't know exactly what Calvin had in mind, but knew he was up to something.

"*Bubla Bolar!*" came the incantation. Instantly an electric bubble formed around Calvin and burst, throwing the praying mantis through the air. Grazlum toppled to the ground and remained motionless. Though fatigued from the effects of casting the spell, Calvin forced himself to move.

"Let's go!" Calvin cried. "We don't have much time." He looked back at Grazlum, who was beginning to come to his senses.

Just as Calvin was about to clear the area he stumbled to the ground, knocking his head against a large, moss-covered rock. Feeling dazed and weak, he attempted to get up, but he couldn't move his legs.

Droplets of saliva fell upon Calvin as Grazlum hovered over him. Grazlum's eyes were glowing with fury. He pounced on top of Calvin and clutched him with his arms and legs. He leaned toward Calvin's head, ready to attack.

Perry watched in horror from behind a tree as his friend was nearing his death.

"Calvin!" Perry cried. "Calvin!"

In an instant, Perry desperately sprung out from behind the tree and drew his wand.

"*Relampago!*" A ball of electricity formed at the tip of Perry's wand and he quickly flung it toward the praying mantis. The lightning bolt struck Grazlum on the head and knocked him back a few feet. He launched another bolt, this time severing an arm. Perry flicked the wand forward again, hurling a streak of electricity, hitting Grazlum on the top of the head, knocking him to his belly.

Wailing in pain, the determined mantis staggered to his feet and took a step closer to Calvin. Another fling and another bolt zinged toward the giant insect, sinking deep into his face. Blinded, the praying mantis felt his way toward Calvin's body and pounced on top of him. The massive Grazlum lurked over Calvin once again. He opened his mouth wide and quickly snapped down at Calvin. Calvin barely rolled out of the way.

Trying to wrestle away from underneath Grazlum, Calvin wiggled his arm loose. "*Sedativo!*" A jolt of energy launched from Calvin's hands and smacked into Grazlum. The praying mantis immediately fell over and did not move.

Not sure how long Grazlum would be asleep, Calvin quickly rose to his feet and made his way over to Perry, who was on the ground, lying unconscious.

"Perry!" Calvin said, gently slapping his companion's face. "Perry! Can you hear me? Wake up!"

Perry's eyes blinked open and met Calvin's. Calvin took his canteen out of his pack and poured some cool water on Perry's face, hoping it would help him come to his senses faster.

He looked over at Grazlum. The slumber charm seemed to be wearing off on the giant praying mantis. His limbs began to twitch.

"We have to get going, Perry. We don't have much time."

Calvin pulled Perry to his feet and draped one of his arms around his shoulder, helping him walk. Though unstable, Perry was mostly able to walk under his own power and was getting stronger by the minute.

As Calvin and Perry hurried away, they heard a nasty growl behind them. Calvin turned his head to look over his shoulder. The gruesome Grazlum was once again on his feet, feeling his way toward them.

Calvin, signaling to Perry to hold still, bent over and picked up a few rocks. He hurled one of them just to the side of the blind praying mantis and made it skip through the bushes. Grazlum immediately turned toward the sound and held still. Calvin threw another rock a little further. Grazlum took a few steps toward the sound and held his head alert. Calvin chucked one more rock even further away. Grazlum followed the noise and finally disappeared behind the thick trees.

As quickly as they could, Calvin and Perry climbed up a steep section of the mountain. They were relieved that they were getting further away from the angry Grazlum.

The rest of the day was uneventful, for which Calvin and Perry were grateful. The night began to darken. Calvin and Perry found a spot that seemed comfortable and decided to stop and rest for the evening. They had had an exhausting day in which they both exceeded their magical thresholds. The idea of getting some shut-eye was a delightful one. But deep down inside, they each knew they wouldn't sleep a wink.

16 • A Yeti Encounter

"Perry!" whispered Calvin.

Perry rubbed his eyes, lifted his head, and turned toward Calvin, who was sitting up staring into a thicket of trees.

"Something's over there."

A heavy foot fell upon some twigs close by, breaking them violently. Perry snapped his head toward the noise, then back at Calvin, frightened.

Calvin got to his feet and ducked behind a tree, peering in the direction of the noise. He hoped it was a deer feeding in the brush but knew it probably wasn't. Maybe it was a unicorn? No. Whatever it was, it meant trouble.

Perry quietly stood up and tiptoed over to Calvin. The moon shone through the trees, but it was not very bright. A steady breeze blew and swayed the treetops, creating a slight roar.

"It's got to be right over there," said Perry, pointing only ten feet ahead.

From behind a nearby tree, a tall, hairy creature emerged. Fangs stuck out from its mouth and curled down its cheeks. A yeti. Calvin recognized it from his book. The yeti let out a snarl and lunged toward Calvin. Calvin slipped aside, but the yeti's claw tore through his coat sleeve.

"Run!" Calvin yelled.

Perry darted behind a clump of trees while frantically reaching for his wand. He stood still in the dark shadows, quietly hoping that Calvin was also safe. As soon as Perry mustered up some courage, he peered from behind a tree in the direction where he had left Calvin and the yeti. It was difficult for him to see through the webbing of low-hanging branches, and he wondered if he should go back to help his friend. He wanted so badly to know what to do, but was so scared that he remained still—and deathly quiet.

As Perry hid, he caught a whiff of a rank, warm breeze from

behind him. He slowly turned around. Directly in front of him was a thick tree trunk that appeared to be covered with long strands of hair. Amazed at the unique tree, Perry began to trace the trunk skyward with his eyes. About four feet above his own head, he noticed the tree had two eyes that stared back at him. A mouth too, which opened and let out a growl. Perry screamed, jumped away from the yeti, and ran through the forest in a blind panic.

"Calvin!" Perry cried, hoping to catch up to him. "Where are you?"

Perry passed by a large tree and felt a hand grab his jacket and yank him to the side.

"No!" Perry shouted.

"It's okay, Perry. It's me, Calvin."

Perry was relieved to hear his friend's voice. He hid quietly with him behind the tree, trying to catch his breath.

"Be quiet," commanded Calvin. "I think I know what to do." Branches that lay on the forest floor snapped as the yeti grew closer.

Calvin brought his hands together and thought in his mind, "*Lucero.*" A bright globe formed between his palms and emitted a glow that lit up the immediate surroundings. Calvin scanned the area and saw two eyes glaring back at him. The yeti stopped and stood still.

With the globe in his hands, Calvin gently molded it into two smaller spheres. He carefully pushed one in the direction of the eyes. The globe slowly floated forward, hovering about five feet off the ground, lighting up everything in its path. It was the first real look Calvin and Perry had of the mammoth beast. The large creature closely resembled a human—it stood on its two hind legs and was covered in hair.

The yeti featured two long, sharp canine teeth that protruded from its mouth. It appeared to be standing about ten feet tall and had feet twice the size of Calvin's all the way around.

"That's strange that he's just standing there," whispered Perry. "I wonder what he wants."

The creature let out a quiet growl and snarled its teeth. Calvin and Perry remained silent as they heard more noise rustling in the trees behind them. Both turned to look, but it was too dark to see anything through the trees. Still holding the other half of the sphere, Calvin gave it a gentle push in the direction from which the rustling came. Stopping just a few feet from a group of aspens, the bright ball unveiled another large, hairy creature.

"Oh, great. He brought his twin with him," said Perry.

"I wish you were right," said Calvin. "But from where I see it, we're not talking twins. Try quadruplets."

Two more towering, hairy beasts emerged from the trees, took several steps toward the ball of light floating in front of them, and then stood still.

"What is going on here?" asked Perry. "Why are they just standing there?"

Perry slowly took two small steps to the side. All four beasts remained still, eyes affixed on the globes floating just a few feet in front of them.

"Perry, are you ready to get out of here?" asked Calvin.

"What do you mean?" asked Perry. "We can't just walk away. They'll see us."

"The yetis are mesmerized. They can't resist the urge to stare into the light. I read about them in *Mythical Creatures*. Yetis are nocturnal and hunt in packs, usually in groups of four to six. My dad made a note in the margin about their weaknesses. He said your best chance against a yeti is to conjure a charm of bright lights. It hypnotizes them. The yetis will gaze into the light for as long as it's lit, or until something distracts them. We need to pick up our things and make our way out of here quietly."

Calvin slowly stepped toward the tree he had been sleeping under. He didn't worry about taking the time to pack everything, but just grabbed up the pile. Perry did the same.

Careful to keep a sure foot, Calvin quietly led the way out of the camp, once again heading up the mountain. He was unsure of the direction they should go in the dark, but followed his gut, hoping it would lead him the right way. One thing he and Perry knew for sure—they didn't mind backtracking if it meant avoiding a confrontation with a pack of yetis.

As soon as the two globes of light were no longer visible

behind them, Calvin conjured another ball of light with his palms. He and Perry stowed their belongings in their packs and slung them over their shoulders. Calvin launched the light forward with a gentle push. It hovered above the ground, effectively lighting the way ahead. When the ball slowed to a stop, Calvin caught up to it and gently pushed it forward again and again.

"Do you think we're headed the right way?" asked Perry.

"I think we are…It feels like we're heading west," said Calvin.

"How long do you think we've been walking?"

"Oh, probably about an hour. At this pace, we've probably only covered a few miles."

"Why don't we stop here for the night?" said Perry. "We are far enough away from the yetis . . . we should be fine. In the morning we can get our bearings straight."

"I think that's a good plan."

Within minutes, the two found a sheltered area in a pocket of trees where they stopped and spread out their bedding. It was a little more secluded than the last spot, which they hoped would be to their advantage.

Calvin held the light in his hands and extinguished it by gently bringing his palms together. The light melted away into the darkness.

"Hopefully we sleep better this time," suggested Calvin.

"Let's just plan on it," said Perry. "See you in the morning."

Calvin lay on the forest floor, gazing up at the starry night through the open spaces between the branches. Amidst Perry's snores, Calvin's eyelids grew heavy. Just as he was beginning to lose himself to slumber, he was awakened by a loud popping sound. He gazed toward the starlit sky and saw twirling lights sparkling high in the air.

"Perry! Perry!" whispered Calvin, shaking Perry's shoulder. "Perry . . . wake up."

Perry woke up, groggily, rubbing his eyes. "Huh?"

"Perry, look at that!" Calvin pointed to the sky.

"Look at what?"

"The lights!"

"Yeah . . . they're called stars. You learn about them in science class."

"Funny. Look at all of them, twirling in the sky," said Calvin.

"What are you talking about?"

Calvin looked up and saw the whirling sparks come together to form the letter B in the sky. The burning lights lasted only a minute before they began to fizzle away into the stillness of the night.

"What do you see?" asked Perry.

"A big, bright B."

"A bee?" Perry took a defensive stance, ready to swat anything that flew his way.

"No, no . . . not a bee. The letter B was illuminated in the sky. It was big . . . and bright."

Perry was relieved and relaxed.

"Why would I be able to see it but not you?" said Calvin.

"Come on. That really surprises you?" said Perry.

"What does it mean? Who is it for?" wondered Calvin.

"Let's ask Grayson when we see him," said Perry. "He'll know."

Calvin and Perry tried to get some rest once again. Calvin gazed up at the night through the thick trees. He couldn't help but replay the image of the B in his mind. He racked his brain, thinking of what it might have meant. The memory of the letter was vivid. It burned in the back of his eyes. When he blinked, he saw a floating B turn green behind his eyelids. He stayed awake for a long time—but not on purpose. His mind kept racing. His last thought before dozing off to sleep was Bordarians.

* * * *

Anna wasn't looking forward to making the journey from Cambria to Wolf Creek alone in the dark, but her parents had gone out for the evening and wouldn't be returning until late, and she wanted to take every advantage she could. She wondered about Calvin and Perry. She hadn't seen them all day. She knocked on Calvin's door several times, but nobody answered—not even his grandpa. She hoped that she would run into them in Cambria.

Yester Year had been closed for a couple of hours now. But Glenburn, the shop owner, always invited her to stay as long as she wanted.

Anna returned a short stack of books to the bookshelf before gathering her belongings and heading for the front door. She passed Glenburn, who was sitting in a rocker reading the most recent edition of *Cambrian Affairs*. Glenburn was exceptionally old but still very lively. He lived alone on the floor above the shop. He was bald except for a ring of hair that grew above his ears and around the back of his head. He wore round-rimmed glasses that made his eyes appear much larger than natural. His nose was long and crooked and came to a point. Glenburn had an unlit black pipe sticking out from one side of his mouth, which he held in place with clenched teeth. An intricately carved wooden cane rested between his legs—a cane he used to favor his right leg.

Glenburn heard Anna approaching and lowered the newspaper.

Anna stopped in front of him. "Thanks again for letting me stay."

"Anytime, Anna. My house is your house."

"Thank you." Anna turned to make her exit when a photo in Glenburn's paper caught her eye. "Glenburn? What is that story about?"

Two images sat side by side. The one on the left was of a strong, good-looking man. He looked brave and confident. The photo next to it seemed to be of the same person, only much more frail. His countenance was evil. His face was sunken, cheekbones prominent. His skin was thin and pale. Eyes bloodshot. Faint, blue veins crawled over his face and neck.

Glenburn flipped his paper around and scanned the headlines. "Which one? This one?" He read a headline, " 'From Bordarian to Zarkon—A Regrettable Transformation.' "

"Yes," replied Anna. "Is that the same person?"

"Sadly, it is," replied Glenburn. "Galigore is heavily recruiting people to join him. The Zarkon have been charged to go after the weak—the vulnerable. When people are down, it doesn't seem to take much to pick them back up. Galigore offers them wealth and power to join him. He picks them up out of their fallen despair and rescues them. They become indebted to him and swear their allegiance to his cause. As you can see by this picture, as one's behavior changes to evil, so does their appearance."

"How sad," said Anna, contemplating Glenburn's response. "Sad that one could be so heartbroken . . . so lonely . . . so down . . . that they would turn to evil to pick themselves back up."

"Yes," agreed Glenburn. "I'm glad you recognize that. The key is to keep your wits when the temptation arises."

"Have you been approached by a Zarkon? Has one tried to recruit you?"

"Yes," answered Glenburn. "It's one thing to say you'd never join forces with the Zarkon now, but it's a whole different story when you are in deep despair. When you are hopeless. When life doesn't seem to matter. I tell you . . . it doesn't take much to change when treasures are thrown your way. You'd do anything to get out of that awful slump."

"So why didn't you become a Zarkon?"

"My heritage. I come from a long line of faithful Bordarians. I couldn't stand the thought of me betraying everything I knew was good. I imagined my parents rolling over in their graves. Memories of the lessons my grandparents taught me came alive inside my mind. My own past gave me the courage to run away from the evil influences that surrounded me. But I can tell you first-hand . . . I can see how people waver and walk into darkness . . . because I nearly did."

"Have you heard of anyone who had become a Zarkon and then changed back to a Bordarian?" asked Anna.

"I've heard it happening. But it's rare. Once you're given power, the tendency to want more power becomes stronger. I'd imagine the thought of becoming good doesn't enter the mind easily. There's too much pride getting in the way."

"How big is Galigore's Society today?" asked Anna.

"I don't know. It is estimated a couple of thousand Zarkon make up his Society."

"I'm glad you were strong," said Anna.

"What?"

"I'm glad you chose to be good, instead of become a Zarkon. I wish I had the good examples in my life to help guide me. I never knew my family."

"You're doing fine with what life's thrown at you, Anna. Your parents love you. It may not seem like it from time to time, but I can assure you they treasure you and want the best for you."

Anna nodded reluctantly.

"And your friends. They're good kids. That boy, Calvin. You're lucky to know him. The Sparks family has deep roots in virtuous living."

Anna thought about how Calvin was doing. It wasn't very often she didn't know where he was.

"Anna?"

She hoped he was okay. His mom wasn't in town and he could get away with anything with his grandpa in charge.

"Anna?"

She thought about asking Priscilla at Fountain Green if she had seen Calvin. Fountain Green was a usual stop for them, especially with Perry.

"Anna?" said Glenburn a third time. "You must be getting tired."

Anna snapped awake. "Oh, yeah. I better get going."

"Come back anytime," Glenburn said.

"Thanks. Good night, Glenburn."

"Good night, dear."

Anna hurried down the dark cobblestone street. It was quiet except for the music, chatter, and loud laughter coming from Fountain Green. She tried not to dwell on the uneasy feelings she had being out so late by herself, and was careful to not make eye contact with anyone. It was bad enough to pass by humans on the street, but now she was dealing with creatures of all sorts giving her funny looks. She quickly made her way up the walk of the old cottage and slipped in the front door. Her nerves began to settle as she was almost home.

Anna peeled the rug back and reached down to pull on the handle to open the creaky door in the floor. She lifted it high enough to duck through and took a step down into the cellar.

"Good evening, Anna." A voice broke the silence. Anna gasped. She didn't see anyone, but someone had seen her. The cottage was dark. Little light from the street lamp out front made its way through the window, but it wasn't enough.

"It's okay, Anna. It's me." The voice was soft and familiar.

Anna turned toward the direction of the voice and saw a figure sitting in a rocker.

"Miss Jasmine?" whispered Anna.

"Yes. It's me."

"What are you doing sitting in the dark? You freaked me out."

"I'm sorry," said Miss Jasmine. "I dozed off sitting here and woke up when I heard the hinges creak."

"So what are you doing here?" asked Anna again.

"I was on my way back from the castle when I saw you were still in Yester Year. I thought I would sit here and wait for you and accompany you home. I remember when I was your age. How I hated wandering these places late at night alone." Miss Jasmine got up from her chair.

Anna began to feel a little more comfortable. She was happy to have Miss Jasmine to travel with. She was right. As brave as she tried to be, Anna didn't like traveling through the woods near The Crossing by herself.

"Well . . . shall we?" offered Miss Jasmine as she held up the door and followed Anna down the stairs.

"How often do you come to Cambria?" Anna asked as they finished descending the last steps.

"Oh, I'm here a little more often these days, now that we're on break for the summer."

"Miss Jasmine? Cambria is amazing. I feel so comfortable there. And whenever I come back to Wolf Creek, it's like something is missing. It's almost like a part of me was left there. Does that make sense?"

"I felt the same way. During my childhood I spent countless hours imagining that I was living in magical worlds. The things I dreamt up . . . I could do anything. And then I discovered the magical world of Cambria myself. It was exciting, and every time I left to come home, I couldn't wait to go back. Now I spend a lot of time here, especially at the castle."

"Where's the castle?" asked Anna.

"It's about twenty miles away. You can barely see part of it in the distance from the town square if you know where to look."

"What's it like?"

"Ah, the castle. It sits on the most beautiful piece of land you could imagine. The grounds are filled with lakes, streams, and waterfalls. There are lots of blooming gardens and walkways, and it's alive with magical creatures. The most vibrant birds, butterflies, and animals around."

"Is there a king in the castle?"

"No king. The castle serves as the headquarters for the Bordarian Army. Ulric Bolt is the Captain."

"What's he like?" said Anna.

"He's like any other Bordarian. He looks the same. Dresses the same. He assigns Bordarians to missions, but he also fights alongside his people. He has a huge amount of trust in his Bordarians and allows them to contribute in ways they feel make sense."

"Who lives in the castle?" asked Anna.

"Ulric lives there full-time. And others live there as needed for different reasons."

"I'd like to go there one day."

"I'm sure you'll get your chance," said Miss Jasmine.

"Are you a Bordarian?" asked Anna.

"I am."

"Wow," marveled Anna. "That's so cool."

Anna continued to fire questions at Miss Jasmine, who graciously answered them all. Before she knew it, they had entered Wolf Creek and were already approaching her home. She loved learning about Cambria and could have talked to Miss Jasmine for hours.

"Keep studying, Anna," Miss Jasmine said, standing in front of Anna's house.

"Hey, this isn't anything like school," Anna said. "I don't need any encouragement learning about Cambria."

Miss Jasmine laughed and nodded.

"Thanks for waiting for me tonight," said Anna.

"It was my pleasure."

They smiled at one another.

"Do your parents know you're out this late?" asked Miss Jasmine.

"No way. If they knew, they'd probably nail boards to the outside of my window."

"We're so much alike, Anna. I did the same when I was younger. I'd sneak out of my bedroom window and quietly slip back in late at night. I'd scramble up a tree and climb into my window."

Anna laughed. "That's the tree I use to climb into my window." She pointed at a window on the upper floor of the house.

"Yes . . . mine was like that, too. Well, I better be off," said Miss Jasmine. "Thanks for the chat."

"Good night."

17 · Bravada

Morning eventually came. The sun rose and warmed the cool, moist, mountain air. Calvin and Perry had tossed and turned much of the night, but they did manage to sleep a little more than they thought they would.

Gauging by the sun rising in the east, Calvin figured they had traveled mostly in the right direction the night before. He thought they would need to retrace some of their steps to find a more manageable trail. They estimated a pretty full day journeying to the summit.

The pathway up the mountain was rugged. Large tree roots broke the surface and ran along the ground zigzagging along the path, then diving deep into the soil only to jut up again several feet ahead.

After a few hours, Calvin and Perry finally made it to the saddle of the mountain. The view from the ridge was spectacular. Thick green trees stretched as far as they could see on the east of Yeti Mountain. On the west, the deep, blue sea was in sight. It was vast and seemed to extend forever before blending into the distant hazy sky.

There were two peaks—one on each side of the saddle. Their destination—the western one that towered atop the ocean—was an exceptionally steep slope.

"That's where we're headed," said Calvin, pointing at the daunting apex. "Do you have one last climb in you?"

"I think so. What do you figure . . . a few hours to the top?" said Perry.

"Yeah. That's probably a good guess."

The two began their climb up the steep slope. Calvin and Perry slid several times, catching themselves with their hands just before falling completely to the ground. Perry began to slow down. "Man . . . my legs are burning," he said, stopping to rest for a second.

"Yeah. Mine are like jelly," said Calvin, kicking his feet out in front of him and shaking them, trying to ease the stiffness in his legs.

"Jelly? Boy, what I wouldn't give for a slice of bread and peanut butter," said Perry.

Calvin hardly cracked a smile and shook his head. "Come on. We must be getting close to the top."

The trail continued to rise steeply. The top was no longer visible from their perspective. They took frequent rests, guessing and wishing that they would reach the summit at any moment.

"You better pass the test and get a dragon," said Perry. "Can you imagine having to find our way back home? We don't have anymore potion, you know. Maybe we can at least talk the dragon keeper into giving us a ride home. I'd imagine a dragon could get us home in no time."

Calvin's thoughts began to wander. Perry was right. Traveling by dragon would be much faster. He thought about how nice it would be to fly home afterward. Or how exciting it would be to knock on Anna's window while sitting upon his dragon. Of course he would have to reserve his dragon flying for nighttime in Wolf Creek, so no one would see him. These thoughts quickly fled from his mind, however, when he realized the impossibility of taking a dragon through The Crossing cellar door. Maybe he would be able to use the portal they had traveled through with Grayson?

Calvin began to dream about his dragon. What would it look like? What would it feel like to fly? Would it be able to breathe fire? How experienced would it be? What about its name? Would it have carried other riders? How would he know which dragon would be his? Would he be able to communicate with it right away? Would it be large? Small? Quick? Slow?

As Calvin awoke from his daydream, he realized he was not straining any longer with each step. The terrain had flattened out and he and Perry were walking atop a plateau in the direction of the sea. The ground appeared to vanish a few hundred feet ahead.

Chills of excitement ran up and down Calvin's spine. "We've made it, Perry!" Calvin moved ahead, shuffling toward the cliff's edge. "You're not scared of heights, are you?" he asked as he cautiously approached the abrupt drop-off. Calvin looked back at Perry, who was on all fours, creeping slowly toward the ledge.

"Holy cow!" cried Perry. "Look at that view."

They felt as though they were on top of the world. Mostly green vegetation covered the walls, but patches of bright colors, including orange, yellow, and red also painted the landscape. Thousands of feet below, they could see the waves crumble and bubble onto the ivory sand. Various valleys could be seen as the coastline stretched for miles in the distance. From one of the lower valleys, a waterfall tumbled down the rocky face, splashing into the ocean hundreds of feet below. Several large animals with wings were basking in the sun near the pool at the top of the waterfall. Dragons were also perched on the cliff walls. Some were close—just beyond a stone's throw away.

"What do you suppose we do now?" asked Perry, backing away from the edge and rising to his feet.

Calvin pointed out over the cliff.

From the valley of the waterfall, an enormous dragon, the size of a semi truck, carrying a rider, quickly soared toward Calvin and Perry. The rider was a large man, dressed in armor. He carried a shield and had a sword at his waist. His hair was long, reaching to his shoulders, and he had a bushy beard.

Calvin and Perry remained still, watching in awe as the dragon landed on the ground near them. It slowed its wings to a stop and tucked them up along its body. The rider dismounted and faced them.

"What brings you trespassers to the Cliffs of Tarnin?" demanded the man sternly.

Calvin tried to sound confident and brave. "We were told to speak with the dragon keeper. We need a dragon."

"I am Pulver, dragon keeper of Tarnin," he said. "Dragons are not for just anyone. The most decisive qualification for a dragon rider is that the rider must be a wizlum." Pulver gestured to Calvin. "Might you be a wizlum?"

"I am."

"And you?" Pulver asked Perry.

"No," said Perry. "We're here for Calvin."

"Calvin?" Pulver asked. "Who are your parents?"

"Miles and Kristal Sparks."

"Yes, I know your family well." Pulver nodded. "Well, you do realize you must pass a certain test before seeing the dragons?"

Calvin nodded.

"I assume you have already had some trying experiences on the mountain. Conquering Yeti Mountain demonstrates your physical capabilities. But I must now test your intellectual skills. I will ask you one question. If your answer is right, I will present you with some dragons. If your answer is wrong, you go home. You can come back and try again, in one year's time."

Calvin and Perry looked at each other, nervously.

"Any questions?" asked Pulver.

"If this doesn't work out, would you fly us home?" asked Perry.

Pulver smirked. "Don't get it wrong, kid."

"Yeah . . . don't get it wrong," encouraged Perry, taking out a candy bar from his pack.

Pulver rubbed his palms together thoughtfully.

"Okay. I've got it," said Pulver. "How about a riddle?"

Calvin wasn't too excited, but he nodded.

"It's better than gold, to underground dwellers. Without it, they die in cellars. Push and pull with all their might, without a turn they'll see no light. A pile of bones shares the name, and with this thing they'll end the game."

"Now, take your time," said Pulver. "Figure it out. I will accept only one answer from you. No help from anyone. I will be back when you are ready." Pulver climbed upon his dragon's back and flew off the side of the cliff into the open air, disappearing from sight.

"Hey," Perry called to Calvin, shoveling the last bite of his candy bar into his mouth. "Wake me up when you're done." He dropped to the ground and used his pack for a pillow.

Calvin walked away from Perry. "What's better than gold? Who are underground dwellers?" Calvin said in a whisper. "Are the underground dwellers prisoners? What do they need more than gold? Food? Water?"

Calvin continued to talk it through. "Okay . . . that works. A glass of water is better than gold because they need water to survive. Without water, they die in cellars."

Calvin traced the word, water, in the dirt with his finger.

"But to push and pull with all your might? What does water have to do with pushing and pulling? Without a turn . . . without a turn for what? I'm not sure that makes sense. What else could it be?"

Calvin started his reasoning from the beginning. "How about a dagger. It's better than gold because you can attack someone with it from inside the cellar. When your plate is brought to you, you can slice the hand. There are always bones in dungeons. Skeletons often have daggers rammed into their chests. The game is over when they are stabbed?"

In such a desperate time, Calvin was surprised at the number of ideas that came to his mind. "What about a bone? A bone is better than gold because that suggests there was food on it. When you're starving to death, you'd rather have food than gold." But the ideas seemed to lack substance.

Calvin worked through more scenarios, throwing out as many words from the riddle that would possibly fit the idea. After more than an hour of internal debate, he found himself back to the drawing board yet again.

Another idea began to materialize. "Maybe I can work backwards," he thought aloud. "And with this thing, they'll end the game. A prisoner's game is over when they either die or escape. There are only two options there. Bones share the name. So whatever this is called, it has something to do with bones . . . perhaps skeletons. Without a turn, they'll see no light. A turn for what? A turn for a fair trial? A turn for justice? A turn for revenge?"

Calvin slowly paced in a circle while he continued to talk through the riddle.

"Or think about something turning. What turns? A wheel? A doorknob? How about something relating to a dungeon cell? If there were a doorknob, you would turn it to open the door. To see the light, you need to get out of the dungeon by turning the handle. And in order to turn the knob . . . " Calvin's voice grew louder. He was onto something. "You would need a key! It's a key! A key is better than gold, because without it, you're not going anywhere. Without a key, you will eventually die. You can push and pull the cellar door all you want, but without that turn of the key, you're not going to get out . . . you won't ever see the light of day."

Calvin's steps became more deliberate and swift.

"A pile of bones shares the name, and with this thing they'll end the game," repeated Calvin. "With this key, they'll end the game. The game is being locked up. Game over. With this key, they'll end the game. Bony skeletons share the name? Bones . . . skeletons . . . share the name? Do skeletons have names? Do skeletons have keys?"

Calvin stopped in his tracks. "That's it!" he whispered. "The answer is a skeleton key. Dungeon masters have a skeleton key . . . one key that opens many doors."

Calvin thought through the answer several times very carefully to make sure it fit every aspect of the riddle. He was convinced he had the answer.

He looked over at Perry, who had awoken from his nap and was sitting on the ground, leaning against a rock.

"How do you suppose we summon the dragon keeper?" asked Calvin.

"He said he would be back when you were ready," offered Perry, biting into a second candy bar. "By the way . . . thanks for packing these for me." He took another bite, easily accounting for a third of the bar.

Immediately, Calvin and Perry heard wings flapping just beyond the edge of the cliff. Pulver, on his dragon, rose steadily to the top of the cliff and landed just in front of them.

"How does he do that?" said Perry with a full mouth, in between chews. "Show up like that, at the right time? You know, that's twice now."

Pulver dismounted his dragon and approached Calvin and Perry. "You've had ample time to think the answer through?"

"Yes," replied Calvin. "I have my answer."

"Are you sure?" said Pulver. "You only have one crack at it."

"I'm sure," said Calvin.

"Well then. If your answer is correct, I will present some dragons to you. I will keep introducing new ones until a match is made. However, if the answer is wrong, I will not see you for another year."

"That's after you drop us off at home, right?" asked Perry, washing his chocolate down with a swig of water.

"We'll see," said Pulver. "It's better than gold, to underground dwellers. Without it, they die in cellars. Push and pull with all their might, without a turn they'll see no light. A pile of bones shares the name, and with this thing they'll end the game."

Pulver stood still, awaiting his answer.

Perry looked over at Calvin and gave him a nod, signaling for him to announce it.

Calvin acknowledged the invitation and looked at Pulver. "A skeleton key," he said. "The answer is a skeleton key."

Pulver stood silently, expressionless. The long awkward silence made Calvin and Perry begin to feel nervous.

"A skeleton key?" Pulver finally repeated. "Are you sure?"

Calvin took a deep breath, exhaled, and nodded. "Yes, I'm sure . . . it's a skeleton key."

Pulver remained silent for another moment. He finally broke the stillness by slowly raising his right arm with his palm facing up. As his hand reached his shoulder, Calvin saw the heads of three large dragons rise from beyond the edge of the cliff. The dragons continued to ascend, flapping their wings, before landing on the edge next to Pulver.

"Now, Calvin," said Pulver. "This is your selection. If you need to see more, I will bring more. Look the dragons over and approach one if you sense a connection. If the bond is meant to be, the dragon will submit to you by lowering its head just below your hand. If you feel that same connection, your hand will be drawn to its head. This will unite you until death."

Calvin looked at the three dragons. They all looked similar, but were different colors. One was made up of blue and green scales. Another was mostly red. The third one was brown and orange. They stood twelve to fifteen feet tall with their tails dangling several feet off the edge of the cliff. Their powerful wings were tucked up close to their backs. Spikes, beginning between their ears, ran down the back of their necks and diminished near the saddle of their backs. They emerged again further back, continuing down to the end of their tails.

Calvin inspected the dragons and was immediately drawn to one. It was the biggest of the three, covered in blue and green scales. As Calvin approached the dragon, the beast began to extend its neck toward him, but immediately pulled back. Calvin extended his hand, reaching for the dragon, holding it still in front of it with his palm facing up.

"It's okay," said Calvin.

The dragon sniffed the air, and again began to lengthen its neck toward Calvin. Just before his hand touched the dragon, it cowered away.

"Amazing!" said Pulver. "That's the closest that dragon has come to anyone in the last thirteen years. I bring her up every chance I get, but she never seems interested."

Calvin approached the dragon again, but this time she turned her body away. On her left hind leg, a mark was visible. It was a crescent moon.

"Pulver?" asked Calvin. "Who was the last person to ride this dragon?"

"Amalga? Why . . . now that you mention it . . . I believe it was your father," said Pulver with a smile. "That explains her behavior toward you. She must sense the connection between you and Miles."

Calvin's face lit up. He thought about his dream where he saw his mother and father embrace before his father departed on a journey. It was the last time his mother would see his father. From his dream, Calvin recognized the crescent shape on the left hind leg of his father's dragon.

"Why don't you see if the others appeal to you, Calvin," suggested Pulver.

Calvin looked the other two dragons over. One of them looked away—uninterested. But the other stared at him intently in the eyes. It too was a large dragon and stood about fourteen feet high. It looked a lot like Amalga, but had reddish scales and glowing blue eyes. It extended its neck forward, suspending its head in front of Calvin.

Calvin continued to peer deeper and deeper into the dragon's eyes. He felt as though he could see inside of its mind. He saw visions of the dragon's past. It was at war fighting other dragons ridden by the Zarkon. He saw it defeat many in battle. He saw it rescue its rider a couple of different times. He saw that it had taken blows while throwing its body in between its rider and the enemy. It appeared to be brave and strong.

Calvin slowly stretched his arm out with his fingers extended, and softly stroked the dragon's snout. The instant he touched the dragon, he felt a warm wave of power shoot through his body. It was an exhilarating feeling—one that gave him confidence and courage.

Still looking into the dragon's eyes, Calvin saw a radiant glow around its head. It seemed as if it, too, was looking inside of him. Perhaps reading into his past—or realizing his potential.

"Calvin," said Pulver. "This is Bravada. She's a good one."

"Hey, Bravada," whispered Calvin. "We're going to make a good team, aren't we?"

"Now, don't get frustrated when trying to communicate with her. In time you two will be one."

"I'll take good care of you."

Bravada acted as if she understood his words and nodded gently.

"Get on," Pulver said. "Take her for a ride."

Calvin looked at the dragon as she crouched down, inviting him to mount. He climbed up her hind leg and scooted to the saddle of the dragon's back. "Let's go, girl," he said softly.

Bravada stood up tall and flapped her wings. With every flap, Calvin could feel the power. It only took a few strokes of her wings before they rose into the air. Two dull spikes stuck out of Bravada's back in front of the saddle that Calvin quickly and conveniently found and used for handles. He had a feeling that he should brace himself and hold on tight. Bravada hovered in the air out over the cliff, tucked in her wings, and swooped rapidly toward the sea below. Calvin screamed in fear as he and Bravada plummeted toward the ocean. The water was drawing near.

"Please, Bravada. Pull up."

Bravada's wings snapped out and she pulled out of the dive, gliding just above the water.

"Woo-hoo!" Calvin yelled, punching his fist into the air. The wind was blowing through his hair as he grinned.

Bravada ascended again. In a matter of seconds they were soaring high, the land far below. There were several islands in the sea just off the coast along Cambria, which he recognized from his map.

As Calvin studied the islands from above, he had a strong urge to visit one in particular. He didn't know exactly why, but knew that Labyrinth would be his next adventure. He had memorized the map completely. And as he looked at the island from above, he could see an aura of light radiating from the rocky mass.

Bravada soared through the air and landed on the edge of the cliff where Pulver and Perry were waiting.

"Calvin," said Pulver, "you have a loyal companion now. You must learn to trust her. She will not lead you astray."

Calvin nodded.

"Very well, then," said Pulver. "My work here is finished." He climbed atop his dragon. "If you ever need anything, Calvin, I will be at Dragon Lookout." Pulver pointed to the beautiful waterfall from where he came.

The sun was beginning to sink toward the horizon.

"How do you suppose we get this dragon back to Wolf Creek?" Perry asked. "It's not going to fit through the cellar door, you know."

"I was wondering the same thing," said Calvin. "I think we should head back to the town square and keep her hidden in the woods there. You and I can get home through The Crossing." Calvin looked over at Bravada. "Come on, girl. We're going for a ride."

Bravada crouched down and Calvin and Perry climbed onto her back. Together they rose high into the sky. It was only a half an hour before they saw the dim lights of the town square. Calvin pointed out the cottage where they would access The Crossing. He figured he would have Bravada drop them off in the woods behind the cottage, and then they would go home through the portal in the basement. But just as he approached the cottage, Bravada bolted skyward.

"Easy, Bravada!" cried Calvin.

"What's she doing?" Perry yelled. He flung his arms around Calvin's waist and held tightly.

Bravada continued to soar. Her powerful wings flapped in a way that began to worry Calvin and terrify Perry. Calvin looked down and saw the earth far below.

Bravada! Please let me down, Calvin commanded through his thoughts.

Bravada plateaued, which eased Calvin's mind a little, but then she began her descent. Plummeting toward the trees below, Bravada fell faster and faster. With every second, she grew closer to what lay below—a lake surrounded by trees.

"Make her stop, Calvin! Make her stop!" Perry yelled frantically.

"Slow down, Bravada!" Calvin began to think that having a dragon was not at all what it was cracked up to be. Maybe it was too soon to take her out. He hadn't even known her for very long. Was it long enough to develop a relationship? Apparently not. She was definitely not listening to him.

The calm water drew nearer. Calvin's life flashed before his eyes. Perry continued to hold onto Calvin, tightening his grip with every ounce of muscle he had. They were both bracing themselves for a mighty crash into water that would feel like cement upon impact. Just a few feet away from the surface, Bravada pulled up and glided only inches above the water. Calvin and Perry were relieved, but only for a moment. Ahead of them was a wall of trees that grew along the water's edge.

"I should have never made you get your dragon!" Perry yelled. "It's all my fault. Now we're going to die!"

"No!" Calvin yelled back. "It's my fault. I dragged you out of bed and made you come with me!" Calvin returned his thoughts to Bravada. "Come on, girl!" he pleaded. "Put us down."

"No, really. It's my fault," Perry argued.

"Perry, drop it already!"

They were approaching the barrier quickly. Only a few

seconds remained before they would smack into the trees. Perry couldn't let it go. "Calvin! I'm the one who made . . . the potions."

Calvin looked back at Perry.

"And . . . wrote the note."

Calvin stared in disbelief.

A bright, blinding flash engulfed the atmosphere.

18 · Labyrinth

The air was thick as Calvin felt himself travel through a wave of energy. Perry's screams turned to a slow, deep crawl. But it lasted only a short moment. Their surroundings became familiar again. Calvin realized instantly that they had just traveled through a portal. He elbowed Perry, trying to silence his morbid cries.

"It's okay, Perry! We're fine!"

The cries began to quiet—barely.

"Come on, Perry," said Calvin. "Look around. We're safe."

Perry finally regained his wits and looked around to find that he and Calvin were alive and well, flying smoothly above the treetops near their homes.

"Bravada took us through a portal," Calvin said. "We're above Wolf Creek. Look!"

He spotted his house, then Perry's, then Anna's. Calvin stroked Bravada's neck. "You knew all along, didn't you?" Bravada turned and acknowledged him as she landed in the woods just outside Calvin's backyard. "You know, one day we'll be able to communicate."

"Hurry up and let me off!" said Perry, breathing hard. He slid down Bravada's side and fell to the forest floor, holding the ground as lovingly as he could.

"Are you hugging the ground?" Calvin asked Perry.

"Just give me a minute . . . alone," Perry said. He whimpered a few more times and then looked up. "I have never wanted to touch the ground as much as I want to now."

"You're fine, Perry. You're fine."

Perry got to his feet and shook his head. "I can't believe we made it."

From the edge of his backyard, Calvin looked toward his home. The lights were on inside. Through the window he could see his grandpa sitting in his usual armchair.

"Are you going to be busted?" Perry asked. "I mean . . .

we've been gone for two days."

"No. I'll be fine," Calvin said. "Grandpa's pretty cool."

"Well, I'll take the blame," said Perry. "It was all my fault."

"I can't believe you actually set me up like that," Calvin said.

"I know. I shouldn't have."

"How did you pull that off?" Calvin asked, amazed.

"Are you mad?"

"No way," said Calvin. "But if I would have died, my mom would have killed you. Come on, let's go inside." Calvin turned to Bravada, and in his mind commanded, *Bravada . . . stay close by, but remain hidden.*

Calvin and Perry entered the house through the back door. Grandpa heard the door shut.

"Calvin?" he called. "Is that you?"

Calvin and Perry entered the room. "Yes. We're home."

"Good. Your mother called to check up on you. I told her you were fine. I didn't tell her that I hadn't seen you for a couple of days. Sorry for not coming home last night. I got held up at the castle. I trusted that you'd be fine on your own."

Calvin couldn't believe it. His grandpa wasn't even home to know that he and Perry had been gone. He decided to just go with it. "Oh, yeah . . . don't worry about us. We're fine."

* * * *

Calvin whispered to Perry a few times but got no response. Perry was asleep. He and Perry had gone to bed an hour ago, and his grandpa had laid down long before that. Calvin quietly laced up his shoes, grabbed a jacket, and slipped out the back door. *Bravada*, he called in his mind. *Where are you? I need you.*

Moments later, a large dragon emerged from the trees just beyond the backyard. Calvin climbed aboard Bravada's back. "Let's go over here." He guided her to Anna's house, just outside of her bedroom window.

Calvin jumped off Bravada and picked up a small stone. He then climbed back onto the dragon and tossed the stone against the glass window on the upper floor of the home. He waited silently.

Finally, the curtains were brushed away, unveiling a pretty

girl behind the window.

At first, Anna's eyes were wide from being startled. But her expression quickly turned to excitement as she rattled the window open.

"Calvin!" she whispered loudly. "Is that you?"

Calvin smiled.

"Come say hello to my new friend, Bravada," Calvin said.

"It's beautiful!"

"Come on, let's go for a ride," said Calvin. "It's amazing."

Anna opened the window wide and sat on the edge of the sill. Bravada stood tall and stretched her neck out for Anna to hold onto. Grasping a nearby tree branch for balance, Anna climbed down the dragon's scaly neck. She sat behind Calvin and threw her arms around him.

"It's so good to see you," she said. "I wondered what you guys were up to."

"Yeah . . . it's been a crazy couple of days," said Calvin, smiling at her. "You're going to love this. Hold on tight."

Anna squeezed Calvin as Bravada flapped her wings, gently rising from the ground. Together they rose toward the stars, leaving the earth far below. Bravada outstretched her wings and gently glided through the sky.

"Tell me, what did you have to do to get such an amazing dragon?" said Anna.

"Perry and I hiked our way up Yeti Mountain. A giant bug attacked us. Then we fought a pack of yeti. We escaped that, and then finally made it to the dragon keeper at the Cliffs of Tarnin. The dragon keeper presented me with a riddle. He said if I got the answer right, he would let me see some dragons. But if I answered it wrong, I couldn't come back for a year. It was tough, but after a long time of going back and forth, I figured it out."

"So what was the riddle?" asked Anna.

Feeling a bit proud, Calvin recited the riddle. "It's better than gold, to underground dwellers. Without it, they die in cellars. Push and pull with all their might, without a turn they'll see no light. A pile of bones shares the name, and with this thing they'll end the game."

Anna thought for a couple of seconds and asked, "A

skeleton key?"

Calvin turned and looked at her, amazed. "You've heard that one before?"

"No. First time. It just makes sense that it would be a skeleton key."

Calvin shook his head, baffled.

"How long did you say you were trying to work out the answer?"

Calvin laughed. "You're amazing, aren't you?"

Calvin and Anna continued to soar through the sky. Anna still had her arms wrapped around Calvin tightly. "This is so cool!" she shouted, as the wind brushed through her long flowing hair.

About an hour passed before Bravada touched down outside Anna's bedroom window.

"I better get back to Perry," said Calvin.

"Does he know you left him?"

Calvin shook his head. "He was sleeping. I tried to fall asleep, but I couldn't. My mind was racing about all sorts of things. I needed to get up and clear my head. That's when I had the idea to come here so you could meet Bravada."

"Well, I'm glad you came tonight," said Anna.

"Yeah, me too," said Calvin, smiling.

"How did you get this thing through The Crossing?" asked Anna.

"It was pretty crazy. Bravada scared us to death. I felt like I had lost control of her, but she knew what she was doing. She entered through a portal near the woods."

Anna didn't say anything. She just sat there, gazing into Calvin's eyes. There was an awkward silence. Feeling red in the face, Calvin wiped his brow with the back of his hand.

"Are you feeling okay?" asked Anna.

"Yeah . . . I'm fine," said Calvin. "I just have a lot on my mind, that's all."

"So, what are your plans now?" asked Anna.

"We need to go to the island of Labyrinth," said Calvin. "According to the map, there is a sword somewhere on the island. I don't know why, but I have a strong feeling that we need to go there. And you need to come with us. We need you."

Anna smiled. "When are we going to go?"

"Tomorrow."

"That might work," said Anna. "My mom is going to be gone most of the day tomorrow. How about picking me up when she leaves?"

"How will I know when that will be?"

"I'll send you a fizzle-gram," said Anna.

"What's a fizzle-gram?"

Anna smiled and looked down at her hands. She formed another ball of light and launched it into the air. The ball popped and sparks twirled again, this time forming letters in the sky. Calvin looked up and waited patiently for the words to appear. Within seconds, the words were visible: *You will know.*

"Cool," marveled Calvin. "Well then, keep me posted."

Bravada straightened up and extended her neck toward the window, close enough for Anna to climb through.

"Thanks for coming to see me."

"Good night, Anna."

* * * *

Calvin heard a loud pop in the room. Sparks suddenly filled the air, dancing and twirling around, forming various shapes. He looked over at Perry, who was still sitting at the table, his arms folded, and eyes staring at his empty plate. It was obvious he was oblivious to the fireworks display inside the house.

When the last sparkly stream formed the final shapes, Calvin made out the words suspended in mid-air right before him: *I'm ready.*

"Perry," said Calvin. "By chance do you see anything odd in this room right now?"

Perry looked around carefully.

"Something over in this area?" Calvin got up and gestured to the middle of the room where the message was suspended in the air.

Perry continued to look around. The message had vanished.

"I don't see anything," said Perry. "Unless you think that big boar's head hanging on the wall looks a bit cross-eyed."

145

Perry could tell that Calvin was having another one of his intuitive moments. "Calvin, what is it?"

"We're going to Labyrinth. But we need to make a quick stop first. Come on. Let's go."

Calvin and Perry mounted Bravada, and Calvin guided her to Anna's house.

"Where are we going?" Perry asked.

"When I asked you if you noticed anything . . . the room was filled with sparks that formed a message. It was a fizzle-gram from Anna telling us that she wanted to come with us to Labyrinth. We are picking her up."

"Really?" Perry smiled. "She's coming with us?"

"Pretty cool, huh?"

* * * *

Anna was watching anxiously out her window and ran outside to greet them as soon as she saw them. She was waiting for them in the same spot Calvin had landed just hours before.

Anna looked over at Perry and gave him a friendly smile as she hurried toward him.

"Hold on," warned Calvin as soon as Anna boarded the dragon. Bravada flapped her wings, and propelled them quickly up into the sky. Within seconds, Wolf Creek was far below.

Although Perry had passed through the portal the night before, he didn't find it any more exhilarating this time. Anna handled the passing through the portal quite well.

Before long, they were soaring over Fiddler Forest and Yeti Mountain. Just off in the distance the land dropped abruptly as they came to the colorful Cliffs of Tarnin. Soon they were flying over the sea. They saw several small islands dotting the waters.

"I think that one," said Anna, pointing, "is Labyrinth."

Calvin nodded and steered Bravada in the direction of the cone-shaped island. As they approached the piece of land, the three examined it carefully. The island appeared to be barren all around except for a thick patch of lush, green vegetation growing near the top of it.

Circling the island, they marveled at its vast craggy cliffs. Several hundred feet up one wall they spotted a long, narrow ledge that protruded out just a few feet. Calvin's eyes were drawn

146

to a pile of rocks sitting atop the ledge. The pile was stacked neatly—so neatly that Calvin presumed it was placed there, not by nature, but by man. Curious, he wondered what was underneath the rubble.

At Calvin's silent suggestion, Bravada flew closer to the ledge. There was not an area large enough for her to land on, but the wall just under the ledge was decorated with several pockmarks. Bravada clamped her claws into the holes while Calvin, Perry, and Anna climbed up her neck and jumped off. Calvin carefully shuffled his way toward the pile of rocks, trying not to look down. A strong breeze was blowing, which made him feel a little unstable, but he managed to keep his footing.

Calvin surveyed the box-shaped pile. The base was made up of two large boulders that were flat on top. The height of the boulders reached Calvin's knees. There was another layer of smaller rocks, each about the size of a basketball. Smaller softball-sized rocks made up a third layer, filling the gaps and completing the peculiar square-shaped pile.

Calvin easily tossed the smallest rocks off the top and was able to muscle the larger ones away. Only the two biggest ones remained. He sat down on the ledge and pressed his back against the wall. Using the wall to push off of, he tried to move the larger boulder out of the way with his feet. It wouldn't budge.

"Perry," called Calvin. "Come help me for a minute."

Perry slowly crawled his way over to Calvin and sat next to him with his back against the wall. Together they placed their feet on the boulder and pushed. The boulder shifted, but their strength wasn't sufficient.

"Need some more muscle?" joked Anna.

Neither Calvin nor Perry answered.

Anna sat down next to Perry and placed her feet upon the boulder. Together, the three pushed with their legs. The boulder rocked a little and scooted just a few inches. Exhausted, the three relaxed and rested from their exertion.

"Yeah . . . about that muscle," said Perry, looking over at Anna. "Do you know where we can find some?"

Bravada flew toward the three of them and motioned for them to stand back by swinging her neck to the side. Calvin,

Perry, and Anna moved away and Bravada turned around and raised her tail, lifting it toward the boulder. She wrapped her tail around the top of the large rock and gently moved it aside, easily clearing it away, exposing an opening.

Calvin moved closer to the hole and cleared several smaller rocks from the area. A cool draft close to the ground seeped through the opening. "This is it," said Calvin. "Let's see where this will take us."

Another boulder was soon exposed and Calvin called to Bravada for assistance. Once again, Bravada dislodged the boulder, this time rolling it off the edge of the cliff. Calvin, Perry, and Anna carefully leaned over the edge and watched the boulder fall into the air, skid off the walls, and finally crash into the sea far below.

The hole was now large enough to squeeze through. Calvin led the way, crawling on his hands and knees, followed by Perry. Anna entered last.

"Ahh!" came a sharp scream.

Calvin heard the sound of rocks cracking and scraping against each other. What little light that shone through the crevice instantly faded.

"What is it?" yelled Calvin. "Anna, are you okay?"

"I'm fine," replied Anna. "The hole just closed itself off. We can't get out. We're trapped."

"What did she say?" Calvin said to Perry.

"She said the entrance was sealed off," Perry repeated to Calvin. "If we're going to leave this cave, we'll have to find another way out."

Calvin continued to slither his way through the hole on his stomach with his hands outstretched in front of him. The tunnel was tight. He could feel his side press against the walls, and in some areas, he could feel the ceiling of the shaft scrape along his back. He hoped that Perry, who was much heavier than he was, was not having problems squirming through the tight passage.

"Perry!" Calvin called back. "You okay?"

"As long as it doesn't get any tighter," replied Perry, struggling to inch forward. "I probably should have laid off the ice cream."

"What are you talking about? When did you have ice cream?" asked Calvin, feeling a little left out.

"The last thirteen years." Perry continued to pull himself forward. "I don't like this," he continued. "When I take a deep breath, I can fill my whole torso press against the rock."

Calvin, surrounded by total darkness, brought his hands together and formed a small globe of light. He gently pushed the globe forward as it floated in front of him, lighting the way ahead.

The tight tunnel only occasionally permitted Calvin to raise his chin from the dirt floor to catch a glimpse of the pathway ahead. On one such instance, he realized he was approaching a fork in the shaft. He was faced with the decision to continue on, or veer slightly to the right. The tunnel to the right seemed to be barely wider. He thought Perry would appreciate that. He chose to follow the tunnel to the right.

After slithering forward for several minutes, Calvin reached a high spot in the ceiling that allowed him to raise his head up. He pushed the globe of light gently forward. It glided ten feet ahead and then bounced back toward him. First impression suggested a dead end.

"You're kidding me," Calvin said softly so only he could hear. He placed his cheek on the cool rock and rested his neck. It was sore from looking up so much. He wondered how he was going to tell the others that they had to go back. He wasn't sure that Perry could even do it. Crawling forward was exhausting. Going backward had to be harder.

Calvin took another look up ahead. This time he noticed that the ceiling appeared to open up. He proceeded to move forward and before he knew it, he was able to stand in a small grotto.

Perry and Anna soon emerged from the tunnel and welcomed the chance to stand up again. Perry took a long, deep breath and filled up his lungs with air. He slowly let it out. "You don't know how good that feels. I couldn't breathe in that thing."

"Where do we go now?" asked Anna.

"We need to go back to the fork and follow the other

tunnel," said Calvin.

"What?" Perry complained. "Are you serious?"

Calvin crouched down to his hands and knees, and started to head back through the tunnel.

"Whoa, whoa, whoa," Perry cried. "Not so fast. We're not in a race here. Can't we take a break?"

Calvin backed his way out. "Of course." He rose to his feet. "Let me know when you're ready."

"Are you sure there's no other way?" said Perry.

"You'll be fine, Perry," Anna said. "You can do this."

"Well, I guess I have no choice, do I? It's not like I'm going to stay here. Just give me a few more minutes." Perry put his hand on the back of his neck and massaged it.

Each one of them had dirt smudged on their faces. Their clothes were covered in dust. So was their hair. Perry appeared to have mud dripping down the sides of his cheeks as his sweat mixed with the dust.

"All right, Calvin," Perry finally said.

"Are you ready?"

"No." Perry sighed. "But let's go anyway."

Calvin led the way down the other passage. The journey was slow and difficult. After several minutes of wiggling and inching himself forward, Calvin felt discouraged. The ball of light that he used to guide him through the burrow indicated another dead end. Calvin lay there motionless, staring at the smooth stone face just six feet ahead. He didn't understand. How could there not be another way?

Feeling defeated, Calvin gave the globe a punch with his fist. The ball of light shot ahead, skipping off the walls, until it hit the wall at the end, and dropped. Hope again filled his body as he frantically wiggled ahead, determined to see where the light had gone. Inch by inch, Calvin maneuvered his body along the tunnel. At the end of the passage, the tunnel became steep. He scooted along and slid down the shaft. He spread his feet wide and scraped his shoes against the sides of the walls to keep himself from sliding too quickly. The chute finally deposited Calvin onto the ground. The room was small, but a welcomed sight, as it allowed him to stand up and stretch again.

A minute later, a head popped up from the tunnel. "This is crazy," said Perry. "It's a good thing we're not claustrophobic."

Calvin gave Perry his hand and pulled him to his feet.

"You know . . . this wouldn't be so bad to travel through . . . if you were a gnome," Anna said, poking her head out. "At least they could comfortably crouch and walk along these passages. It would be easy for someone like Osgar Ivins to explore these tight holes," said Anna.

"You think he made these tunnels?" Perry said.

"It only makes sense that he did. If he is the creator of the orbs, he's the one who hid them. According to the map, the sword is supposed to be on this island. I'm sure Osgar had something to do with it."

Calvin pushed the ball of light along the top of the room. The room was dome shaped. It was about ten feet across—the ceiling was six feet high in the tallest part. Rocks were scattered about the dirt floor. Looking around the room, they could see no way out.

Calvin walked over to the wall and placed his hand on the rock surface. He put his ear to the stone. He could sense nothing. Perry walked over to the opposite side of the room and scanned the walls, up and down. He looked at every inch, trying to be open to anything peculiar, sticking his fingers in every crack and hole they passed, hoping to find a secret button.

Anna sat down on a flat rock in the middle of the floor. "Is anyone else cold?" she said, rubbing her hands together, trying to warm them up. "I feel cold all of a sudden."

Calvin immediately stopped what he was doing and looked over at Anna sitting on the rock in the center of the room. He knelt beside her and felt a faint, cold draft coming from the base of the rock.

"Get up for a second," said Calvin, scooting her to the side.

Anna stood and stepped away. Calvin pushed against the rock. It wouldn't budge. He leaned his shoulder into it—this time feeling a slight movement.

"Perry, come over here. I need a hand," Calvin grunted.

Perry knelt by Calvin, ready to help him move the rock. There was a wall within reach that he used to push off of with his feet.

"On three . . . ready?" said Calvin. Perry nodded.

"One . . . two . . . three."

They braced their shoulders against the rock and pressed their feet against the wall. Their faces strained. The two grunted and exerted as much power as they could. The rock finally budged a couple of inches and they rested to catch their breath.

"This is the way!" said Anna, waving her hand over the small opening. The draft became more pronounced and emitted a steady stream that blew through Anna's hair.

Perry looked at Calvin and nodded as if to ask, "Are you ready?"

Calvin pulled himself up and got into position.

"One . . . two . . . three."

Together they pushed from one side while Anna pulled the rock toward her from the other. The three managed to slide the rock away another six inches before resting again. The hole was large now, but not quite big enough for them to fit through. Calvin guided the globe of light into the hole—it lit up the cavern below, but cast too many shadows to get a decent look.

"One . . . more should . . . do it," said Calvin, out of breath.

The three worked together one final time and successfully slid the rock away. Perry looked inside and found that he could lower himself into the hole onto a ledge, just a few feet below. The ledge was the top step to a set of stairs that descended into the darkness. The others followed.

Without notice, the entrance sealed itself off as the large boulder they had just shouldered out of the way had moved back into place.

19 · Abreyla

The three descended the steep, stone staircase carefully, trying not to look down off the edge. There was no handrail to hold onto, and there was a sheer drop on either side. The stairs were uncomfortably shallow, extremely close together, and very awkward to tackle one by one. Calvin led the way one sure foot after another. Perry slid down on his bottom, one step at a time.

At the bottom of the staircase, there was only one way to go. On the opposite side of the room, dangling against the vertical wall was a rickety ladder made of frayed rope and wooden planks. The top of the ladder disappeared through a narrow hole in the ceiling.

"Are you kidding me?" Perry said. "Now we have to climb a ladder? Anyone ever heard of escalators? Now, that would have been a novel idea."

Anna walked over to the ladder and tugged on the ropes. "How old do you think this is?" She rolled a frayed portion of the rope between her fingers.

"More like how *safe* do you think this is?" Perry offered.

The ladder seemed like it would be awkward to climb. The rungs were made of wooden planks, just six inches wide. The planks had two holes—one on each end—that the ropes were strung through. Knots in the rope above and below each plank kept the rungs in place. Each board was spaced four inches apart. Clearly the ladder was designed for small people, most likely gnomes.

Calvin took the rope in his hands and tugged—it had some flex to it but seemed sturdy. He placed one foot on the first plank of weathered wood, about six inches off the floor, and stepped onto it. The rope became taut, but only after the board sunk to the ground. Calvin skipped a few planks and climbed another step—and then another. On his fourth step, as he pressed his leg down to lift himself, the old board splintered in half. Calvin was caught off guard. His body spun out of control and his back smacked against the rock. Determined, he straightened himself out and continued to climb—still skipping three or four rungs at a time. Perry and Anna held their breath as they watched from below.

Calvin climbed higher and higher, approaching the tight opening above. Perry and Anna saw Calvin's body disappear into the dark shadows.

"Ahh!" Calvin shouted as he caught hold of the rope, holding his weight with his right hand only, twisting and swinging, banging his body against the wall.

"Calvin?" Anna shouted. "Calvin? Are you okay?"

Calvin collected himself. He made sure his footing was secure once again.

"Calvin?" Anna said. "Are you okay?"

Calvin finally answered, "Yeah."

"What happened?" asked Perry.

"Another board broke. I'm fine."

Calvin created a globe of light so he and the others could see as they climbed the ladder. He noticed that the rope continued upward, but there was a platform that he could step onto.

"I'm off the rope. Who's next?"

Perry and Anna looked at each other. "You go," offered Perry. "I'm heavier."

Anna didn't say anything, but she approached the rope and began to climb.

"I'll catch you if you fall," Perry assured her.

Anna had little trouble making her way up the ladder. Occasionally her foot would slip off one of the planks, which would startle Calvin and Perry more than her.

Near the top, Anna found herself suspended in the middle of the shaft.

"Give me your hand," Calvin said.

Anna kept a firm grasp of the rope with one hand, and extended her other hand for Calvin. He took hold of it and helped her easily step onto the platform.

"Okay, Perry," Anna said. "I'm off."

"You can do it, Perry," said Calvin.

Perry didn't want to climb the ladder, but he really had no

choice. He took a deep breath and inched his way up, awkwardly, step-by-step, careful not to make any movements that would apply unnecessary weight to the ropes.

"That's it," said Anna. "Steady."

"Just like when we were kids, huh, Calvin?" said Perry. "Climbing up to our tree fort."

"That was a ladder made of metal rungs, Perry," said Calvin. "And those were attached to the tree trunk."

"You're not helping," said Perry.

"It's just like it, Perry," Anna said, elbowing Calvin in the ribs. "Just like it."

"Thank you," said Perry, forcing a smile.

Perry was approaching the shaft where Calvin and Anna stood. He strained as he slowly pulled himself up. He could see Calvin and Anna just a few feet above. He was fatigued. His calves and his forearms were burning. As he stood upon the next worn wooden rung, one of the frayed ropes suddenly snapped.

"Ahh!" Anna screamed.

Perry caught hold of the rope, just above the break, and the larger portion of the ladder whipped wildly below him, the rungs uselessly dangling from the one remaining rope. Perry's legs flailed. Desperately holding on for his life, he began to reach higher. The muscles in his forearms were about to fail.

"Come on . . . you're almost there," said Calvin.

Shaking furiously, Perry wrapped his legs around the rope, trying to provide some relief to his arms. He slowly reached up and pulled his body a couple of feet higher.

"That's it!" said Calvin.

Perry was finally high enough to dismount. "Give me your hand," said Calvin.

Perry wrapped his legs tighter around the ropes to help him adjust his grip. He clutched the rope with his left hand, and pinned a portion of it against his body with the inside of his arm and elbow.

"That's it," said Calvin. "Now give me your hand."

Perry began to reach for Calvin's hand. His weight shifted. The rope snapped near his waist. And the rope ladder plummeted to the ground.

155

Anna screamed.

Perry gasped as he instinctively grabbed onto the rope again. He hung—arms outstretched—with his feet dangling freely below.

"Hold on, Perry!" Anna called.

"I'm going to die," he cried.

"No, you're not!" said Calvin. "You hold on!"

Perry's knuckles were white as he strained to retain his clutch.

"Hold on!" Anna repeated.

"Listen, Perry," Calvin said. "You have to give me your hand."

Perry shook his head. "I can't . . . I can't do it."

"You have to!"

Perry tried to adjust his grip, but he couldn't pull his body up high enough. His fingers slipped further.

"Just do it!" said Calvin. "Reach for my hand!"

Perry shifted his eyes toward Calvin. He saw Calvin's hand nearby.

"Come on, Perry," Anna said. "Grab hold of it."

Perry swallowed and then quickly released the rope with his weakest hand and reached for Calvin. Calvin caught Perry's hand and immediately pulled back as hard as he could, swinging Perry toward the ledge. Perry let go of the rope and his body flung through the air toward Calvin.

Together the two tumbled to the ground. Calvin landed on his back and Perry toppled directly on top of him. They found themselves staring face-to-face, their noses an inch away from each other.

Anna ran to Calvin and Perry and dog-piled them, screaming with excitement. "You did it!" She threw her arms around each of them.

Calvin and Perry were both breathing hard. "Yes, Perry," Calvin said. "You did it."

"Thanks."

Anna made her way off the pile.

"Perry?" said Calvin.

"Yeah," answered Perry looking into his eyes, still catching his breath.

"You can get off me now."

"Oh, yeah . . . right." Perry rolled off of Calvin and onto his back.

A narrow staircase, carved out of rock, spiraled upward.

"Looks like that's the way," said Anna.

"Who designed this place?" complained Perry. "This is insane." He rose to his feet.

Calvin led the way up the staircase. He continued to push his globe of light forward, illuminating the path immediately in front of them. Calvin rounded the corner and stopped at once. A full skeleton lay on the steps to one side—a dagger rammed into its chest.

Anna gasped, covering her mouth with her hand.

"This makes it all seem real, doesn't it?" said Calvin.

"This?" said Perry. "This makes it seem real? I think almost falling to my death seemed pretty real to me."

"I know," said Calvin. "But I'm talking about these people. Others have been here looking for the same thing we're looking for. This guy . . . he didn't make it."

"Yes, but others have been searching with evil intentions," said Anna. "We aren't after power. We are fighting for freedom and there's . . . there's a difference—a real difference. We just might succeed, when others have failed."

"Who do you suppose killed them?" asked Perry.

The three carefully stepped over another skeleton lying on the steps, its hand still clasping a sword that was covered with rust.

Another skeleton laid across the stairs several steps ahead.

"There had to have been a winner," said Perry. "Did he escape? Did he find the sword? Did he find an orb? Or did he die in here—a slow, painful, starving death?"

"Listen," said Calvin, putting his hand up. The three of them stopped immediately. "I heard something up there."

Perry drew his wand.

Calvin quietly led them forward, carefully listening. The staircase continued to spiral upward, offering limited visibility. The bodies adorning the steps became more frequent with every turn.

"Shhh," said Calvin.

They heard a faint noise ahead that sounded like squeaking door hinges—and then a lock.

"Someone's up there," said Calvin. "Come on."

They continued up the stairs, trying not to dwell on the masses of bones underneath their feet. Minutes later, the staircase ended. In front of them was a solid, wooden door encased in an iron frame with an iron loop for a handle. But there was no place for a key—no handle to turn.

"Maybe you pull on it," said Calvin.

"Maybe *you* pull on it," Perry fired back.

Calvin forced a nervous smile and reached for the loop. He gave it a tug, but it was locked. Calvin closed his eyes and reached again for the handle. A word came to his mind. "*Abreyla*," he said. After a couple of clicks, he pulled the door open.

Calvin gave a gentle push to the globe of light that had been so helpful on their journey so far, but as soon as it entered through the door, it fizzled out. He tried to conjure another ball of light, but nothing happened. Apparently their magic would be ineffective inside.

On the other side of the door, torches adorned the walls and lit up the spacious, circular room. The ceiling was nearly one hundred feet tall and the room easily stretched the same distance from wall to wall. Directly in the middle of the room was a large fountain. Water trickled into a pool below. Without warning, a loud slam came from behind them. They spun around and saw that the door through which they'd just entered had vanished.

20 • Tobran

Calvin retraced his steps to the door and felt the wall. He pushed against it and pounded it with his fist. It was solid rock.

With his wand still drawn, Perry walked toward the pool of water and looked in. The water was clear and deep. The floor of the pool was lit, and it illuminated treasures unimaginable. There were thousands of gold bricks and statues. Large diamonds were scattered about, shimmering in the rippling water. Jewel-decorated swords, helmets, and breastplates were strewn across the floor. Surrounding the pool was a short stone wall that had numerous gold coins on top.

"Look over here," said Anna pointing at the wall. "There is something written in the stone."

Anna read the words aloud, making a full circle around the pool:

> *Of all the treasures within your sight*
> *Choose the ones that will help you fight;*
> *Skilled you may be with spell and charm*
> *But against the guardian they do no harm.*
> *Each person who enters is allotted two*
> *Hoard any more and you will be doomed.*

"Choose the ones that will help you fight?" repeated Anna. "A weapon? Armor?"

"What I want to know is where's the guardian?" said Perry. "And how tough is he? Maybe my two pieces can be a sword and that gold statue over there." He pointed in the water at a golden sphinx. "You know how much that is worth?"

"The keeper of this treasury knows that most people would be eyeing the treasures," said Calvin. "Most people would try to pack out the heaviest pieces they could . . . because they're worth more. But somewhere along the way we will be facing something dangerous. A gold statue you can hardly lift will do you no

159

good."

Perry bent over the edge of the pool and dipped his finger in the water. "It's freezing!" he said. "How are we going to get the armor and weapons if they are on the bottom of the pool?"

"We haven't got a choice," said Calvin, looking into the water. "We need weapons . . . and the only place to get them is down there." He took off his jacket, threw it to the floor, and climbed atop the ledge.

"What do you want, Anna?" Calvin asked.

"I can use that shield." She pointed.

Perry and Anna watched Calvin take a deep breath, extend his arms over his head, and dive into the calm water. He had expected an immediate, unbearable freeze, but was surprised as the water comfortably warmed his body. The bone-chilling water in the pool had immediately become as warm as a soothing bath.

Calvin kicked and propelled his body downward, stretching his arms forward. The richly decorated shield lay before him. He reached out and grabbed it, then kicked off the bottom, shooting himself upward to the surface of the water. When he broke the surface, he gasped for breath.

"Here, Anna . . . take it," said Calvin, bringing the shield out of the water. Anna took the shield from Calvin.

"Perry? What do you see?"

"I need a sword."

Calvin disappeared beneath the water again.

"He's crazy!" said Perry. "How's he doing that?"

A few moments later, Calvin broke the surface again—this time with a sword. Perry reached out for it and examined it.

"Anna?" said Calvin. "What weapon do you want?"

"There's a dagger down there."

"Hey," said Perry. "If you see something to protect my heart, why don't you grab it? I'd hate to die of a heart attack." He smiled and playfully hit Anna.

Anna didn't seem amused.

Calvin disappeared again. He found a pointed dagger he thought would be manageable for Anna. He picked it up, along with a breastplate, and swam again to the surface. Anna took the dagger from Calvin and Perry took the breastplate.

"Aren't you freezing?" asked Anna, concerned.

"The water's perfect," said Calvin, treading water near the edge of the pool. "A little too warm, actually. I'll be back." He plunged into the water one final time and examined the floor. Treasures mostly caught his eye, but he tried to sift through the golden sparkles, looking for the weapon of his choice. He reached for a helmet and another sword and promptly kicked his way to the surface anticipating a fresh breath of air. When he emerged out of the water, he saw Perry and Anna standing close by, still holding their pieces of armor and weapons.

Calvin grunted as he tried to lift the heavy helmet out of the water and onto the edge of the pool. Recognizing his struggle, Perry reached out his hand to assist him.

"No, Perry!" said Anna. "You're already holding two!"

The warning was too late. As Perry took the helmet into his hands, the floor began to shake. Pieces of rock fell from the ceiling and crashed to the floor. Calvin hurried and climbed out of the water. They all ran to the edge of the room and pressed themselves against the wall. Debris continued to fall as the three crouched together underneath Anna's shield.

Directly across from them, on the other side of the pool, a large crack formed in the middle of the wall. The opening grew wider and the room began to shake more violently.

The light grew dim amid the dust from the fallen rubble and a roar sounded from the far side of the room. Emerging from the large crack in the wall opposite them was a giant, descending a stone staircase. The ground vibrated with his every step. He was heading in their direction.

Anna readied herself with the dagger and shield. Calvin and Perry also held their swords firm.

As the giant drew closer, they got a sense of how big he really was—easily ten feet in height. His face was scarred. His hair was snarled. His clothing was worn and tattered. The enormous figure carried no weapons; it clearly relied on brute strength.

Calvin, Perry, and Anna, even armed with swords and a dagger, felt outnumbered.

161

As the large man approached the pool, Calvin, Perry, and Anna ran in the opposite direction, keeping the fountain between themselves and the enemy. This seemed like a decent plan—to keep their distance—until the giant stood atop the edge of the water and sprung to the fountain that was in the center of the pool. He let out another intimidating roar.

Terrified, Calvin, Perry, and Anna split up. In just a matter of seconds, Perry and Anna were on one end of the pool and Calvin on the other, with the giant in the middle.

"What business do you have coming here?" the giant growled.

"I was wondering the same thing about you," said Perry. "We were doing just fine until you showed up."

"I am Tobran. And I have sworn to Master Osgar that I would not let anyone past this point."

"And if we happen to get past you, what would we find up ahead?" asked Anna.

"Nothing of use to you," growled Tobran. "The sword cannot be removed by anyone lest he possess the means to unlock its clutch."

"And how does one unlock this sword?" said Anna.

"The secret lies in a magical stone that Osgar fabricated long ago," said Tobran. "Unless you have that stone, you cannot remove the sword."

"And what if we have the stone?" asked Calvin.

Tobran laughed. "You don't expect me to believe that?"

"Anna," said Perry, "we came all this way, putting our lives in danger, for nothing. I mean . . . who knew that we would need a stone to unlock the sword?"

"Tobran?" said Anna. "Is there another way out? Please don't make us go through that tunnel again."

"Oh, don't worry, dear. I won't make you do that," said Tobran slyly.

Perry sighed with relief.

"You see . . . this is the end of the road for you," said Tobran. "Stone or no stone—my job is to destroy anyone who crosses my path. I am under oath to do everything in my power to protect it. I have been appointed to terminate any persons I see."

"Why not let us pass?" said Anna. "I mean . . . if we can't remove it, there is no harm done."

"You know too much now. But it is remarkable that children such as you have made it this far. No one has ever made it as far as you. You should be proud."

Perry and Anna looked at each other, somewhat helpless.

"Now," said Tobran, "any more questions before I destroy you?"

"Where's the sword?" Perry asked. "Not that it matters . . . I mean, clearly we don't have the magical stone, nor do we have the strength to get by you."

"I'm sorry to have to put you to death," said Tobran.

Tobran jumped across the water, swinging his fist through the air, targeted at Calvin's face. Calvin instinctively jerked his head to the side and the giant's hand bashed into the wall behind him.

Calvin quickly swung his sword at Tobran, but Tobran moved out of the way.

"So . . . what is the best way to defeat someone like you?" asked Calvin, backing away from him.

"Being alive is evidence that I have never been defeated," said Tobran. "So the best way is yet to be discovered."

Calvin noticed Perry and Anna quickly sneaking up behind Tobran. Calvin stuck to his tactic and continued to distract the giant. "How did Osgar talk you into spending your life in this hole?" Calvin asked.

"Osgar is a good man," said Tobran. "He gave me all of this for payment." Tobran pointed to the mounds of treasure that filled the pool.

"But what good does it do you if you can never get out of here?"

Perry and Anna were close now—almost within striking distance.

"I mean, really . . . this treasure makes you wealthy beyond measure, and it is very remarkable," said Calvin. "Tobran, the richest giant in the world." Calvin raised his hand and moved it through the air as if he were reading a headline of a newspaper.

"Yes. It sounds very nice, doesn't it?" said Tobran.

"Yes, it does . . . to a brainless mammoth like yourself!"

Perry and Anna shot Calvin confused looks. This clearly wasn't the way to get on Tobran's good side.

"Listen," said Calvin. "You are locked up here with the charge to destroy anyone who trespasses, and your reward is a pile of treasure. Treasure you will never get to use...You're wasting your life away in this hole."

Tobran continued to pursue Calvin. Perry and Anna were closing in behind him.

"Come with us," said Calvin. "We have a better cause we are fighting for. It's one that you can help us with."

"What are you talking about?" said Tobran.

"Evil is winning the war out there. Every day more people are turning to the dark side. Galigore is manipulating good people . . . persuading them to follow him to a so-called better life. His followers are recruiting anyone they can get."

"You've mistaken me for a bad person," said Tobran. "Don't you understand? That's why I am here: to fight against evil. Osgar hired me to protect the sword at all costs. If the sword were to get into the hands of the wrong person, prevailing against evil would be that much more difficult."

Calvin backed his way up the staircase. Tobran followed.

"Stop!" yelled Tobran with a roar that echoed loudly through the room. "You are not allowed up there."

Calvin quickened his pace but slipped on the front edge of a step and landed on his back. Anna gasped.

Tobran charged with a flailing right hand. Calvin barely skirted out of the way as the giant's fist crushed the stone step. Tobran swung once more. Again, Calvin dodged the forceful blow—another step shattered.

Calvin quickly raised the point of his sword toward Tobran's face.

"You don't get it, do you?" said Calvin desperately, his voice stern. "We all want the same thing. We . . . are on . . . the same . . . team!"

Calvin quickly scrambled to his feet and bolted up the last remaining stairs. At the top was a small, empty chamber with three corridors branching off in different directions.

"There's nothing for you up here," said Tobran. "And might I remind you, there is no exit. You're trapped . . . and you're mine."

Out of the corner of his eye, Calvin saw Perry and Anna sneak out of the room and hoped they would find their way to the sword.

"You're better than this!" Calvin said. "Join us."

"I can't," said Tobran. "I made a vow. I am a man of my word. I cannot break it."

"You're wrong," said Calvin. "If you promise to do something, and later learn that what you promised to do was not right . . . you can go back on your word. We're fighting for the same thing. We need you to help us fight Galigore."

"Osgar told me of your kind," said Tobran.

"And what is that?"

"He said that people would come here and try to manipulate me. He said I should not fall for any of their tricks."

"Listen to your heart," said Calvin. "What do you feel you should do? What is right?"

"I will not. I can't."

Tobran continued to follow Calvin through the corridor. It eventually opened up into a beautiful room of gleaming crystals. The floor, the walls, everything was made of translucent solids that mimicked sheets of clear ice. In the center of the room was an elevated platform that had steps leading up to a large diamond, three feet tall by three feet across. Wedged in the center of the diamond was a sword. The diamond emitted a magical glow.

Calvin quickly turned to run up the steps.

"You think you're the one, do you?" said Tobran, laughing under his breath. "You think it's as easy as pulling the sword and suddenly being endowed with mighty power? Go ahead . . . give it a tug." Tobran continued to walk toward Calvin, hastening his pace.

Calvin took a firm grip on the handle of the sword in the diamond. A jolt of electricity shot up his arm, which made him immediately grimace in pain. He pulled with all his might, but to no avail.

Calvin caught a quick glimpse of the hilt of the sword. It was beautifully decorated with carvings that wrapped around the handle. A dragon's mouth was formed at the butt of the handle. The mouth was empty; however, it appeared to be just the right size to hold the orb Calvin had hidden in his pouch.

As he stood there, marveling at the sword, his body became weightless. Tobran's hands were wrapped around his waist, and he found himself flying through the air, being hurled down the stairs, and then landing hard on the ground below. Tobran chased after him.

His vision was blurred for a second and blood trickled down the side of his face. Calvin scrambled to his feet. Backing away from the giant, he knew that he wasn't going to be able to persuade Tobran to let him go. Calvin needed to buy a little more time to dig out the orb from his pouch and insert it into the dragon's mouth.

"I could have killed you just now," said Tobran.

"Huh?" said Calvin.

"I could have killed you, instead of throwing you to the ground."

"Then why didn't you?" said Calvin.

"Because I like you. I haven't had anyone to talk to in years."

"So you'll let me go?" said Calvin.

"No. I just won't destroy you so quickly. I see our relationship much like a cat playing with a mouse before making it its meal."

Calvin made his way around the large diamond and scurried up the steps to where his sword from the fountain had fallen before he was thrown from the platform. He quickly picked it up and raised the tip toward Tobran.

"Calvin!"

Perry and Anna entered the room.

"Yes . . . I wondered how long it would take before you joined us," said Tobran.

"Back off!" said Perry, raising his sword and walking toward the giant.

166

Tobran turned to Perry and took a step toward him.

"You know Osgar would rather have that sword be in the hands of someone who would use it for good," said Perry.

Calvin knew what Perry was doing. It was just what he needed to find the orb.

"I told you," said Tobran. "No one is taking that sword."

"What if we really do have the stone?" asked Anna.

"Osgar hid them away in places that no one could find," said Tobran.

"If no one will ever find them, why are you guarding the sword?" asked Anna.

Tobran looked confused for a minute but quickly recovered. "Osgar is the mastermind behind the magical triad. He is the only one who knows where the artifacts are hidden."

Tobran suddenly interrupted himself and asked, "How did you three know the sword was on this island?"

"Perry and I heard about it from a friend," said Anna.

"A friend? What friend is this?" said Tobran.

"Calvin told us about it," Anna said, pointing at Calvin.

Tobran turned to look at Calvin, who was holding a small magical orb that was now glowing.

"No . . . it . . . it isn't!" said Tobran. "It can't be!"

"Yes, Tobran. We knew where the sword was because we have a secret map that identified it," said Calvin. "But I have news for you. Galigore also knows about this map. He already has an orb and a staff that have made him very powerful. If he were to obtain another orb and this sword, his power would increase. And his power is not being used for good, but for evil. We need to stop him. And we need your help."

Tobran turned to Perry and lunged toward him. Perry dodged the attack, raised his sword, and pierced Tobran in the arm.

Calvin quickly inserted the orb into the dragon's mouth on the hilt of the sword. At the moment he inserted it, the dragon's mouth closed around the orb, securing it tightly, and the diamond that housed the sword turned a bright white. Calvin grasped the handle and easily slipped the sword from the giant jewel. The sword glowed. Calvin was amazed at how light it was.

As if it weighed nothing, he raised his arm into the air.

Without warning, the ground began to shake. The ceiling broke apart and large pieces of rock tumbled, crashing to the ground. Daylight began to sneak through the cracked ceiling as debris continued to fall to the floor. Calvin, Perry, and Anna scurried about to find a wall they could stand against. The three huddled together, trying to cover their heads. Each of them took blows from falling debris.

After several minutes, the room grew quiet and the dust began to settle. The light of day shone through a crevice near the ceiling. A pile of rubble formed a ramp leading up to the exit. Calvin, Perry, and Anna brushed themselves off and headed toward the light.

Calvin heard a groan. He turned and saw Tobran lying beneath a pile of wreckage. He was conscious but couldn't escape. Calvin immediately went to him and began to throw rocks from off his body.

"What are you doing?" said Perry.

"Help me," said Calvin, still frantically uncovering Tobran.

"He wants to kill us," said Perry.

Calvin continued to remove rock that was concealing Tobran's body. Perry and Anna reluctantly joined in the rescue.

When Tobran was finally free, the three helped him to his feet. He didn't say a word but slowly hobbled toward the light. Calvin, Perry, and Anna followed. Together they climbed up the rocky terrain and slipped through the crevice. The warm sunlight was inviting, and Tobran stopped for a moment to soak it in. Tears filled his eyes as he looked around at the sun and the ocean. "I have missed the world," he said.

"It's a beautiful day, Tobran," said Calvin.

Perry and Anna looked at each other, smiled, and then turned to the giant.

"It is," said Tobran.

The three continued gazing out on the horizon from atop the island. The cool ocean breeze was salty and fresh. The waves were roaring far below as they crashed into the rocky shore. In the distance, Calvin saw Bravada soaring toward them—their only way off the island.

"Thank you," said Tobran. "My loyalty now resides with you, Calvin. You have saved my life. I will do all I can to repay you."

"But what about your contract with Osgar?" asked Calvin.

"The agreement was made void when the sword was removed from the diamond," said Tobran. "I no longer have an obligation to Osgar."

"Hey, Tobran," said Perry.

Tobran looked over at him.

"Sorry about your arm."

"Don't worry, Perry," said Tobran. "I'll get even."

As Tobran walked past Perry, he pointed to the horizon. "What's that?" he said.

Perry looked. And as he did so, Tobran playfully cuffed him on the back of the head. Calvin and Anna laughed. Even Perry cracked a smile.

21 · Trixel Strait

The natural saddle on Bravada's back was not big enough to get everyone off of the island at once. It took two trips. But within a few hours, Calvin, Perry, Anna, and Tobran found refuge at Stone's empty cottage. Calvin spread the map over the dining table to plot their next journey. He traced his finger from one island to another. He remained quiet, with his eyes focused on the various lands protruding from the sea. The others crowded around the table and quietly observed. Tobran's massive body took up one full side of the table. The low cottage ceiling forced him to look on in a crouched position, with his hands on his knees. Even then, his head was just inches from the ceiling.

"We're going to Peril Cove," said Calvin.

The others looked at the map with curiosity, trying to locate the island. Calvin reached in his shirt, lifted the key from around his neck, and tossed it onto the map. The key clunked as it hit the table, spun a few times, and landed on top of Peril Cove.

Perry coughed under his breath, "Lucky throw."

Anna laughed.

"Let's find out what this key goes to," said Calvin. "I think we should leave in the morning."

"But what about your grandpa?" Perry asked. "Should we let him know that we're staying at Stone's? And what about you, Anna? Your parents would kill you if they knew what you're up to."

"Yeah, you're right," Anna said. "But at this point, I think I'll suffer the consequences. This is where I feel I need to be."

"My grandpa would be fine with us being here. He'd probably be a little jealous, actually."

* * * *

In the family room, Calvin sat on the old leather armchair—flames flickering in the fireplace. He held the sword in

170

his hand and slowly twisted it around. It was the first opportunity he'd had to really examine it since removing it from the diamond.

Along the blade he noticed some characters that he could not decipher. "There's something inscribed along the blade," said Calvin. "It's in some kind of runic language."

Anna stood up and walked over to see it for herself, focusing on the eight characters etched along the base of the blade.

Perry also moved to survey the sword and thoughtfully examined it as it lay in Calvin's hands. "Hmmm . . . yeah . . . looks to me like it's written in some sort of . . . runic language."

"Nice observation," said Calvin, rolling his eyes.

"Let me have a look," said Tobran, who was sitting on the floor. He pushed himself up to his knees. Calvin stood up and held out the sword so Tobran could see. "It's written in Gnomanic."

"Gnomanic?" said Calvin. "What's that?"

"It's the magical language of the gnomes," said Tobran.

"Can you understand the language?" asked Anna.

"My knowledge is limited . . . but I know enough to get by."

"What does this say?" asked Anna.

Tobran peered intently at the characters for a moment. "It says Tavanari."

The room was silent. Calvin held the sword out with the blade tip pointed upward and repeated the word, "Tavanari."

As he spoke the word, lightning bolts discharged from the base and rippled up the blade. The lightning crackled and the electricity extinguished when it reached the tip.

"Whoa . . . can I try?" asked Perry.

Calvin handed the sword to Perry and the tip fell to the floor. "It's so heavy," said Perry. "How do you hold this thing?"

Perry grasped it with two hands and lifted the tip up, but not without a struggle. "Tavanari," he said. Nothing happened. "Tavanari," he repeated. Nothing. "Tavanari."

Calvin reached for the sword. He took hold of the handle and easily raised it with one hand. He swung the sword swiftly, from side to side, cutting the air.

"It's weightless," said Calvin. "It feels like I'm not holding anything."

Perry looked frustrated. "Why should I be surprised?"

* * * *

In the morning, Tobran insisted that Perry and Anna stay behind while Calvin took him to the island first. He thought he could spend his time looking for clues that would help them on their quest while Calvin went back to retrieve Perry and Anna. Plus, Tobran had said that it would be safer for the others to come after him so they would not be left on the island alone.

Bravada flew south of the Cliffs of Tarnin toward the rocky shoreline of Peril Cove, which was largely made up of thick tropical forest. The island had sheer cliffs running the length of one side. Thick forest covered the entire island, except for black lava rock that was sprinkled along its shores.

Bravada landed on top of the cliff. Calvin had mixed feelings the minute he stepped foot onto the island. He looked over the edge and peered down at the crashing waves hundreds of feet below. But that wasn't what made him feel uneasy.

"What is it?" Tobran said. "What's wrong?"

"I don't know," said Calvin. "I feel uncomfortable. On one hand I feel scared, but I also feel excited."

"Scared about what?" asked Tobran.

"I don't know. . . Maybe the journey will be hard, or dangerous. But I also feel excited to see what the key will unlock."

"So unlocking whatever it is the key goes to is a piece of the puzzle to defeat Galigore?" Tobran asked, and Calvin nodded.

"Whatever happens, Calvin, it will turn out right in the end," said Tobran. "Evil will not prevail. We'll make sure of it."

Rain began to fall lightly. "Will you be okay here?" asked Calvin.

"Yes. Don't worry about me. Go get the others."

* * * *

Calvin, Perry, and Anna approached the area where Tobran was supposed to be waiting. He was not there. "Let's circle the island again," Calvin told Bravada. The sky remained overcast, the air humid. Flying high and low, they saw no sign of Tobran.

Perhaps he had found something for them to pursue?

Bravada made one last swoop along the ocean's surface before gliding up the face of the cliff, and landing on the ledge where she and Calvin had left Tobran. They dismounted the dragon and scanned the area.

"Bravada, go circle the treetops and see if you can spot anything," Calvin commanded. Bravada immediately soared into the air.

Just as Bravada flew out of sight, six pale-skinned, hooded Zarkon emerged from the trees. Their faces were sunken in, their cheekbones prominent. Their hands and fingers were bony. The sky grew darker; the wind blew harder. Lightning clapped and thunder rumbled nearby.

"Give up, boy," commanded one of the Zarkon with a sneer. He had long, greasy, black hair. His robe flickered in the wind. "You have no business interfering in our affairs."

"I know what you're up to," said Calvin. "Nothing good will come from your work."

One of the Zarkon raised his wand and flicked it toward Calvin, who immediately drew Tavanari from its sheath. A blue flash shot from the wand tip in Calvin's direction. Calvin instinctively reflected the flash with his sword and watched the streak ricochet into a rock close to where the Zarkon stood. On impact, the rock shattered.

Perry waved his wand and flicked it at the Zarkon. "*Fuegero!*"

A waist-high wall of fire danced around the Zarkon, encircling them in flames. The fire would last for only a moment.

"*Aquaro!*" A thick stream of water sprayed from one of the Zarkon's wands and effectively doused the fire.

Calvin bravely took a step toward the enemy. One of the Zarkon drew his sword and lunged toward him. Their steel blades clanked together. Calvin realized he was exerting much less energy than the Zarkon. His sword was weightless and he swung it speedily and with little effort. The Zarkon, however, was becoming slower and slower, tired from lifting his weapon. Calvin found his opportunity and pierced the Zarkon in the chest. The Zarkon fell to the ground, lifeless.

Perry and Anna joined in the battle, trying to attack, but found themselves mostly on the defensive. Perry fought with his sword while Anna relied solely upon her magic.

Calvin picked off another Zarkon, and a second body dropped to the ground.

Two separate battles ensued. Two of the Zarkon surrounded Calvin, while two more battled Perry and Anna.

One of the Zarkon fighting Calvin showed a toothless, evil smile and turned toward Perry. Flicking his wand, he muttered, "*Immoboli.*" A wave of energy shot from his wand and struck Perry. He fell to the ground motionless.

"No!" Calvin looked over and ran toward Perry.

"*Tirovista!*" came an eerie cry.

Calvin's body flew through the air backwards. He saw his friends' bodies get smaller as he was getting further away from them. It took him a moment before he realized that he had been hurled off the cliff.

"Bravada!" cried Calvin. She did not come.

Calvin looked down at the water that was fast approaching. Before he could think too much about anything, he plunged into the ocean below.

The impact was solid. His body went limp and sunk into the black depths of the sea. Calvin was relaxed. He had an incredible feeling of peace as he drifted weightlessly through the water. He passed through what seemed to be a dark tunnel. He could see a light at the end of the passage that was beautiful and calming. As he drifted along, every hardship was taken from him. Every pain was gone. He felt so liberated, so light.

He continued to pass through the dark space toward the light and he just let it happen. It felt so good. Drifting—comfortably. Effortlessly. Not a worry occupied his mind. Any feelings of anger were gone. There was no sadness. No happiness. Just tranquility. And he let it take control. For a moment he had no thought of where he had been. He didn't care where he was going. He just allowed whatever was happening to happen. And it felt good.

The state he had found himself in was heavenly. Is this what it was like to die? He didn't entertain the idea. He wasn't concerned about that right now. He wasn't concerned about anything, except to remain in the state of bliss. Images began to break the barrier of his consciousness. *No*, he thought. *Don't let this feeling go away*. In and out of peacefulness, he saw in his mind a flash of Anna. Then an image of his mom flickered. Thoughts began to come back, blatantly distracting him from the sea of tranquility he drifted through.

A horrific face came into focus in his mind. Galigore. Why Galigore? The journey to death was more peaceful than he could have imagined. Why did this malignant image of evil appear? Anna's face erased the image of Galigore. Then he saw his mom again. Then Perry's face came into view.

The thoughts and images of the world he had just left brought him into a state of semiconsciousness. He knew he had a decision to make. He realized he had not yet lost control of his fate. He could continue to drift away happily—which he felt would be perfectly fine—or he could choose to survive.

His decision was a quick one. Calvin suddenly fought to regain consciousness. He quickly recognized his surroundings. He immediately noticed his sword was still gripped tightly in his hand. He sheathed it and then began to kick and pull himself toward the surface of the water. He longed for a breath. He never wanted anything so badly. Just moments before, he was in a state of serenity. Nothing mattered. But now, he was knocking on death's door, struggling to find a breath of air. The ocean's surface was in sight, but still far away. It seemed too far to wait for that next breath of air. Why did he do it? He traded peacefulness for torture. He continued to reach and kick upward. He was determined to make it.

Another stroke. Another kick.

Finally, he broke the surface and gasped violently for air. He forced air in and out of his lungs—while choking on water—until he returned to normal breathing.

All around him were steep walls. He could see nowhere to pull himself out of the water. He looked up high above him from where he fell. No one was in sight. While he feared for his friends' safety, he had to worry about saving his own life now.

Treading water, Calvin looked all around for a place to rest.

Rough, dark waves crashed over his face. He felt his heart pound in his chest. His breaths became shallow and fast. He was afraid. How was he going to escape the power of the sea? Recognizing that his mind was creating this anxiety, Calvin took slow, deep breaths and tried to calm himself.

He swam to the nearest wall, hoping to find a piece of rock that would protrude just far enough that he could use to rest on. But the rocks were slippery and offered no support.

In the distance, Calvin noticed a small crevice. It was just what he needed. At a minimum, it would give him something to hold onto while he caught his breath and rested his arms.

As Calvin approached the crevice, he found that it was a gap larger than he had anticipated. He rested for a moment and then swam through. The opening led him to a dark, dome-shaped cavern. There was a natural stone shelf that jutted out just above the surface of the water. Calvin pulled himself onto it, relieved to be on solid ground. It was dark, and it appeared that there was nowhere to go.

"*Lucero.*" Motioning with his hands, the area filled with light and Calvin surveyed every nook and cranny on the surface of the walls. Thick moss clung to the low, damp ceiling and crawled down the sides. Cracks were prevalent and numerous on all the surfaces. He continued to scan the cavern, looking for knobs that could be prodded—perhaps revealing a secret passage—but found nothing.

Across the small chamber, Calvin noticed something strange. The wall was covered with black and green moss, but it seemed to be growing in sharp lines that formed letters. He entered the water, pushed off the wall behind him, and glided to the peculiar growth. Calvin picked at the moss with his fingernails and peeled away chunks from the wall. He discovered letters that had been etched deep into the rock: P-O-I-N-T.

"Point?" said Calvin under his breath. "What does that mean?" he wondered.

Calvin continued picking away at the moss. He uncovered another line of letters: O-F-N-O.

Ofno? he thought. It didn't make sense. Calvin unveiled a third line just above the water's surface: R-E-T-U-R-N. "Oh.

Point of no return."

Calvin held onto a nearby knob that stuck out from the wall. It made a nice handle and allowed him to keep his head and shoulders up out of the water. He imagined someone many years earlier clinging from the same knob, etching the words into the wall using a sharp metal object and thousands of repetitive strokes to make the grooves as deep and distinct as they were.

Calvin searched the area. He felt with his foot under water along the wall beneath the message. The stone was solid for a few feet below the water, but his foot slid off the wall as he examined deeper. Calvin discovered there was a hole, large enough for him to enter. As he explored the size of the orifice with his feet, his legs were being sucked in. The current was steady and he was sure it would lead him somewhere.

Calvin found a solid surface he could use to push off from that would help propel him into the opening below. He took several deep breaths to expand his lungs. After one final inhale, he completely submerged himself into the chilly, salty water, and kicked himself through the hidden underwater passage. He felt his body being forced through the hole by a strong current.

The message on the stone wall flashed through his mind, "Point of No Return." He knew he was not getting out the same way he was going in. The current would not allow it.

Calvin opened his eyes, but saw nothing. Everything was black as he continued to glide quickly under the water. He had no idea how long this tunnel was, and he was beginning to wonder when he would get another breath of air. As he cruised along, he had a troubling feeling. He wished that he had never entered the hole, and thought that he should have waited for Bravada to find him. At least then he would be safe—not worrying when, or if, he would ever breathe again.

Calvin felt something scrape against his leg. A sharp pain pierced his calf. Bubbles quickly burst from his mouth as he exhaled a shrill scream. Feeling panicked, Calvin began to kick and stroke faster. Reaching farther and kicking harder, he swam on. His lungs were longing for a breath. He feared he wouldn't get one.

In the distance, the black water seemed not so dark. A

murky, yellow glow began to get closer and brighter. He continued to swim frantically. Finally, he saw the mossy floor below him. A few more bubbles escaped his mouth when he passed a skull resting within the plant life below. Pushing off the ocean floor, he thrust himself up out of the water and gasped desperately for air. He pulled himself out of the water and rolled over onto his back, trying to catch his breath.

Calvin turned and looked toward the water. A long tail broke the surface. It rose high, then lowered, disappearing into the dark water. Calvin raised his pant leg and looked at his calf. There was a deep gash about three inches long. Blood poured from the wound and pooled on the rock surface below him.

"Calvin Sparks . . . wounded?" came a high-pitched voice. Calvin looked around and saw a familiar gnome sitting on a nearby boulder.

"Trixel?" asked Calvin. "Is that you?"

"No time for introductions. You need to stop the bleeding," the gnome said.

"I have nothing to use," said Calvin.

"May I?" The gnome winked and then jumped down off the boulder.

The last time Calvin had seen Trixel was when he and Perry exited Fountain Green on their first visit to Cambria. Trixel had an unusually large hump on his back that day that seemed to weigh him down. But today the hump was gone and he stood straight with good posture.

The gnome walked toward Calvin. Calvin figured he would do no mischief. Otherwise he would have jumped him when he wasn't looking. Had Trixel known he was coming? Was he expecting him? Waiting for him?

The bearded gnome was even smaller than Calvin had remembered. He approached Calvin and knelt beside him, reaching into a leather pouch strapped around his shoulder. He pulled out a glass vial that had a silvery liquid inside.

"Pull up your pant leg," said Trixel.

Trixel unstopped the vial and tipped the bottle downward to allow a few drops of the liquid to fall onto Calvin's calf. "A topical elixir to heal."

The droplets plunged into Calvin's wound. Within seconds the deep cut began to smoke. Calvin grabbed his leg and winced in pain.

"You're almost finished, child. It should feel better now."

To Calvin's relief, the violent sting did begin to die down. The blood around the wound slowly, but completely, vanished. The raw flesh smoothed over and became new, healthy skin—as if nothing ever happened.

"What was that?" Calvin asked amazed.

"My family recipe . . . centuries old. Consists of various hard-to-find ingredients."

"Why did you heal me?"

"That's what life is about." Trixel winked again. "The more we give, the more we get. A simple principle, really."

"What is it that you get?" asked Calvin.

"Gold, treasure, stones. You can never have too much." Trixel seemed to slip into a daydream.

"Where did you come from?" asked Calvin.

"I came from a magical world."

"A magical world?" asked Calvin. "Aren't we in the magical world?"

"Oh, right you are. I come from another land. My world is beyond this world. The world of the gnomes. It's a world similar to this, but scaled to our size."

"I'm not sure I follow you," said Calvin.

"There are thousands of gnomes that live their lives in our world, which is, as I have explained, beyond this world. Just as you go to school in Wolf Creek, we go to school in our world. You learn about science and math and history. Our math is music. Our science is magic. And our history is ancient treasure."

"Does your world have a name?" asked Calvin.

"Some refer to our world as Paragon."

"I've heard of that name. It's on one of the doors at The Crossing."

"We have several portals that only a few of your kind know about. Most are small entrances that humans could not fit through. But there are a handful of larger ones around—big enough that even you could pass."

"The door to your world was locked," said Calvin.

"Yes, it was. And so it shall remain." Trixel brought a finger to his chin. He sat pondering and then spoke again. "You have already located an alternative portal to Paragon." He paused, then winked, and continued. "One that would grant you immediate access. Perhaps you didn't know it when you saw it."

"What are you talking about?"

"Every time a portal to our world is accessed, music fills the air."

"I still don't get it," replied Calvin.

"Tell me, have you ever heard music near The Crossing?"

Calvin remembered the time when he, Perry, and Anna had followed the sound of music into the forest behind The Crossing. "Are you talking about the Wishing Well?"

"I don't know . . . am I?"

"The Wishing Well is a portal to your world?" asked Calvin.

"Is it? I must not disclose that information. If a gnome tells someone from another world where one of our portals resides, that portal loses its magic . . . never to be accessed again. Imagine . . . if we couldn't keep a secret, we would lose all contact with outside worlds. I cannot tell you where any of the portals are located."

"But you already did," challenged Calvin.

"Did I? I believe you drew your own conclusion. I only asked a few questions."

"How does the portal work?" asked Calvin.

"I have complete confidence that you will figure it out."

"Why are you so interested in me?" asked Calvin.

"Just as you are concerned with Galigore erasing anything that's good in this world, Paragon is equally distressed."

"Yes, but what does that have to do with *me*?"

"We have kept a close eye on you your entire life, hoping that the circumstances would line up as they have. You possess innate skills that we haven't seen in anyone for over a hundred years."

"Why are you so interested in what Galigore is doing? Does it also affect Paragon? I mean, can't you just stay in your world and never come here? Just destroy the portals so no one can get in. I don't understand your interest."

"You're a bright one, Calvin. Inquisitive, too," said Trixel. "We are anxiously engaged in this cause because we're largely responsible for the evil that has invaded your land. Gnomes are magical creatures. And we are very wise. Tell me, Calvin. What is my age?" Trixel gave another wink.

"I don't know."

"Just take a guess."

"Okay, don't take this personally, but I would say you are about ninety-five."

"That's a little older than I thought you'd say," said Trixel.

"Hey, you're the one that made me guess."

"I know. I deserve it. Actually, I am two hundred and fifty-three years young. It is common for us to live five hundred years or more. Imagine the time we have on our hands to collect treasures. And imagine the time we have to devote to learning new things, such as the art of magic.

"That healing potion is only the beginning of our knowledge of plant life. Now, to our detriment, I admit, we may have a little too much time on our hands. One of our own, Osgar Ivins, would attest to this. Osgar became so well rehearsed in the arts that he fabricated some very powerful artifacts. They were so powerful they began to change his persona. He became greedy, arrogant, and proud. To his credit, he recognized his deviant behavior and disposed of his artifacts before it tore his family apart.

"He scattered the artifacts throughout Cambria, hoping they would never come together again as one. If any person were to possess all the artifacts at one time, the desire for power would be nearly impossible to resist. He would become immortal and rule in pride, always striving to become more and more powerful."

"Why did the map lead me here?"

"You have the key still wrapped around your neck, I presume?" asked Trixel.

How did he know about the key? Calvin pulled the key from his shirt and watched as it dangled in front of him.

"Good. Now go unlock whatever it is that's waiting for

you. I will visit you at another time."

"What do you mean? Where are you going?"

"This is something you need to do alone, Calvin. Trust me." Trixel smiled, gave one last wink, snapped his fingers, and disappeared in a cloud of sparkly dust.

22 • Key to Peril Cove

Calvin noticed the glass vial that Trixel used to heal him still sitting on the boulder. He grabbed it and stuck it in his front pocket. Looking around, he found himself in a dark cavern. He could see only one trail to follow—a narrow corridor with a high ceiling. A thin stream of water ran down the center of the trail and emptied into the sea. Along its edges, the stone path was lined with skeletons.

Calvin quickly made his way up the tight, stony passage. The further he traveled, the narrower the path became. His progress was stopped when he came upon a large, moss-covered boulder that blocked the entire passageway. A steady stream of water flowed over the top of the rock, and wound its way toward the sea. Scaling the slippery boulder, Calvin shimmied his way to the top.

On the other side was an open shaft above him with a rope ladder dangling down in front of him. "Another rope?" he complained. There appeared to be no other passages—nowhere else to go but up. Calvin gave the ladder a firm tug and began to climb. He continued to climb higher and higher. To his relief, the rope seemed to be in good shape. It stretched upward and disappeared into the darkness.

At the top of the rope, Calvin wiggled his way onto a platform where the ladder was fastened by two rusty stakes, driven into the rock. At the end of a short tunnel, Calvin came to a fork. He chose to go right and followed the path up a steep, zigzagged incline. Ahead of him he was met with a closed chamber door. It had iron bars, which would allow him to see through to the other side. He hesitated for a moment but didn't know why. He tried to go but couldn't. Calvin had a distinct impression that he should be careful when proceeding. His feelings were of excitement, fear, and confusion. He took a deep breath and then advanced a couple of steps.

Calvin looked through the bars. He couldn't see much of

the chamber on the other side. The contour of the walls was lost in the shadows. He continued to peer cautiously, then jumped when he realized there was someone sitting in the corner. The figure was hunched over, leaning against the rock. His knees were brought to his chest and he had his arms wrapped around his legs in front of him with his hands clasped. He stared ahead at a spot on the floor in front of him. Calvin noticed the man was slightly rocking back and forth. His hair was long and tangled, and ran down his back.

"Please, come in, won't you?" said the weary voice.

Calvin wondered how he knew he was there. He hadn't looked up.

"I haven't had visitors in years," said the figure. "Matter of fact . . . I've never had a visitor."

"Who are you?" Calvin asked.

"Oh . . . you're a young one, aren't you?"

Calvin wasn't pleased to hear his comment. He considered himself pretty brave. He thought about making a smart remark, but he held his tongue. "How long have you been here?" Calvin asked instead.

"I don't know. Ten years. Perhaps more," said the man. "There's not much light to count the days, but I do my best."

"Who put you in here?" asked Calvin.

"The devil himself . . . Galigore."

"Who are you?"

"A Bordarian."

Calvin's feelings of worry slowly began to fade. He felt an immediate connection with the man. He could rescue one of Galigore's prisoners—a real Bordarian.

Calvin waved his hands across the chamber door handle. "*Abreyla*." Nothing happened.

"It's no use," said the man. "It's charmed. It's impossible to do magic in this room. I suppose once the door is opened, the charm will be broken."

Seeking approval from the man, Calvin wanted to show him just how good he really was. Without the man seeing, he took the key from around his neck. He looked at it—comparing it to the lock. It appeared to be of similar size. Calvin slowly insertcd the key into the lock as far as it would go. As he turned the key, Calvin said loudly with extreme confidence, "*Abreyla*!" The internal latch clicked loudly and the dead bolt disengaged.

The disheveled man turned toward Calvin, standing in the doorway, and stared incredulously, wide eyed. "Boy . . . how'd you do that? I've tried that same spell thousands of times."

Calvin entered the dungeon dangling the key.

"I came to this island specifically to unlock whatever it was this key was guarding," said Calvin. "I must admit I was hoping it would have opened a treasury. That I would have found a magical orb or an artifact."

"Don't sound so disappointed, kid," said the Bordarian. "How do you know about the lore of the orbs?"

"I don't know much, really. But I did manage to find this the other day." Calvin unsheathed his sword. The Bordarian was in awe as he affixed his eyes on the precious possession—the dragon's mouth on the pommel grasping the glowing orb.

"That's something special, kid," marveled the Bordarian. "What's it called?"

"This is Tavanari." He held it up in the air. Vibes of electricity emanated from the base of the handle and crawled slowly up the shaft. The crackling of the sparks diminished at the point of the sword.

"You don't know much, huh?" The Bordarian chuckled. "Looks like you've been around the block a time or two."

Calvin smiled. He could tell he was gaining approval from the Bordarian.

Calvin tucked the sword safely back into the sheath and took a few steps through the room.

"What's all of this rubble?" he asked.

"After a few days of being in here, I decided to tunnel my way out. I began to chip away at the wall. But it was no use. This stone is hard and these walls are thick. All I had were a couple of weapons." Calvin crouched and looked into the hole near the floor of the dungeon. It was hardly a tunnel. The opening was about eighteen inches round and it extended only a few feet back. Calvin saw a couple of handles inside the burrow that had once been a sword and dagger. "Magic has never worked in here. . .

Galigore placed a charm inside of this chamber," the Bordarian continued. "I thought I could dig far enough to break the charm. But if that didn't work, then maybe I would dig far enough to get myself out of here."

Calvin looked around the dungeon cell. It was a large room with high ceilings. Near one of the torches on the wall, Calvin saw some words etched into the rock. He rubbed his fingers across the words and read:

Right prevails. Evil fails.

Calvin continued walking and saw another engraving:

Never abandon hope.

In the flickering light, Calvin read another:

I am in control.

And another:

I am alive.

And one more:

Tomorrow will come.

"Let's get out of here," suggested Calvin.

Calvin reached out his hand toward the Bordarian and helped him to his feet. The man's hand was rough with calluses. Calvin looked him in the eye—he felt he could trust him. If the key had led him here, this man must be someone important. The two of them exited through the door.

"Wait," said the Bordarian, stopping suddenly. He turned back toward the door, waved his hands, and chanted, "*Cantello Fuegero!*" A ball of fire launched from his hands and violently crashed into the dungeon wall. "Yes . . . I've still got it! After all these years . . . you don't know how good that feels!"

Calvin retraced his steps through the corridor to where the passage forked. "Do you remember how to get out of here?" he asked.

"It's this way," the Bordarian said.

"I was hoping you'd say that," said Calvin. "We don't want to go back the way I came."

Calvin led the way through the twisted corridor. They came upon some doors that were locked, but a simple unlatching spell allowed them to pass through easily.

After several minutes of trekking through the tunnel, one

final turn introduced them to outside light in the distance.

Daylight shone through a gap in the rocks. The opening was only a couple of feet wide, but stretched nearly six feet tall. With every step, the outside world grew closer. Freedom was within grasp of the Bordarian, who had tears in his eyes.

"I've missed so many years," he whispered under his breath. "So many years."

Calvin was the first to slip through the exit. The Bordarian followed. Full of emotion, he reached for Calvin and embraced him. Calvin thought about how awkward he should have felt, hugging a stranger. But it wasn't awkward at all. It was comfortable. It was like he knew this man. After all, he was a Bordarian.

"Thank you," he whispered in Calvin's ear. "Thank you."

* * * *

Anna was losing her stamina fast. She was greatly outnumbered as the remaining Zarkon surrounded her and Perry, who remained on the ground. He had not moved in the slightest since being struck with an immobilization spell.

"*Bantarlo!*" cried one of the Zarkon. A silvery, transparent bubble formed from the end of his wand and engulfed Anna and Perry.

"*Temperna,*" said Anna, throwing a bolt toward a Zarkon, but it fizzled out when it hit the inside of the wall.

"*Obscuro!*" came another incantation from a Zarkon. The spell of darkness cast over the bubble, and Anna could no longer see outside. Everything went black.

Their bodies became weightless as they hovered across the sky in an unknown direction.

"We'll be fine," said Anna to Perry, unsure if he was aware of his surroundings. "They want us alive . . . otherwise they would have finished us off by now."

Several minutes passed. Still airborne, they continued to travel in silence and in total darkness.

"Ugh," said Perry groggily as he began to come to. Anna quickly put her hand on him and spoke, "It's okay, Perry. I'm here. We've been captured by the Zarkon."

Perry groaned a few more times. "Where's Calvin?"

"I don't know. The Zarkon threw him off the edge of the

cliff and he fell into the water."

"Off the cliff?" said Perry. "That . . . that drop must have been a couple hundred feet!"

"I know," said Anna. "One of the Zarkon peered over the edge and told the others that he never surfaced."

Tears began to well in Anna's eyes. She couldn't stand the thought that Calvin might be dead. "He can't be gone."

The bubble finally slowed to a stop. While they had no idea where they were, they could tell that they were no longer in the air. Their surroundings remained quiet and still.

Perry forced his hand through the bubble, and when he brought it back in, a glimmer of light softly penetrated through the membrane. Slowly, the surface became translucent.

As the charms wore off, Perry and Anna found themselves sitting inside of a dungeon cell. There was an opening high above them on the ceiling through which they could see daylight—but it was not large enough for either of them to squeeze through. The room was spacious, but gloomy, dim, and cold. The only door in the room had two windows that were latched shut. One was at eye level, big enough only to communicate through. The other—long and thin—was located at the bottom of the door.

Perry drew his wand and waved it toward the dungeon door. "*Abreyla.*" Nothing happened.

"I'm sure this place has been charmed," said Anna. "Magic won't work in here."

On the floor in the corner of the room there was a single tin container—the chamber pot. It was empty, but well used, and not cleaned very well. The stench stayed mostly in the corner.

"You're telling me that's our toilet?" Anna said, disgusted.

The clattering of latches sounded from the door. The two of them looked over and saw the bottom window slide open. A hand reached through the opening, scooting a scroll just inside the door. The window quickly slammed shut and was locked.

Anna picked up the parchment, slid off the tie, and unraveled it. The paper was old and weathered. The handwriting was neat. Anna read aloud:

" 'You have arrived at the Isle of Desolation. As you probably already know, this chamber is enchanted. Any form of magic within its walls is impossible. Food will be served twice a day if your empty dishes are within reach of the lower window. When the chamber pot is full, set it by the door for disposal. You each have a wool blanket, which should almost suffice on the cold nights. If you step out of line you will be severely punished. You have been sentenced to Desolation indefinitely. I am your dungeon keeper. I cannot be bribed.' It's signed, 'Brawn, Desolation Dungeon Master.' "

The lower window opened and two round, deep dishes were pushed through the portal—their contents emitted steam. Two thick, wool blankets were also crammed through the small opening. The window quickly closed and the latches were locked.

"Wow . . . impressive service." Perry examined the contents of the bowls and gagged. "I'm not eatin' that!"

"What is it?" asked Anna.

"It's foul is what it is. Look!" Perry pointed at something in the bowl. "What do you think this tail belonged to?"

A thin, tubular piece of meat wrapped around the inside of the bowl. The thickness tapered and finally ended in a point.

"Looks like snake to me," said Anna.

"That would be better than rat," said Perry.

"Well, do you think tonight's dinner will be better than tomorrow's breakfast?" asked Anna.

"Let's hope not," said Perry. "I am willing to wait and take the chance . . . I'm not touching that."

Dumping the contents of their bowls into the chamber pot, they decided to go without food that evening and trust that breakfast would be more appetizing.

As the hours passed, Perry and Anna sat on the dungeon floor, cold and hungry. Anna was beginning to wonder how bad that tail really would have been. At least it would have been something warm in her tummy.

* * * *

Calvin waited for his new friend to gather himself from the emotions he was feeling—not having been outside for all these

189

years. The Bordarian took several slow, deep breaths of the cool, salty air.

Although it was still overcast, the brightness of the day was fading fast. The clouds grew darker and gloomier.

"Let's get going," said Calvin. *Bravada . . . I need you. Where are you?*

In the darkening distance, Calvin saw his winged beast soaring toward him. Calvin felt safe with Bravada around. She landed in a small clearing between the trees. He approached her and embraced her. "How are you, girl?" Bravada nuzzled Calvin with her snout.

"Shall we get out of here?" asked Calvin, turning to the Bordarian.

"If only you knew how many times I've dreamed about this moment."

The man began to climb aboard Bravada as a fierce roar bellowed from another creature in the air. A large, winged dragon, with blue and green scales, hovered in the sky high above them. As it descended near them, the Bordarian laughed aloud. "Can it really be?"

The large creature drew closer. "Is it really you?" cried the man.

The dragon landed near the Bordarian. Calvin glanced down at its left hind leg and saw a distinguishable mark in the shape of a crescent moon.

"Amalga?" Calvin asked.

The Bordarian glanced over at Calvin, nodding vigorously, sporting an incredulous smile.

Calvin's eyes grew wide. His jaw dropped.

The man looked overwhelmed with joy at being reunited with his old sidekick. "Never take them for granted, these drag-ons," he said as he continued to stroke the neck of Amalga. "They will be loyal companions and will never forsake you. They're with you until the day you die."

He looked over at Calvin, who continued to stare at him in disbelief.

It was quiet for a moment.

"Boy, are you okay?" asked the exhilarated Bordarian.

Calvin looked deep into the man's eyes. It was a look so piercing, that it commanded immediate attention from him. Through glossy eyes, Calvin finally responded. "Dad?"

23 • Premonitions

Miles looked at Calvin. Tears immediately filled his eyes. He stretched out his arms invitingly. Calvin stepped forward. He wrapped his arms around his father's back and rested his head upon his shoulder.

"I've replayed in my mind thousands of times the day I would be free," Miles said amid tears. "But never did I imagine a scenario where my own son would save me."

Miles broke the embrace. "Let me look at you."

Calvin smiled.

"You're all grown up," said Miles.

"All my life people have told me that I look like you."

Miles ran his hands through his hair and looked down at his filthy hands and tattered clothing. "I'm sorry."

Calvin laughed. "I'm sure you'll clean up nicely."

"No . . . I mean I'm sorry I've missed it," said Miles.

"Missed what?"

"You. Your life. I'm sorry I haven't been around."

"You know, there's a lot of life left in me," said Calvin. "In fact, my best days are still ahead."

Miles smiled. "I'm proud of you already."

"Come on, let's go," said Calvin. He climbed up Bravada's leg and onto her back. "We need to go find some people."

Calvin flew above the island, looking for any sign of Perry and Anna. He flew high and low but saw nothing. He landed his dragon at the place he last saw them—the place from where he plunged into the sea.

"Who are we looking for?" his dad asked.

"My friends," said Calvin. "This is the last place I saw them before we got split up."

Calvin walked into the cluster of trees and called their names. He heard no reply. He walked further in, still no sign.

They flew around the island again and again. Still nothing. Dusk was falling rapidly. Calvin felt helpless. Perry and Anna could be anywhere.

* * * *

Calvin and his dad stopped at Stone's for the night. Before Calvin went to bed, he had explained everything to his dad. He patiently answered questions as his dad tried to catch up on the past thirteen years.

In his slumber, Calvin dreamt that he saw a rocky, barren island somewhere at sea. He saw Perry and Anna locked inside of a dungeon cell. Perry was standing alone, no doubt trying to devise a plan. Anna was sitting down on the stone floor with a single blanket wrapped around her. She looked cold.

A guard sat outside the dungeon door. A second guard entered the scene and muttered to the other, "I just received word. Galigore will be here soon to interrogate these two."

One of the guards shivered. "Oh, how I'd hate to be in their shoes."

"So I guess I should notify the ditch diggers?"

"About what?"

"You know what will happen after Galigore's done with them." He moved his hand across his throat as if slicing it with a knife.

"Good point. Tell the diggers to prepare two more holes."

Calvin tossed and turned. When he finally settled down, he found himself drifting through another setting. Tobran was surrounded by primitives who were holding spears. He was lying over a flat stone table—his eyes closed. Was he sleeping? The native islanders danced around, raising their spears, chanting, and beating their drums. Alongside the body was half of a coconut shell, filled with blood—Tobran's blood. Perhaps Tobran wasn't sleeping after all.

* * * *

Calvin awoke early the next morning. He stoked the smoldering fire that was burning in the fireplace. The sofa his father had slept on was vacant and the blankets he had used were neatly folded and stacked on the arm of the chair. Calvin saw lights down the hall coming from the bathroom. He turned to the refrigerator to see what his options were for breakfast.

With the assistance of a little magic, Calvin soon had

freshly-squeezed juice in a pitcher and bacon and eggs frying perfectly on a cast iron griddle. He dropped two pieces of bread into the toaster. The delicious smell filled the air. Considering where his dad had been the last several years, Calvin was determined to treat him to a breakfast fit for a king.

Calvin almost didn't recognize the figure that entered the room. His matted hair that had hung down his back was now clean and straight, and fell just above his shoulders. His long scraggly beard was neatly trimmed. He'd donned crisp, clean clothes from Stone's wardrobe.

"Much better," said Calvin approvingly.

"Smells great," his dad said taking a deep breath. "I haven't smelled bacon in a long time."

Calvin watched, eager to see his father take his first bite of real food. His dad popped the egg yolk with his fork and mixed it around a bit, and then piled it onto a piece of buttered toast. He then topped the egg with pieces of bacon that he had torn into manageable sizes. His dad brought the toast up to his mouth and bit down.

Calvin watched his dad chew slowly, savoring every bite. He washed each bite down with a swig of cold juice.

"Very good, Calvin." He placed another smashed egg on top of his toast. "Your mother has taught you well."

"Why do you think Mom never told me about magic?" asked Calvin. "She never told me about The Crossing, or Cambria. She never told me about Amalga."

"Your mother is as much at war as we are. I imagine she didn't want you to know about it because she was afraid you would get involved at too young of an age. She lost me . . . and she didn't want to lose you, too. That's probably why she moved away from Cambria."

"What's she going to think about me now? I mean, with the map . . . the orb . . . with the magic I have learned."

"She will support you, Calvin. It was only a matter of time before you'd be involved. Although I must admit, we never fathomed that you would be involved at this level. The way the cards are falling, you're going to have a lot of responsibility."

They sat in silence for a minute until Calvin's dad admitted,

"You know, Calvin, your mother is one crafty magician herself. I wouldn't be surprised if she knew what you've been up to."

"She does know that I left with Grayson. Grayson told her that he was going to take me in as his apprentice," said Calvin. "But she doesn't know about the map, orb, or key that I have."

"Yes. I imagine she suspects that you are learning a lot about the magical ways."

"Is mom a Bordarian?"

"She is."

"Why haven't I ever seen her leave mysteriously?"

"A Bordarian's first priority is his or her family. If, for instance, in your mother's case, she has young children at home, she needs to be there for the family. I'm sure over the years she has seen the call for Bordarians, but because she was caring for you, she was excused from the call."

"Has she ever been on a mission?"

"Lots of them."

Calvin wore an expression of disbelief and pride. His mom was a Bordarian! Maybe one day he would also be appointed Bordarian.

"Have you had any more thoughts about your friends? Where they might be?"

"Last night I dreamt that they were locked in a dungeon," said Calvin.

"Do you know where?"

"No."

"Were they safe?"

"Yes," said Calvin. "But Galigore was coming to see them soon."

Calvin's dad thought for a moment. "We must act on these premonitions. We should notify Ulric immediately."

"How do we do that?"

"By fizzle-gram."

24 · Betrayal

The dungeon door rattled open and a hooded figure entered, compounding the prevailing atmosphere of gloom. The dim dungeon cell became darker. Perry and Anna huddled close together, trying to remain brave. The figure glowered at them suspiciously, shadows disguising his facial features. Anna whispered into Perry's ear, "Galigore."

Galigore held a long staff with a familiar orb clinched in an ornate fist at the top. "What have we here?" the fiend scowled. "A younger generation trying to disrupt my triumph? Some talented adolescents you think you are? I sense that only one of you exhibits significant potential. But your heritage is of no threat to me. As for you, Perry, you have no hope alone. A lowly wizard is all you'll ever be. But, with the help of the right master, you can become powerful. You see, that is where I come into play. I can become your liberator."

Perry and Anna stayed calm, seated against the cold, hard wall of the stone room. "Come with me, Perry," the cackling voice commanded.

Perry did not move.

"Do you need some motivation? I said, come with me!" The cell echoed gloomily.

Perry remained at Anna's side, frozen in fear.

Galigore raised his staff and pounded it on the heavy stone floor. A reverberation of electricity formed a ring around the bottom of the staff that grew bigger and bigger as it traveled toward Perry. As the ring hit Perry, he writhed in pain, clawing at the stone floor. Anna was unaffected.

"You haven't got a chance, Perry, of doing it your way. You might as well be accommodating, or I will make you oblige my command."

The intense pain diminished and Perry lay on the ground gasping for air.

"Now, let's try this again," roared Galigore. "Perry, come

with me." Galigore turned and walked toward the cell door.

Frustrated by the pain Perry was suffering, Anna shot him a look, jerking her head in Galigore's direction, telling him that he needed to go. Perry didn't want to, but knew he was powerless in the struggle. He staggered to his feet and followed Galigore out the door.

For the first time, Anna was convinced that her little team was in over their heads in the battle. Heavily outnumbered, her hopes began to fade as she saw the dungeon door slam shut with her friend, Perry, on the other side in the hands of the most powerful villain to ever have existed.

Perry followed Galigore through the winding corridors of the dungeon. He thought about running, but the reality of being able to escape at this point was hopeless. Perry only understood the slightest amount of power Galigore possessed with the magical orb slotted into its matching staff. He remembered hearing the stories from Grayson at Fountain Green about Galigore's power. He now had no doubt that every story was true.

Galigore made one last turn down a narrow passage that dead-ended with a single iron door. A wave of the staff made the door rattle open on its own. Perry followed the evildoer into the lair and the door locked behind him.

"Have a seat, my young friend," Galigore directed.

There were only two places to sit. Two rigid thrones, made of stone, were situated in the middle of a spacious round room. They faced one another about ten feet apart. Between them was a low, flat-topped block. Perry sat on the throne to his right. Galigore took his seat on the left. It was the first time Perry got a good look at Galigore's face. It was a hideous sight. His skin was pale and scarred. His teeth were jagged and yellow. His hair seemed to be black—about shoulder length.

"Please forgive me for the display of power back there, Perry. I didn't think it would take much to entice you to follow me."

Perry made no expression at Galigore's words.

"Let me begin by telling you a little story." Galigore tried to sound friendly but his voice still pierced the room with devilry. "I was once young, as you are today. I had acquaintances I thought were my friends. But through the years, I found myself growing further apart from them. The more I hung around them, the more I realized we were different. Tell me, how much do you have in common with Calvin and Anna?"

Perry didn't say a word. He sat still, expressionless.

"Answer me." Galigore raised his staff.

"We have lots in common," Perry replied.

"Have you ever had dreams about what is to come?"

Perry shook his head.

"Have you ever had intuition strike you—warning you with absoluteness what was about to happen?"

Perry shook his head again.

"What about magic? I see you carry a wand. Has that come easily to you?"

Perry did not respond.

"Do your friends carry a wand?"

Perry said nothing.

"I didn't think so. But you do . . . because you are a lowly wizard. Tell me . . . how do you really feel around your friends?"

Perry's head was beginning to feel hot. He could sense beads of sweat forming on his forehead. He thought about the times when he lacked confidence. The time he was scared to go into the trap door of The Crossing. Or when he first entered Fountain Green. Calvin and Anna were coolheaded. But he lacked confidence. He replayed the experience of passing through the portal with Grayson. He was such a crybaby. He must have looked like a fool. They were so calm. He was in a panic. He saw himself climbing off Bravada after what Calvin thought was an exhilarating ride. All he could do was roll over and kiss the ground.

"You're not as similar as you may think, Perry. Have you ever felt jealous of your so-called friends' innate powers and the lack of yours?"

"What are you getting at?" Perry asked, defensively.

Galigore rose to his feet, walked around the altar, and motioned for Perry to stand. "I have been labeled the bad guy, and for good reason, I admit. But I have a good side. I can help you."

Galigore raised his staff and waved it in front of Perry. A

wave of exhilaration perked him up.

"Here, Perry. Take my staff for a moment. Let me show you what is possible."

Perry held the staff up. It was heavy but uplifting. He twirled it in his hands and gazed at the orb. A continual stream of energy radiated from the staff making him feel invincible. Powerful. All of his worries faded.

"You see, Perry? Can you feel your potential?"

Perry was mesmerized by the power and suddenly found himself craving for more.

"That's it," encouraged Galigore. "Let it build. Let it escalate. Jealousy is a thing of the past. This is your future."

Perry continued to soak in the feelings of power. His countenance slowly changed from confidence to pride. He loved what he was feeling. Not a care in the world. He wanted more of it.

Galigore ripped the staff from Perry's hands. The energy in the chamber ceased immediately, and Perry dropped to his knees, panting for more.

"There has been much misunderstanding about me, Perry. I am a kind person. I want to give you a piece of what I have. As possessor of this staff, I have power to allow even a wizard like yourself to taste of its strength. You have experienced only a small amount of what you can expect. But believe me, you shall receive much more. Everything you can imagine will be yours . . . that is, of course, if you desire to have it."

"I want it," said Perry.

"Do you? I'm not sure you can fulfill your end of the bargain."

"What do you need me to do?" inquired Perry.

"As you know, there are three sets of orbs and their respective artifacts. Calvin has one set; here is another." Galigore raised his staff in the air. "We must find the third. And when we do, it will be yours. But in the meantime, I need to possess the set Calvin has. That is where you come into the equation. You see . . . Calvin will be coming for you and Anna sometime soon. When he frees you, I want you to lead him to me. That's it. I will worry about the rest."

"But . . . Calvin's dead."

"No, Perry. He is very much alive."

"But the Zarkon chucked him off a cliff. They said he was dead."

"Not true."

Perry considered for a while.

"Where will you be?" asked Perry.

"Lead him to me here. As you saw on our way into this chamber, there was only one other way to go after winding through the corridors. Near the end, we turned right, which led us here. A left turn will eventually lead you outside, which would upset the plan. Do not allow him to go left, Perry."

"I can do that," affirmed Perry.

"If you succeed, I will give you my staff, and I will take over the sword. Then together we will search out the bow. Believe me, the reward is far greater than one can imagine. You will have it all."

Perry stood, deep in thought, dreaming of what could be. The power he felt was undeniably attractive. He yearned for it. For once he was able to feel what it was like to be powerful.

"Very well," grunted Galigore. "I must get you back to your cell so you can await your rescuer. I'm certain he'll come in the next day or two."

"What about Anna? Will she be safe?"

"Perry, in the long run, you'll dictate her safety. You'll have power to do as you please. But, to ensure her immediate protection, I will have her removed from your cell and taken to another chamber given to prisoners who have exhibited insurmountable cooperation. We cannot risk her skewing our plan when Calvin comes. We will isolate her but provide her with exceptional living quarters. You do understand the need?"

"I do," said Perry.

"I knew I could count on you, Perry. We'll make a good team."

25 • The Castle of Cambria

A loud clap rang from outside. Calvin's dad went to the window and pulled back the drapes.

"Come here, Calvin."

Calvin looked out the window toward the sky. Fizzling amid the gray-clouded background was a bright, gleaming letter B. As soon as Calvin was able to see it clearly, it began to fizzle away.

"Did you see it?"

"Yes," said Calvin. "That's the same B I saw in Yeti Mountain."

"This is the call for all Bordarians to report to the castle."

Calvin's suspicion was right. When he saw the signal light up the mountain sky, he guessed that's what it meant—a call for Bordarians.

* * * *

The castle was easy to spot. He had seen pictures of many old castles in books. This one was similar. The exterior was made of large gray stones. Green and black moss grew upon the lower half of the castle walls. Several towers shot skyward from the main body of the structure with guards standing at every lookout. The flag of Cambria flew from the highest tower.

It was surrounded by a ten-foot stone wall that easily enclosed one thousand acres. Guards were sprinkled about generously. The castle's towering spires were majestic. A layer of low clouds stretched thinly across the spires about halfway up. Watchmen stood guard from the turrets.

As Calvin approached the walled kingdom, he noticed several buildings resting within the castle grounds. A huge lake sat to the east and a large meadow adjoined the water where dozens of dragons and other creatures rested. On the other side of the castle were several acres of gardens with brick paths winding throughout. The vegetation was dense and the terrain varied in elevation—hundreds of feet.

Calvin and his dad arrived by dragon at the main security entrance. It was situated at the rear of the grounds where the trees and shrubbery were the thickest.

"State your name and your mission," said the castle guard in a surprisingly high voice. He stood about four feet tall and was chubby, with a pointed nose that stuck out from his face. The tops of his ears were also pointed. He wore glasses with lenses that were perfectly round and had a lot of hair that hung well below his stocking cap. His hair was long and white and seemed connected to his beard. A second guard, whose appearance was nearly identical to the other's, stood nearby.

"Miles Sparks. Bordarian of Cambria. Summoned to report to the castle."

Calvin glanced over at the guards, who were conversing among themselves, sifting through a list of names. Then, finally, the first guard replied, "No entry granted . . . Step aside . . . Next?"

"Wait . . . there must be a mix up," Miles said.

"I'm sorry, you're not listed as an active Bordarian."

"Do you have a list of inactives?" asked Miles.

"We do . . . but you probably won't be on this list," said the second guard holding up a thick, leather-bound book. "All of these names are Bordarians who have died or have been decommissioned due to disloyalty. Those who have died obviously wouldn't be inquiring to enter. Likewise, those who have been expelled would not be granted entry."

"Please," said Miles. "Look for my name among the deceased."

The guard looked a bit confused but thumbed through the pages anyway. He advanced to the section where surnames began with the letter S.

"Okay, we're almost there . . . Sparks, you say?" His finger slowly skimmed down the page on the right side. As soon as he got to the bottom, he flipped the page.

"S-M . . . S-N . . . S-O . . . here we go . . . S-P. Yes . . . Sparks. Miles, you say?"

"Yes, Miles Sparks."

"You don't say . . . " The second guard motioned with a

short jerk of his head for the first to look at the entry. Both watchmen carefully examined the photo in the book. In unison they looked up from the page and glanced at Miles—then back to the photo.

"That's him all right. It's not very often Bordarians come back from the dead. I guess there's a first for everything."

"I was held prisoner at Peril Cove for years. I was presumed dead shortly after my encounter with Galigore."

"Place your hand here," said the guard, holding out a stone tablet.

Miles placed his hand on the marble surface. A white light began at the top edge and moved toward the bottom as it scanned the print. After the scan, the tablet glowed green.

"Miles Sparks. Entry granted," he pronounced.

Miles passed through the gates and waited on the other side where he could see Calvin through the iron bars.

"State your name and your mission," came the command.

"Calvin Sparks. Summoned to report to the castle." Calvin's expression was an awkward one. He wondered if he was doing this right—after all, he wasn't really a Bordarian.

"Were you dead as well?"

"No, sir. I should be in the living book," he said confidently. He didn't even know if it was called a living book.

The book did not list his name.

"No entry granted. Step aside. Next?"

Calvin turned and looked behind him. There was no one there.

"But I was summoned this morning," said Calvin. "I saw the B in the sky."

The two guards looked at each other in surprise. "You saw the sign, but you're not a Bordarian?" they asked.

"That's right," responded Calvin. "I've seen the sign twice now. My friend didn't see it, but I did."

"Say . . . could this be one of those special cases?" one whispered to the other. "Just a moment," he said to Calvin.

The two guards huddled together in their security booth. Calvin wondered whether or not he would be able to enter the castle grounds. He could see his dad waiting for him on the other side of the gates. At least he would know if he were not granted access.

"Okay . . . Calvin Sparks, right?" asked the guard.

Calvin nodded.

"We just communicated with the head of security," he explained. "We have been instructed to let you enter the grounds as a visitor. I suggest you head straightway to the castle. Captain Ulric will be looking for you."

"Place your hand upon the tablet," said the guard.

Calvin held still while the bright light scanned his hand, and he smiled when it finally turned green.

"Calvin Sparks. We hereby grant you access to enter the castle of Cambria."

Calvin hastily entered through the gates and met his dad. The path they walked on was made of rough cobblestone. The short tunnel brought them to a beautiful courtyard. Lush plants in baskets hung from pillars surrounding the yard. The spacious, green lawn was lined with meticulously groomed hedges that reached to Calvin's waist. Strewn throughout the lawn were walking paths that were lined with trees. Along the paths, Calvin could see benches placed in shaded areas.

"Ulric will be in the Gathering Hall," said his dad. "It's this way."

They walked along paths that intertwined through acres of flowers, lawn, trees, and exotic plants. Several large fountains decorated the intersections between pathways. Calvin thought the grounds were heavenly. Large hummingbirds hovered in front of flowers, filling up with sweet nectar. Colorful butterflies danced from bud to bud. Two unicorns were grazing in the grass. Honeybees buzzed from flower to flower.

The castle sat on a hill, much higher than where they were. As they continued on the path, it turned into a long flight of stairs. They quickly climbed them.

Two large cyclopes stood in front of the heavy wooden entrance doors. Their size reminded Calvin of his lost friend Tobran, but the comparison ended there. They each had only one eye, and it was in the middle of their foreheads.

They each spoke in a surprisingly low voice. "The Captain

received word that you were here. Please come in. I will take you to him."

"Tagron?" asked Miles, recognizing the other cyclops standing guard.

Tagron looked over. "Miles? It is true? You're still alive?"

Miles walked over to Tagron and clasped his hand. "It's good to see an old friend."

"Why don't I take this one, Groban," Tagron said. The other cyclops acknowledged Tagron's request.

The door opened and Tagron escorted Miles and Calvin into the castle. The entry was spacious with ceilings that reached several stories high. A huge chandelier, illuminated with hundreds of candles, dangled fifteen feet from the floor. On one side of the entry, portraits of brave Bordarians adorned the wall. It was a reverent tribute to the many stalwart Bordarians who had lost their lives in battle. Though there were hundreds of heroes displayed, Calvin immediately spotted the painting of his dad and read the caption.

"Well, I guess we don't need that one . . . do we?" said Tagron. He waved his wand in front of the portrait and it vanished while all of the others hanging on the wall shuffled around and filled in the vacant spot.

"Follow me," said the cyclops as he motioned for Miles and Calvin to walk through the door into the Gathering Hall. There was a buzz coming from several conversations taking place. The room was round. A continuous row of tables encircled the hall. Most of the chairs were filled. At the head of the room sat Ulric, the Bordarian Captain. Next to Ulric were three empty chairs.

As Miles entered the hall, the sound of chimes began to fill the air. Ulric had started the signal, while those who noticed joined in by picking up their silver utensils and tapping them against their crystal goblets. Within seconds, all talking stopped and everyone in the room joined in the melody. Ulric raised his hand and the clanking ended.

"Thank you," said Ulric. "I want to re-introduce you to someone many of us knew long ago." Ulric's voice was deep, bold, and confident. He was younger than Calvin expected—

about the same age as his grandpa. He was fit—his arms strong and muscular. His hair was short, wavy, and brown. His dress was not regal. He wore no crown. He fit in with everyone else as far as appearance was concerned.

"Please . . . come forward." Ulric motioned for Miles and Calvin to come up front and occupy the vacant chairs next to him. Everyone turned to watch as they made their way up to the front of the room. Calvin heard a few gasps and observed some whisperings.

"As my friends make their way up to the front," said Ulric, "let me take you back in time. Thirteen years ago."

Miles and Calvin continued to walk forward.

"As many of you may recall, I sent a few of you on a dangerous mission to Shadow Gorge. I sent my most skilled team. Galigore had built up his Society of Zarkon to ward off our Bordarian Army. Two Zarkon pursued Grayson and Stone. Galigore himself chased after Miles. It was the last time we saw Miles Sparks, who left behind a dear wife and baby. Thought to be destroyed long ago . . . ," Ulric said, his eyes welling up, "we now have the honor of hearing from our old friend, hero, and survivor . . . Miles Sparks."

The Bordarians jumped to their feet and the room erupted in applause. Miles and Calvin now stood up front, next to Ulric. Miles glanced over on the other side of Ulric where Grayson and Stone stood. Miles made eye contact with Stone. Stone smiled and discreetly pumped his fist in the air.

Ulric lifted his hand, aiming it at Miles, inviting him to share a few words. The room was still filled with energetic applause as Miles tried to quiet the hall. The commotion slowly died down as the Bordarians took their seats.

"Thank you," Miles began, speaking over the hushing hoopla. "Thank you. Every day . . . every day over the past twelve years I hoped that this day would come. I believed it would come. I believed I would one day get out of that awful dungeon. I believed I would enjoy my family again. And this belief, after thirteen long years, has finally become a reality." The hall burst with energetic acclamation. After a moment, Miles continued, speaking over the clapping and whistling. "And through this long period of wretched affliction, I learned that the mind is more powerful than you might suspect. I am a firm believer of that. Each one of us chooses our feelings. We choose how we will respond to certain situations. When we are down, we choose to either shut down and give up or pick ourselves up and press on.

"I had all the reason in the world to fall into despair, to let go of hope. To permit myself to die. But I chose not to let go . . . not to give up. And I am glad I realized that early on. I am glad I instilled a belief within myself that I would see the sun again . . . that I would hold my dear wife again . . . and that I would come to know my son. And as it turned out, he was the one who rescued me." Again the hall roared in approval. "If there is one lesson I learned while being isolated in an awful prison, it is this: while we may not always be able to control our circumstances, we can always control our attitude."

Fierce applause filled the hall. Miles waved to the group. Ulric motioned for silence as Miles took his seat next to Calvin.

Calvin thought back on the tour of his dad's dungeon cell. He recalled the many positive statements that were etched into the wall that he must have leaned on to give him hope. Hope that one day he would be free.

"Thank you, Miles. It is so good to see you again, my friend. We look forward to rubbing shoulders with you anew. Now, we have some business to take care of."

A dwarf entered the hall and waddled up to Ulric. He handed him a piece of parchment.

"Excuse me." Ulric unrolled the note.

"Please converse amongst yourselves for a moment. I have something important to take care of. Miles. Calvin. Follow me."

Miles and Calvin rose to their feet and walked out of the hall with Ulric.

"What is it?" asked Miles. "Is everything okay?" They walked down a corridor.

"Everything is quite fine," said Ulric. "There is someone I think you should see."

"Ulric?" Miles stopped in the hall. "Is it her?"

"Who?" Ulric asked.

"Is it Kristal? Is she here?"

Ulric smiled. "She just arrived."

Excitement ran throughout Calvin's body. He had wondered, since freeing his dad, what this reunion would be like.

Ulric stopped in front of a door. "Are you ready?"

Miles took a deep breath. "Yes."

Ulric opened the door and ushered Miles and Calvin inside. Kristal was sitting on a sofa. She immediately turned and stood up.

"Kristal?" Miles said.

Kristal stared in disbelief. "Is it really you?" Tears streamed down her face.

"Kristal . . . it's me." Miles held out his arms. "I'm free."

Kristal put her hands to her face.

"Come give him a hug, Mom," said Calvin.

Kristal ran to Miles and threw her arms around his neck. "All these years . . . I-I thought you were . . . " Kristal didn't finish her sentence. She squeezed Miles tighter.

"I was being held prisoner." Miles wrapped his arms around Kristal's body and placed his cheek on hers. He closed his eyes. They embraced for a long time. Neither of them seemed to want to let go.

Calvin looked at Ulric. "Did you plan this?" Ulric nodded. "I tracked her down in a cabin near Wolf Creek. She was with a bunch of her friends."

Calvin sat back and quietly admired the reunion. He never knew what it was like to be a complete family with a mom *and* a dad.

"Come here, Calvin," said Miles, standing next to Kristal with his arm tightly and lovingly wrapped around her shoulders. Kristal laughed and cried as Calvin made his way over. She reached and squeezed him into their circle.

Ulric gave them a few more minutes and then broke up the reunion. "Miles, let's all go back into the hall. I have something you won't want to miss."

The four of them entered the hall. Miles, Kristal, and Calvin took their seats up front. Ulric clanked his utensil against his crystal goblet. Within seconds, every person followed his lead.

He raised his hand and the hall was silent.

"As you know," Ulric began, "Miles has developed high marks in several areas. He broke many records and became a Bordarian at a very young age. Let me tell you . . . the apple doesn't fall too far from the tree. Today, it is my privilege to appoint a new Bordarian. Calvin Sparks will become the newest member of our order, and the youngest to ever be appointed to the call."

Calvin's eyes grew big. He looked over at his mom. She gave him an affirming smile. He then turned to his dad.

"You've earned it, son."

"Calvin Sparks . . . please come forward," said Ulric.

Calvin walked over to Ulric and stood next to him, on his right side.

"Calvin, if you desire to become a Bordarian, raise your right hand and take the Bordarian Oath."

Ulric twirled his hands and formed letters that floated in the air in front of him. He gently pushed them toward Calvin. The letters arranged themselves into words that only Calvin could see.

Calvin brought his arm up and began to read.

"I, Calvin Sparks, promise to preserve, defend, and uphold the laws of Cambria, and to promote the general welfare of our people. I promise to faithfully perform all the duties pertaining to this office to the best of my ability. I promise to keep secret all that may be entrusted unto me. I pledge my loyalty to this, the Bordarian Order. And to this cause I dedicate my life."

"By the authority vested in me," pronounced Ulric. "I now present to you Calvin Sparks, our newest member of the Order of the Bordarians."

Ulric leaned into Calvin and whispered in his ear.

Calvin then faced the Order, clenched his fist, and extended his right arm in the air. Everyone in the room rose to their feet and extended their fists in the air in the same manner. Calvin put his hand down, and the Order followed him and took their seats.

"I will be making assignments shortly. But I need a few minutes alone with our newest Bordarian. Brunch will now be served. Please, make yourselves comfortable."

Conversations emerged instantly. People rushed up to the front to see their old friends, Miles and Kristal. Ulric exited the room with Calvin.

"You did well, Calvin," said Ulric. Together they walked down a long corridor, passing many wooden doors. The first one they passed was the one where his mom had been waiting to meet his dad. Calvin wondered what was behind the others. He imagined some were the servants' quarters. He almost asked, when his thought was interrupted. "Here we go . . . this way." Ulric opened a door at the end of the hall. "Please come in; make yourself comfortable."

Calvin entered Ulric's living quarters and gazed in awe. The spacious room was divided into sections. In one nook Ulric had his desk. It was messy, with lots of papers stacked in several different piles. Behind the desk was a large bookcase that spanned from wall to wall and floor to ceiling. It was filled with books.

In another nook off the main room was a sitting area that stepped down two stairs. Furniture was arranged neatly around the fireplace.

"Let's have a seat," said Ulric.

Calvin sat on the sofa and reserved the armchair for Ulric.

"Your father briefed me on everything. You've been on some remarkable adventures, Calvin."

Calvin nodded.

"You have also become a target. When the Zarkon saw you had the sword and orb on top of that ledge, you became Galigore's goal. We must keep a watchful eye over you. And until we find more answers, you and your family will make your home here in the castle."

"What about my grandpa?"

"We need to keep him safe as well. Actually, I'm a little surprised he's not here already. He's usually one of the first to respond to the Bordarian call. I'll have a team of Bordarians go and check on him."

Calvin hoped that he was safe.

"Your father said your friends were in trouble."

"Last night I had a dream that my friends were locked up in

a dungeon cell. Two guards outside the prison door were talking. They said that Galigore would be there soon to interrogate them."

"Calvin," Ulric said in a serious tone. "We must find your friends before Galigore does something."

Ulric stood up and started toward the door. "Stay here for a moment. . . I'm not quite finished with you."

26 · Desolation

Ulric left the room and Calvin sat in silence, gazing around at the vastness of the captain's quarters. He wondered what his room was going to be like here at the castle.

"Every time I see you, you are deeper involved, aren't you?"

Calvin spun around quickly to find Trixel sitting near him on the hearth of the fireplace.

"Trixel? How did you get in here?" asked Calvin.

"Oh, we gnomes have our ways of doing things."

"Why have you come this time?" inquired Calvin.

"You are my assignment, Calvin. I am to look after you. My master says it is imperative that you remain safe from harm."

"Your master?" asked Calvin. "Who's your master?"

"Osgar, of course." Trixel winked at Calvin. "I don't have much time, Calvin. But take this. It shall help you on many journeys to come."

Trixel dropped a round, polished stone, about the size of a small marble, into Calvin's outstretched hand. He held it up in front of his face and examined it. Streaks of smoky matter swirled within its core. Thin wire strands wrapped around the stone, encaging it in its grasp. There was a loop at the top with a leather tie threaded through it. The swirling matter seemed to form the letter M.

"What does it mean?"

"It stands for a word that is associated with secrecy."

"What does it do?" asked Calvin.

"It turns one invisible."

"How does it work?"

"Certainly you know what to do with a necklace?" asked Trixel.

"No, I mean, how does it turn one invisible?"

"Always wear the necklace, Calvin. When you need to access its powers of invisibility, say the word *Murdrum* and you will become invisible. To reverse its powers, pronounce the word backwards and you will become visible again. It's quite simple, really."

Calvin slipped the necklace on over his head.

"Remember Calvin, this gift of invisibility only works if you have virtuous intentions. One time a gnome stole a necklace similar to this, intending to unlawfully acquire treasure from another. As soon as he took what was not rightfully his, he became visible, right in front of the keeper of the treasury. Needless to say, he is no longer with us and that particular stone lost its power."

"I will use it for good."

"I know you will. Oh, there is one more important thing. Anyone you touch while you are invisible will also turn invisible. And I suppose I should point out the obvious. While you are invisible, do not let this slip off from around your neck, or you will immediately become visible to all around you. Be good, Calvin." Trixel winked again, snapped his fingers, and vanished behind a display of sparks.

Calvin walked around Ulric's quarters. There were various doors he thought he should probably not enter, but his curiosity got the best of him. One solid wooden door with an arched top and blackened iron trim caught his eye. He twisted the lever and pushed the creaky door open.

The room was empty. There was a second door on the opposite wall. Above the door, carved in the stone, was an inscription. Calvin stepped inside the room and read the message:

With this pool, one might wish to follow his life sublime.
Be it bright, or be it glum, this water will not lie.
Place a hair into the pool and watch with real intent.
But be aware that once submerged, the truth will sometimes hurt.

With this pool? thought Calvin. *What pool?*

The room began to shake. The walls cracked where various vines penetrated through the stone. The plants spread out, became interlaced, and created a thick web of vegetation that clung to the walls. The stone floor Calvin was standing on had turned to rich soil. Large trees grew from the ground and shot upward. Branches fanned out and filled the room. Thin stone slabs materialized and sat on end with a low mound of dirt extending out in front.

Although Calvin could not read the inscription upon the tablets, he recognized them as headstones. The floor in front of him crumbled and formed a gaping hole. Calvin looked up and saw the ceiling extend skyward as trees stretched as far as he could see. The words on the wall became entangled in greenery. The sound of water gurgled from below. The rumbling subsided as the deep hole that opened in front of him was now an effervescent pool of magical water.

Calvin pondered in amazement as the room he had entered had completely transformed into an isolated cemetery nestled within a lush forest. He reached up to his head, yanked out a single hair, and held it in his fingertips. Stretching as far as he could, out over the pool, he dropped the strand into the sparkling water.

Rippled rings formed around the hair. As the water became still again, the surface showed scenes from Calvin's life. He saw himself become a Bordarian exactly how it had happened earlier that day. He saw himself at The Crossing in the woods behind his house. He then saw his mom and dad embrace the night his dad rode off on Amalga. It happened just like he had seen it in his dream. The archive then showed his mom and dad embrace him as a baby just minutes after he was born. The scene changed again to his parents' wedding day. Time continued to go backward. The imagery then showed his grandpa becoming a Bordarian. He saw his grandma and grandpa dancing at a gala. She was clear as could be. His grandma had died when he was two years old. He had only seen old photos of her, but now he was looking at her as if she were alive and well. His grandparents faded away as a new image appeared. It was another elderly couple Calvin assumed were his great-grandparents.

"You have deep roots, don't you, Calvin?"

Calvin jumped. He turned to see Ulric standing in the doorway. "I see you have found the Pool of Lineage. If you stand there long enough, you will see ancestry dating back several generations—all the way to the beginning of time. But I'm not sure we have time for that."

"What does it mean . . . the truth will sometimes hurt?" asked Calvin.

"I'm afraid life is not rosy for everyone. Some people have come here and learned about their past, uncovering dark secrets kept by their ancestors. It has destroyed people. They would have been better off to never have known what their distant relatives did."

Calvin contemplated Ulric's response.

"There are two other pools similar to this," Ulric continued. "This one unfolds the lineage of any person whose hair is dropped into the water. There is another one called the Pool of Veracity that detects truth. That one is also kept in the castle. But the Pool of Destiny—a particularly dangerous one as it reveals the future—is kept locked away in a safe place."

Calvin looked around and found himself standing in the same empty room as before. The pool was gone, the floor was stone again, and the vines had vanished, leaving the walls unbroken.

"I just sent your mother and Grayson back to the house to retrieve your grandfather. I have another assignment for you. I need you to lead the way to find and free your friends. You will go with an experienced team. Let's go. Time is of the essence."

Ulric escorted Calvin out the other door that was underneath the message on the opposite wall. It led to a main hallway of the castle. Inside the Gathering Hall, most had finished their meals and were polishing off dessert as they visited with one another. Ulric made his way to the front of the hall and clanked a spoon against his goblet. Almost immediately the entire hall joined in on the signal. The room grew quiet as Ulric raised his hand, preparing to speak.

"Stone Stryder and Miles Sparks, please rise," commanded Ulric. "You are to join Calvin Sparks on a quest to free two prisoners who were captured while battling the Zarkon at Peril Cove. We don't have much time. You must locate them and free them from bondage before Galigore reaches them. Have you any questions?"

Stone raised a finger. "Where are they exactly?"

"It is up to you to find and rescue them. I wish I had more details, but that is all. Calvin can tell you who it is you will be looking for, and I suspect you will use his resources to point you in the right direction. You must leave immediately."

* * * *

Dozens of dragons and other beasts of various shapes and sizes were engrossed in eating at the feeding grounds. Fresh raw animal flesh was strewn about the lawn where groups of dragons gathered around and picked chunks of bright red meat from the carcasses. In his mind, Calvin called for Bravada. She stuck her neck high above the other dragons that were intently chomping their chow. Bravada jumped into the air, flapped her wings, and headed for her rider.

Miles looked over the mass of dragons. He saw his dragon emerge from a cluster that was gathered around a watering hole. Amalga was holding a large trout in her claws. She quickly crunched the fish down and came to him.

Calvin noticed a beast from the corner of his eye that startled him. He had seen pictures of the feldinari before, but had never seen one in real life. It was a vicious, three-headed animal with a powerful body. Two block-shaped heads resembled that of a French Bull Mastiff. Its razor-sharp teeth protruded from the perimeter of its mouths. The noses were flat and the eyes intimidating. From the feldinari's large paws emerged sharp, curled claws. Its sturdy wings appeared to be adequate to carry many more times its body weight. Its tail was thick, scaly, and lengthy, and it extended over the top of its body. The end tapered a little, transforming into the head of a serpent with green, glowing eyes and two long, sharp fangs. Its back bowed downward, perfect for a saddle.

"That's it. Come on, boy," said Stone as his beast made its way to him. It had thick, slimy drool hanging from the corners of its mouths. As the beast turned from one side to another, the thick drool whipped around, flinging the strands from its jowls.

"A feldinari?" said Calvin in amazement.

Stone nodded. "Calvin, meet Ramsey."

Calvin stretched his hand toward the beast. Ramsey

brought a head near Calvin's hand. A large, wet tongue emerged from the beast's mouth and saturated Calvin's palm. He cringed in disgust.

"Let's go, Ramsey," commanded Stone.

Calvin continued to stand there with his arm outstretched. He held a pool of sticky drool with chunks of chewed meat in his hand. Wondering how he would clean it, he gave his arm a strong flick, whipping the sticky mess to the ground. Calvin's nose turned up, but his face exhibited half a smile.

Each of them mounted their beasts. Calvin led the way, soaring as high as he could, out of sight from civilization below. He flew to the place where he last saw Perry, Anna, and Tobran. Calvin rehearsed everything he knew, including what he saw in his dream regarding Galigore.

"Describe again what the dungeon cell looked like," said Miles.

"It was barren. Everything was stone . . . the floor, walls, and ceiling."

"Were there other prisoners there?" asked Stone.

"I never saw any, but there were multiple watchmen."

The three of them sat in silence, thinking. Calvin took his map out and laid it on the ground. He placed a rock at each corner to keep the breeze from taking it.

"I'm certain that's the same one I had . . . before someone stole it," said Stone. "But I knew it wasn't meant for me. Interesting how it ended up in your hands. The orb, as well . . . I felt nothing when I handled it. How about you, Calvin? Have you ever felt any energy come from it?"

"The instant I touched the orb, I felt its energy. A painful jolt shot up my arm. My hand was sore and swollen from a spider bite I got earlier that day. And the orb completely healed my hand."

"Well, there you go," said Stone. "I guess that's why you have it today, and not me. It was meant for you."

Calvin drew his sword and held it out over the map. He closed his eyes and concentrated. He thought about where his friends were located. He felt energy building up at the handle and vibrating down to the tip. Miles and Stone silently looked on.

The tip of the sword began to sway in circles. His eyes still closed, he felt the sword hover over the map, slowly moving from one location to another. After several seconds, the swaying became tighter and more focused. The sword tip crackled with energy as it hovered motionless over the Isle of Desolation.

* * * *

Calvin knew the island when he saw it. Desolation was barren, with no trees or other vegetation. No sign of life was present. On the south side of the island, there was a cavity that appeared to be an entrance to a cave. The arched opening was large enough for small boats to maneuver their way through, barely avoiding the jagged, low ceiling.

Stone noticed a boat making its way toward the opening. Another boat followed in the distance. He thought for a moment and then broke the silence. "We're going in."

Calvin and his dad turned and looked at him.

"We'll follow those boats inside," Stone said.

"Gauging the speed at which the boats are approaching the island," Stone said, "I figure we have maybe twenty minutes to devise a plan."

"Do we hijack one of the boats?" asked Miles.

"No . . . the other boat would surely see us," said Stone.

"So what if we take over both?" suggested Miles.

"We don't know what their purpose is for coming to the island," said Stone. "Are they bringing provisions? Are they bringing prisoners? How many guards are inside the entrance? If we happened to take over the boats successfully, without the island guards noticing, we're sure to fail once we talk to them."

"What do you think, Calvin?" asked his dad.

"Can we make our way into the water and swim out to the boats? If we can wait underwater until the second boat passes, we can grab on to it and let it tow us in."

"Creative," said Stone. "Not a bad idea."

"Do you know of any charms that would allow us to breathe under water?" asked Calvin.

"Yes. I know of a few," said Miles. "Come on, let's go."

Calvin, Miles, and Stone flew down to the shore and hid

behind a large, jagged rock that stuck out of the water. The sea was very cold and took their breath away when they jumped in. The boats were getting closer and would be passing soon.

"*Vortexum.*" Miles conjured a spell over the three of them. At first, nothing seemed different. But as Miles submerged himself into the water, a small whirlpool connected from the surface of the water to his mouth. The small vortex formed a straw through which he breathed easily. Calvin and Stone plunged into the sea and followed Miles.

Calvin was amazed at how natural it felt to breathe under water. As he dove deeper, he saw the small swirling tube of air extending from his mouth to the surface of the water. He and his dad and Stone kicked their way to where the boats would pass.

As they were waiting under the sea, they saw a dark shadow above them. The first boat rushed by. A few minutes later, Calvin pointed at another dark shape as it glided closer to them. He spotted a rope hanging from one side, dragging through the water, and caught hold of it as it passed. Stone spotted the rudder and quickly latched on. Miles reached for a second rope dragging through the water, and barely caught it. All three of them kicked to help move the boat forward so as to lessen the feel of the drag.

The turquoise tint to the water suddenly turned black. Calvin knew they had entered the dark cave. The boat slowed and began to turn sharply, back and forth. They must have traveled a few hundred feet before the water lightened up again. Calvin peered from under the boat and noticed, through the water's rippled surface, a distorted, muted cavern. The boat came to a stop next to a dock. Calvin had an idea and motioned for his dad and Stone to follow him. The three carefully moved away from the boat and found refuge underneath the wooden platform. They determined they were out of sight and released their vortexes. The dock floated about a foot off the water. It was made of wooden planks spaced half an inch apart. One man stood on top of the dock, the rubber soles from his shoes just inches away from Calvin's face.

"Making the rounds, Sandoval? What do you have for me

today?" It was a gruff voice that came from a stout, middle-aged man.

Sandoval stepped off the boat. His footsteps were heavy as they thudded against the floorboards. "Aye, Laszlo. I brought me treasures tuh barter wit."

"What do you have in mind?" asked Laszlo.

"I need me some help. I'm lookin' fer a maidservant."

"Yes. It looks like your boat can use a good cleaning. I have a pretty one that just came in. What are you willing to pay for her?"

Sandoval held up a leather pouch. "This bag o' gold should be more den enough."

"Give me a minute. I will be back with your slave." The heavy footsteps faded away as Laszlo disappeared into a dark cave.

"He better bring me a good 'un," said Sandoval quietly under his breath, but loud enough that Calvin heard.

Recognizing the opportunity, Miles quietly whispered to Calvin and Stone, "If that's Anna they're talking about, one of us needs to take control of the boat and sail out of here with her."

"What are we going to do with the pirate?" asked Calvin quietly.

"I have an idea. Let me handle it," said Miles.

Miles took a deep breath and disappeared into the water. He swam along the bottom of the vessel, making his way to the stern of the boat. Quietly, his head broke the surface of the water. He looked up and saw Sandoval with his back to him. Grabbing onto the edge of the boat, Miles slowly pulled himself up out of the water and looked inside. There were heavy blankets strewn across the floor—perfect to hide under. He continued pulling himself up and threw one leg over the side. Footsteps and clanking chains echoed in the hall. Caught off guard, Miles quickly lowered himself back into the water and remained hidden.

"I have your lady," Laszlo said, entering the cavern. Anna walked ahead of the keeper. She had a chain wrapped around her wrists and a short chain cuffed around each ankle that prohibited her from taking long strides. A piece of cloth was tied around her mouth, making it difficult for her to speak.

"She's a perty one, she is," said Sandoval. "Me thinks she'll work out fine fer me needs. 'Tis nice doin' bizness wit you."

Sandoval tossed the bag of gold to Laszlo, who immediately checked its contents. "Sorry, Sandoval . . . nothing against you . . . it's just that I have been stiffed so many times . . . I've made it standard protocol."

"Me understands. No worries."

Laszlo handed Sandoval a set of keys on a large brass ring. Sandoval took it and placed it in the pocket of his coat.

He reached out for Anna's arm and helped her step onto the boat. One step rocked the boat gently from side to side.

"We jus' bought us some help, Indy," Sandoval said to a pirate sitting inside the boat.

Miles was shocked to hear of another pirate. He never saw him and felt lucky that the pirate hadn't seen him either.

Indigo raised his eyebrows and whistled. "You dun good, Sandy." He helped Anna find a seat. The boat was messy. Several blankets were piled on one end, and four twenty-gallon drums were situated on the other. Sandoval took his place at the oars. Indigo sat behind Sandoval, facing the same direction.

"Now, if ye can untie us, we be off."

Laszlo untied the boat from the metal cleat bolted to the dock and threw the rope inside. He then gave a big push with his foot and the boat slowly drifted away. Sandoval began to work the oars. Still clinging to the boat, Miles was careful to remain hidden. He inched around the perimeter, toward the bow, trying to keep the boat between himself and the dock so Laszlo wouldn't see him.

Sandoval maneuvered the boat through sharp rocks until he exited the cave and entered the deep, open waters.

Miles pulled himself up, high enough to get a quick peek at Sandoval, sitting on a bench in the middle of the boat. The pirate, Indigo, was sitting on the floor, leaning against the side. He had a pistol he was playing with, twirling it around his fingers.

As Miles lowered himself back down out of view, he made eye contact with Anna. She gasped quietly. Miles quickly brought his finger to his lips, urging her to remain quiet. Anna, looking a bit confused, nodded in agreement.

Anna waved her hands in a circular motion and swished them toward Indigo. A loud thud came from Indigo's head smacking against the wood as he fell over.

Sandoval looked back and saw him lying on the floor of the boat. He put the oars up and scrambled to the front of the boat to check on his shipmate. As he stood over his friend, Miles pulled himself up out of the water and threw a charm at Sandoval. The pirate fell over onto Indigo in a deep slumber.

Anna turned quickly to Miles, who was pulling himself out of the water and into the boat. He unsheathed a knife that was strapped to his boot and cut through the cloth that was tied around Anna's face.

"Who are you?" asked Anna.

"You wouldn't believe me if I told you," said Miles, emptying water from his boot.

"Are you a Bordarian?"

"I am," answered Miles.

"You look familiar," said Anna. "Do I know you?"

"I can assure you we've never met." Miles grabbed the key ring out of Sandoval's pocket and unlocked the chains that held Anna in bondage.

"I'm looking for Anna. Might that be you?"

Anna seemed surprised that the stranger knew who she was. She remained quiet.

"I hope you are indeed Anna. Otherwise, I just wasted my time."

"You're here to rescue me?"

"Okay," said Miles, "let me explain. Do you know a Calvin Sparks?"

Anna's eyes lit up. "Is he okay? Tell me, where is he?" The last time Anna had seen Calvin, he was falling off the edge of a cliff, plummeting into the waters far below. The Zarkon had assumed he was dead.

"Calvin's fine. Look, Anna. My name is Miles Sparks. . . . I'm Calvin's dad."

Anna's eyes widened and her mouth dropped. "But I

thought you were—"

"Dead?"

"Yes . . . dead."

"That seems to be the common notion."

"So, where did you come from?" asked Anna.

"I've been locked up at Peril Cove," said Miles. "I assume you know about the key Calvin has?"

"Yes," Anna nodded.

"That key led him to me."

Anna sat there speechless.

"What about you?" asked Miles. "You've known Calvin long?"

"Yes. We go to school together. And hang out a lot."

"And your parents? Who are they?"

"I don't know my real parents. I'm adopted."

"Do they know anything about your birth parents? Their names?"

"Not a thing. They don't know who my birth parents were. I guess I was only a couple of days old when my adoptive parents took me in."

A groggy moan came from the floor of the boat. "Come on," urged Miles. "We haven't got time for this right now. We'll catch up later. These guys will be waking up soon. And when they do, I imagine they're going to be quite upset."

Amalga swooped down to the boat and carried Miles and Anna away. The dreary pirates continued to snooze while their boat drifted aimlessly to sea.

27 · Murdrum

Through thin wooden slats, Calvin and Stone peered up at Laszlo as he took a seat on a stump on the dock. Heavy footsteps echoed from the nearby corridor.

"Oh hey, Jacco," greeted Laszlo.

"I saw you sold the young lady to Sandoval," said Jacco. "What did the first boat want?"

"Just inquiring. He was a first-timer here. Wanted to know what we had to barter for. He'll be back."

A constant trickling of water crawled down the wall and splashed onto the ground, emptying into the sea. A steep, craggy bank, high enough to conceal them, stretched along the shore. Calvin and Stone scaled along the rocky surface to one side, away from the guards' direct line of sight.

They clambered toward an embankment where they would easily be able to climb out of the water. "You wait here," Calvin whispered to Stone.

Stone grabbed onto Calvin's arm and shook his head. "I'm coming with you."

"I'll be fine," Calvin said. "You keep an eye out and be my backup. Whatever you do, don't take your eyes off me." Calvin smiled. Stone nodded, appearing a bit confused.

Slowly climbing out of the frigid sea, Calvin hoped the guards wouldn't hear the water dripping from his clothes, splashing onto the stone floor. He looked into the water and saw his reflection among the undulating ripples. "*Murdrum,*" he whispered. Within seconds, he saw his body fade away into nothing. He walked toward the dungeon keepers while his wet, squishy shoes squeezed out a generous puddle of water with every step. Stone became nervous as his eyes followed the trail of water to the guards. Calvin had stopped directly in front of them.

"What in the . . . " Laszlo pointed to the floor in front of him. A pool of water swelled before their eyes. It grew steadily bigger as water continued to run from Calvin's sopping clothes.

"Is it springing up from the floor?" wondered Jacco.

"No, that would be impossible," answered Laszlo.

The two stood and looked around at the peculiar circumstance.

"There . . . it's coming from there!" exclaimed Laszlo, noticing the trail of water leading to the edge of the shore. "Someone's in here!" The two guards drew their swords. Stone looked on tentatively, unsure as to when he should rush to Calvin's side.

"We know you're here. Show yourself!" cried Jacco, cutting his sword through the air.

"I'm here!" cried Stone, climbing out of the water with his hands raised above his head.

"You've got a lot of nerve coming in here unannounced," said Laszlo. "You know what this place is, don't you? Trespassers face a stiff penalty. I'm afraid you've seen your last bit of daylight for a while." He approached Stone with his sword tip aimed at his face.

"What's your business here?" demanded Laszlo.

Jacco fell clumsily to the floor in a deep slumber.

"What happened to him?" asked Stone, acting afraid. "Who did that? Is this place haunted?"

"I've wondered the same thing," said Laszlo, nervously looking over at Jacco on the floor.

"You had a boy that just came in . . . where is he?" asked Stone.

"Why would I disclose that information to you?"

"We'll find him sooner or later," said Stone. "It might as well be sooner."

"We?" asked Laszlo.

"Well, I'm sorry to ruin your plans of locking me up," said Stone. "But I do admire you for your diligence."

"What are you talking a—" Laszlo fell heavily to the floor next to Jacco.

"*Murdrum.*" Calvin reappeared.

"Don't take my eyes off you?" asked Stone.

"Yeah . . . I thought you'd like that."

"Obviously you get it from your father. Come on," said Stone. "Let's get going."

Shadows danced along the walls as Calvin and Stone scooted through the torch-lit corridor. The long tunnel wound back and forth. It was a minute before they came to the first dungeon cell. Stone opened the latched window and peeked in. No sign of anyone. Up ahead on the other side of the hall was the next door—Calvin was already peering inside. Stone was making his way to the next. He opened the window—he saw no one. Calvin reached up to unlatch the next window. For an instant there appeared to be nobody inside, but then a hairy, dirty, creature jumped to the window and roared a toothless scowl. Calvin jumped backward and slammed the window shut. Calvin leapfrogged Stone, continuing on to the next cell door. Just as he reached up to unlatch the window, he had an impression to proceed to the next cell. Following his intuition, he pressed on.

"Stone!" Calvin whispered loudly. "It's this one."

Stone caught up to Calvin. "*Abreyla*." The lock clacked and Calvin muscled the heavy door open. Inside, Perry was sitting on the floor with his back against the wall. His complexion was ghostly white. He looked scared. Distraught. His eyes were affixed on a crack in the floor in front of him.

"Perry!" said Calvin. "Perry, let's go."

Perry snapped out of the trance. "Calvin! Boy, am I glad to see you. How did you find me?"

"We'll explain later. Let's get you out of here."

"Where's Anna?" asked Perry. "Did you find her too?"

"She's safe," said Calvin. "My da . . . " Calvin stopped mid-word. He knew he would have a lot of explaining to do if he continued his thought. He decided to save the explanation for later. "She's fine."

Perry looked at Stone. "And you are?"

"Stone Stryder." He held out his hand.

"Oh yeah. I've heard about you," said Perry. "That's a nice house you have. By the way, I used your toothbrush. I hope you don't mind. I rinsed it off really good, though." Perry looked over at Calvin. "Boy, I've wanted to get that off my chest for a while."

Calvin noticed color coming back to Perry's face. "Do you feel okay?" asked Calvin. "You looked a little upset."

"Me? Oh, no. I mean, yeah. Well, you can imagine being locked up all alone in a cold dungeon, never knowing if or when you'll get out. Your mind starts to play tricks on you. You begin to have conversations with the walls. You imagine seeing things in the dark shadows. There's such an eerie feeling in here. . . . Can we leave?"

"Yeah. Let's get outta here," said Calvin.

Calvin turned down the hall to go back the same way he and Stone had just come.

"Wait. It's this way," said Perry.

"Are you sure?" Calvin stopped.

"Let's just say I had a guided tour of the dungeon. There's an exit up ahead."

"How far up ahead?" asked Stone.

"Just a few minutes along this corridor," assured Perry.

Calvin knew the guards he put a sleeping charm on would be waking up soon, if they hadn't already. He trusted Perry and let him show the way.

The three of them set off at a quick pace. The narrow tunnel zigzagged just as Perry remembered it. They hustled through the angled passage and came to a fork.

Calvin turned to go right. Stone quickly followed.

"Wait!" Perry cried. Calvin and Stone stopped. "I know something about this fork." Perry looked down and ran his fingers through his hair. He clenched his fist and closed his eyes. Flashbacks of him holding Galigore's staff flooded his mind. The powerful feelings came back and they felt real, as if he was reliving the experience again. This was a turning point for him. Would it be betrayal and power? He had made his mind up earlier that he would do it. The immediate gratification was liberating. It made him feel invincible. Confident. But now, it was a more difficult decision with his lifelong friend in his presence. The disappointment. The regret. The guilt. Would it be too much to handle?

Calvin knew there was a struggle going on inside Perry's mind. "Perry, we need to get out of here. Which way do we go?"

Perry looked right and imagined Galigore sitting behind the door, waiting to attack. It would be that simple. Choose to go right and walk into a world of power. Or go left, avoid Galigore entirely, and maintain his integrity.

"He looks confused," Stone said to Calvin. Voices and footsteps were lurking in the distance. Stone thought that Jacco and Laszlo must have awakened from their slumber charm. "Just choose a way!" he commanded. "We don't have time for this!" Stone looked back to see if he could see the guards closing in on them.

Calvin headed down the right side. For a moment, Perry was relieved that Calvin chose for himself. That would make it easier for him when he encountered the evil Galigore. Chills ran up and down his spine, but Perry could not decipher whether they were chills of relief, anticipation of what was to come, anxiety, or guilt.

"Stop!" Perry shouted. Calvin and Stone turned. Perry didn't realize he had said the word. It was as if something had control over his body for a split second. Perhaps it was his subconscious prompting him to do what was right. "It's this way. If you continue ahead, something horrible awaits you. But if you go back this way, we'll find a way out of this dungeon."

"How do you know?" asked Stone.

Perry was still visibly flustered. "Let's . . . let's just go this way and . . . and I'll explain later. Please . . . just believe me."

"Let's go, then," Calvin said, leading the charge back the other way.

Perry felt better about the whole situation. He was convinced that he had made the right choice and, while he yearned for the power he had possessed for just a moment, he talked himself into believing that his friends, his loyalty, and his character were most important to him. He knew that Calvin and Stone thought he was acting strange, but if he could just lead them out of the dungeon and get off the island, he would explain, and everything would be back to normal. He wished he had time to explain now, but he didn't.

The three rushed through the corridor that began to climb. They ascended several short staircases broken up by twists and turns. They kept walking quickly until the corridor dead-ended. The pursuing commotion behind them grew louder. A door at the end was visible—the door that would lead them home.

"*Abreyla*," Calvin muttered while sweeping his hand across the latch. The bolts disengaged and the door opened by itself. The other side of the door was haunting. The room was mostly dark except for a fountain of gloomy, green water emptying into an emerald pool.

"Are you sure this is the right way?" asked Calvin.

"Yes," said Perry. "Let's go."

Jacco and Laszlo were approaching quickly. "Hurry, you two," said Stone. "Go inside. I'll hold these guys off."

Calvin hesitated. He wasn't sure he wanted to enter. The evil feeling was strong.

"Hurry!" yelled Stone. "I'll be fine."

Calvin bravely took a step inside the dark room. Perry followed. The room was spacious. The low light illuminated around the fountain, and didn't stretch beyond. Blackness filled the top of the room. Calvin wondered how high the ceiling was. He also wondered which way was out. Nothing resembled an exit.

The door slammed shut behind them. The room was quiet. Too quiet. But the silence was snapped by a cold, shrill voice. "At last we meet."

The room slowly began to light up, just barely enough to see the surroundings. A black-robed figure emerged from behind the fountain. He wore a large hood that covered most of his face. The shadows made it too dark to see any facial features, although Calvin knew they would be hideous.

"Well done, Perry. Well done. I knew I could count on you."

Calvin turned swiftly to Perry. "You knew about this?"

"Calvin, I swear. I didn't know!"

"Of course he knew about this. I told him I would be waiting for you. You did just as you were directed. Unfortunately, I won't be needing you anymore." The voice was chilling. Galigore raised his staff and threw the tip toward Perry, emitting a red, fiery bolt, striking him in the gut. He doubled over, writhing in pain and holding his stomach. Another swish of the staff sent Perry airborne, twisting and twirling before smacking his back violently against a rock wall. Perry's limp body lay motionless upon the ground. Blood trickled out of his stomach, soaked his shirt, and pooled around him on the cold, stone floor.

Calvin drew his sword from its sheath and held it up in defense. Blue strands of electricity traveled from the handle to the tip.

"Hand it over, Calvin." Galigore's screechy voice sent a chill down Calvin's back. Galigore held his hand out. "Obviously, we're after the same thing, but unfortunately for you, you're outnumbered."

Two of Galigore's Zarkon stepped out from the darkness. One stood on either side of their leader. "Give it up, boy."

Galigore threw the tip of his staff toward Calvin. A blue bolt of electricity shot from the end. Instinctively, Calvin shielded himself with his sword. The bolt bounced off the blade and shot to the ceiling, causing large pieces of stone to fall to the battleground between them. A second bolt tore through the air, aimed at Calvin. His sword deflected it again easily, this time casting the jolt to the side. One more streaked toward him. The angle of the deflection pointed perfectly at one of the Zarkon standing beside Galigore. The skeletal figure fell in a heap on the hard floor.

Calvin's fear turned to confidence. He wasn't sure he had seen the extent of Galigore's powers, but he was pleased with the outcome so far.

"Impressive," muttered Galigore. "But don't get overly excited. Let's heat it up a bit."

Before Galigore could muster up a spell, Calvin quickly shot a bolt at Galigore, who lunged out of the way. A cloud of dust puffed up from the impact behind.

Galigore shot a bolt at the ceiling above, dislodging a large fragment of rock. Calvin skirted out of the way as it came crashing to the ground. Again came another wave of artillery. Calvin jumped behind the fallen boulder as multiple shots blasted away at the stone.

The remaining Zarkon and Galigore attempted to surround Calvin, but Calvin backed up, keeping both of them in his view. The three of them stood twenty feet from each other, forming a triangle.

Calvin thrust his sword tip at Galigore. Bright orange flames streamed forward and encircled the fiend. A gentle movement of Galigore's staff, however, easily extinguished the flames with a gush of water.

Galigore shot a streak of energy at a large rock and lifted it into the air. Calvin glanced up and saw the boulder hovering above him. He quickly pointed his sword and used its energy to force the boulder in a different direction. The Zarkon shot a blast that united his energy with Galigore's. Three strands connected with the mammoth stone. Calvin was clearly overpowered. The boulder was moving steadily in his direction. Clasping the sword handle with two hands, Calvin strained mightily. He was losing ground. He looked over at Perry with hopes he would somehow be in a position to help. But he still lay on the ground motionless. Bleeding.

"You're finished!" bellowed Galigore. "Give it up!"

Calvin continued to fight. He was afraid Galigore was right. The heavy rock was in the air, immediately above him. Thoughts streamed through his mind. Would he have enough time to break the bond and scramble out of the way? Was there another spell he could use to his advantage? Usually incantations just formed in his mind, and they always seemed to be the right ones at the right time.

Calvin was losing the struggle. He had to break the connection and dodge the plummeting rock. Without thinking, he muttered, "*Murdrum,*" and dove to the ground, escaping the car-sized boulder collapsing down on top of him.

"Where did he go?" said the Zarkon. "Is he under the boulder? Is he behind it?"

Galigore stared intently at the boulder. "Well? Go and see!" he yelled.

The Zarkon cautiously walked around the massive rock, disappearing from Galigore's view.

"He's not here," the Zarkon reported.

Sedativo. Calvin didn't need to speak it. The Zarkon dropped to the ground.

"What do you see?" roared Galigore. "Tell me, what do

231

you see?"

Calvin held still behind the barricade.

Galigore walked toward the boulder. He peered around the edge and saw his Zarkon slumped over in a heap. Galigore used his staff to topple the rock over. When the boulder overturned, to his dismay, he found that Calvin was not squashed after all. The Zarkon was.

"Reveal yourself!" shouted Galigore.

The room was quiet.

"I know you're in here. I can feel your presence."

Galigore walked past Calvin, nearly brushing him with his cloak.

Crazed and reckless, Galigore wandered the room and cast spells randomly in all directions, pulverizing the thick walls. A heavy rock thwacked Calvin on the head near his temple and knocked him to the ground. Dazed, Calvin did all he could to keep his senses and stay conscious. With his face to the ground, he continued to watch the mad man's exhibition as the room filled with dust.

The deadbolt on the chamber door unlatched and the door burst open. Ulric led the way, with Stone and Miles following behind. Through the thick dust, Galigore cursed the men and shot spells in their direction. They missed.

"Where's Calvin?" Miles demanded.

Galigore replied with a cackle.

"Where's Calvin?" Miles repeated sternly.

"He's gone," Galigore said coldly.

"No!" Stone charged at Galigore, but Galigore simply threw a fireball at him, knocking him back.

"Impeccable confidence," Galigore retorted.

Calvin fought to rise to his knees. He mustered up enough strength to fling a rock behind Galigore. It bounced and tumbled along the ground, banging off the walls. Galigore turned and peered into the dark corner.

Calvin quickly launched an attack of fire bolts in Galigore's direction. One struck the back of his shoulder and knocked him down. His staff flew out of his hands and rattled to the ground. Calvin threw another round in his direction. The barrage of attacks knocked the staff further away from Galigore.

Ulric quickly ran in hopes of retrieving the artifact, but Galigore stumbled to his feet, lunged for the staff, and held it, once again, tightly in his grasp. Ulric stopped and slowly retreated.

Calvin cast another spell in Galigore's direction. The fireball struck him in the leg and Galigore dropped to the ground.

Exhausted, Calvin collapsed.

"You have only seen the beginning of me," hissed Galigore as he stood up, painfully, favoring his shoulder, and wiping blood from his face. He hobbled toward the emerald pool. "I will destroy you." He climbed on top of the fountain, placed his staff in front of him, and bowed his head. The green water turned bright as vapor rose, engulfing the figure. Bright sparks surfaced and Galigore was gone.

Ulric went over to Stone and helped him to his feet.

"Oh, no . . . no . . . no . . . no," cried Stone, looking over at a fallen body across the dark room. Ulric ran to see who it was and discovered Perry was lying in his own blood.

"*Murdrum*," Calvin managed to speak the word, revealing himself, lying wounded on the ground. His strength had almost left him entirely as he groaned one last time. It was loud enough to draw the attention he needed.

"Calvin!" Miles ran to his side. "Calvin, stay with us."

Calvin reached into his pocket and pulled out the small vial that Trixel Strait had given him after passing through the Point of No Return. He took a sip, gave it to his dad, and then looked over at Perry. Miles quickly turned to Perry and poured a few drops into his wounds. He then drizzled a few into his mouth. The gash on his stomach began to fizzle and bubble. It looked worse before it began to show signs of improvement. Within seconds, the charred skin became pink and smooth.

Unable to keep his eyes open any longer, Calvin fell into a deep slumber, thankful to be alive.

28 · Pool of Veracity

Calvin awoke hours later lying in a bed in a room he was not familiar with. Anna was sitting by his side, along with his mom and dad.

"Calvin!" whispered Anna. "How do you feel?"

Calvin slowly sat up and glanced around the room. Ulric was standing off to one side in quiet discussion with Grayson and Stone.

"Where am I?" asked Calvin.

"You're in the castle," his mom replied. "In the Recovery Room. You're safe now. How are you feeling?"

Calvin sipped ice water from a fancy glass that was sitting beside him on a bed stand. He noticed that the vial, the one he had given his dad to heal Perry, was also sitting on the table. It was about a quarter full.

"I feel fine. A little tired. It looks like that stuff healed me pretty good." Calvin pointed to the vial.

"Helped me out too." Calvin's grandpa wheeled around the bed, sitting in a wheelchair.

"What happened to you?" asked Calvin.

"I was attacked by some Zarkon and left for dead," explained his grandpa.

"The house was ransacked when we got there," said his mom. "The sofa and chairs were broken apart, pictures thrown about, holes all over the walls, scorch marks throughout the place. Your grandpa was barely alive amid the mess."

"Luckily your mother and Grayson were on their way to the house, or I wouldn't have made it."

"Why the wheelchair?" Calvin wondered.

"I'm still a little weak."

"Where's Perry?" asked Calvin.

Ulric approached the bedside. "Calvin, it's good to see you are feeling well. It's evident that your tolerance for spell casting is increasing. The amount of spells you ignited from your hands

234

would have depleted the energy from many experienced wizlums. Remember . . . you're building up a tolerance. Next time you should be able to withstand more."

Calvin nodded.

"There have been a lot of developments over the past few days and we're still trying to put meaning to what has happened," said Ulric. "We have reason to believe that Perry has conspired against us. We have heard Stone's side of the story. Clearly, there's concern that Galigore had interacted with Perry before you reached him."

"He *was* acting a little strange," confirmed Calvin.

"Tell me, Calvin, what happened after you and Perry separated from Stone?"

"Perry seemed confused," explained Calvin. "But I thought he told me the truth . . . that is, until Galigore showed up. Galigore thanked Perry for bringing me to him. I looked at Perry but wasn't sure what he was thinking. He seemed scared . . . confused."

"What happened next?" asked Ulric.

"Galigore said he didn't need Perry anymore and attacked him," said Calvin. "Ulric, why didn't Galigore try to attack you?"

"He was hurt. You struck him in the back of the shoulder with a spell. He didn't know where the barrage of fiery darts was coming from. He was dazed. And I suspect he felt outnumbered."

"So what is that fountain Galigore disappeared into?" Calvin asked.

"That is one of several portals in existence," said Ulric. "I didn't know that that one was there, but then again, there are many others I am unaware of."

"So how do we figure out what's up with Perry?" asked Calvin. "Where is he?"

"Perry is safely held in Erewhon," answered Ulric.

"Erewhon?" Calvin repeated.

"Erewhon is the dungeon on the castle grounds that is home to the most evil villains. I know that sounds a little harsh for Perry, but he is in his own cell. He is occupying one of the soundproof blocks, isolated from any contact. We needed a place to keep him until we can give him a fair trial."

"You haven't talked to him yet about what happened?" asked Calvin.

"Not yet," answered Ulric. "We wanted to get everyone's account first before we heard his."

"How will you know he's telling the truth?" asked Calvin. "I mean, he sounded pretty convinced that the door on the right was not safe. He tricked us into thinking that the exit was through the left door."

"Our judgment will require the use of an apparatus," said Ulric. "Are you strong enough to take a walk with me?"

Calvin scooted to the edge of his bed and dropped to his feet. He held up his own weight comfortably and followed Ulric through a door off the recovery room. "Please excuse us for a moment," Ulric said to everyone as he and Calvin exited the room.

"How does it all work?" asked Calvin as he and Ulric walked down a tight corridor.

"What do you mean?" answered Ulric.

"If one collects all three orbs, and their matching artifacts, it makes that person immortal. Is there a way to destroy them? Why can't we just destroy the sword and orb that I have? Then there would be no way Galigore could attain ultimate power."

"Those are good questions for Osgar."

"Have you ever met him?" asked Calvin.

"I met him long ago. It was believed for many years that these magical artifacts existed, but no one ever found them. People tried, but failed. When Galigore stole the orb from the treasury and uncovered the staff, we knew we had a long battle ahead of us," explained Ulric. "I went to Osgar for advice. He felt it was a little premature at that point to get involved. I asked if I could help him reclaim them and disarm their powers. He said it would be impossible. The artifacts have been bound with an unbreakable charm. They cannot be destroyed individually, but must be disposed of all at once."

"If they need to be destroyed together, that means someone, at some point, will have to have all three in their possession?"

"Yes, Calvin. That seems to be correct."

"Why does the orb respond to me and Galigore, but not you? You're a wizlum."

"A good question that is still unanswered. Obviously, Osgar understands the intricacies surrounding the lore of the orbs."

"Is he friendly?"

"Osgar?" asked Ulric.

Calvin nodded.

"He has a reputation of being difficult, but sensible." Ulric stopped in front of a door and turned to Calvin. "There are many more questions we can discuss surrounding Osgar and the orbs, but we need to take care of something else right now."

Calvin and Ulric entered a room that looked familiar, although Calvin was sure he had never been inside before. This room was also empty, and there was a second door located on the opposite wall. There was a message inscribed in the stone above the door—only it was a different message from before. Calvin read the words aloud:

Look inside this water round,
To disclose the sights and sounds.
All that's hoped to be discovered,
Only perfect truth uncovered.
Drop a tear or two within,
To reveal virtue or sin.

Calvin thought about the water round. He didn't see it, but as he anticipated another magical transformation, the floor began to rumble. The stones shifted and piled on top of one another, forming a large, raised ring that spanned across the middle of the room. The walls crumbled and dissipated into blackness, while a series of thick, iron bars rose from the floor and connected with the receding ceiling. The sound of water bubbled from below, and within seconds, the stone ring was filled to the rim with a sparkling liquid that illuminated the room. Calvin found himself standing in a room that resembled a dreary dungeon cell. As the transformation completed, the air inside the cell turned cold.

"As I mentioned before, Calvin, there are believed to be three of these pools in existence. You are familiar with the Pool of Lineage. This is the Pool of Veracity, a valuable tool used for detecting the truth. This will help us determine where Perry's loyalty lies. Let me show you how this works." Ulric stood aside the pool and motioned for Calvin to join him. From his robe, he withdrew an onion and a knife. "Usually, the culprits we interrogate are so convinced that they are telling the truth, they naturally drum up a few tears. Most of the time it's all part of the act—an emotional plea. I can't say I blame them. The dungeon we have here on the castle grounds is heavily guarded. The gates are impassable. Most prisoners are sentenced to life. Because of this, prisoners spill their guts, lying if they need to, to convince us that they do not deserve a life in Erewhon."

Ulric tossed the onion up and caught it. "But, because we will need a little help producing tears, I thought this onion would suffice. If these little buggers make you cry half as much as they make me cry, we'll have more than enough to drop into the pool."

Ulric handed Calvin the onion and the knife. He placed the onion on the floor and began slicing it into thin rings. He knew onions affected him. His mom frequently cooked with onions and within minutes of her slicing them, he would feel the sting in his eyes—even from a different room.

Calvin felt the initial sensations of a burn. The slight prickling in his eyes grew stronger before turning into a substantial sting. Calvin rubbed his eyes with the backside of his hand and blinked. He felt tears welling up inside his eyes. Moments later, the salty droplets began to dribble down his cheek.

"Very good," said Ulric, teary-eyed. "Now watch this. It's remarkable." Ulric wiped his nose and sniffled. "Place your face over the pool and allow a couple of drops to fall."

Calvin tilted his body forward until he saw the reflection of his face gleaming in the mirror-like liquid. One teardrop plummeted into the pool, creating ripples in the still water. A second one fell, making the lustrous liquid begin to glow.

"Now stand back and watch," instructed Ulric.

As the shimmering ripples softened, an image of Calvin appeared inside. He was at the Isle of Desolation with Stone and Perry. The events unraveled before their eyes from Calvin's point of view. Just as Calvin had explained earlier, he and Ulric watched as Perry acted out of the ordinary. Perry looked confused and frustrated—indecisive. They heard Perry tell Calvin and Stone with absolute certainty that they should go left at the fork, because the passage to the right had danger lurking ahead of them.

Calvin asked Perry if he was sure. Perry insisted that he was. Calvin and Perry entered a door at the end of the hall. Once they were inside the room, the door slammed closed. Galigore appeared and they heard his words as clear and accurate as Calvin had explained earlier, "Well done, Perry. Well done. I knew I could count on you."

Calvin saw the surprise and confusion on his face as he looked over at Perry. He saw himself turn to Perry and ask, "You knew about this?"

"Calvin, I swear. I didn't know!"

"Of course he knew about this." Calvin and Ulric continued to watch and listen to Galigore. "I told him I would be waiting for you. You did just as you were directed, Perry. Unfortunately for you, though, I won't be needing you anymore."

They saw Perry topple over onto the stone floor.

"I had only heard the story from Stone," Ulric said as the images in the bowl faded away. "But I felt his description of what had happened was enough to isolate Perry for a while. I'm glad to have heard your account as well. Stone said you might have more to tell, and as you have done so brilliantly, I am a little more convinced that Perry did side with Galigore."

The stones began to shift and the water from the pool vaporized. The cell bars disconnected from the ceiling and slid back into the ground, while the ceiling elevated back to its original height. Stone slabs slid back into place, forming smooth walls again.

Calvin watched as the room returned to its original state. "You know . . . there is one way we can be certain," he said.

"How's that?" Ulric asked.

"We need a couple of Perry's tears."

"Indeed." Ulric smiled.

29 • Interrogation

Perry found himself in total darkness. He was able to stand up in the tight cell and felt the ceiling just a foot above his head. His outstretched arms were able to touch the walls on either side. The room was about five-and-a-half feet square. All of the walls were stone except one, which was made up of a heavy iron gate.

Trying to escape was pointless. He called for help. No one came. Occasionally, he would see a faint light coming from the corridor, but it always dissipated into blackness. After seeing several small glimpses of light, and not having anyone come to his rescue, he began to ignore any sign of radiance, no matter its brilliance.

"Perry!" came a whisper. "Perry, is that you? Wake up!"

Calvin shone a ray of light through the iron bars. Perry shielded his face with his hands.

"Come on, Perry," Calvin said, unlocking the iron door. "We're going to get you out of here." Calvin grabbed Perry by the arm and helped him to his feet. Perry staggered alongside Calvin and Ulric as they escorted him out of the cold cell. Light slowly began to fill the halls as Ulric, Calvin, and Perry worked their way toward the dungeon gate. Perry's eyes were still trying to adjust to the light.

"What's going on?" Perry asked. "Where am I?"

"We're taking you to the castle," said Calvin. "A lot has happened over the last couple of days. We need to figure some things out. But don't worry. You're safe now."

Calvin knew Ulric was still questioning Perry's loyalty. Even he had his doubts. Would his best friend really betray him? Was he telling the truth? Had Perry really thought he was leading him safely out of Desolation? All of his questions would be answered shortly. Perry's fate would now lie in the genius of the Pool of Veracity.

Ulric led Calvin and Perry back to his quarters. He directed

Perry to sit in a chair. Calvin and Ulric sat in the sofa facing him. It was a comfortable setting—perfect for interrogation. It was quiet for a moment before Ulric began. "Perry, what is the last thing you remember at Desolation?"

"I remember being attacked by Galigore."

"Do you remember? Why did he strike you?" asked Ulric.

"Because I went against his plan."

Calvin sat quietly and listened as Ulric fired questions at Perry.

"Against his plan? But didn't you bring Calvin to Galigore, just as he requested?"

"No . . . yes . . . no." Perry was becoming frustrated. "Galigore wanted me to lure Calvin to him, but I wouldn't do it."

"Wouldn't do it? But you did do it."

"I know. It probably seems that way. But I didn't bring Calvin to him on purpose."

"Tell us, Perry, why did you hesitate while you were leading Calvin and Stone through the dungeon?"

"I was trying to remember where Galigore was going to be waiting. He told me he would be waiting for us down the right passage. So I insisted we go left."

"It's a simple thing to remember, isn't it?" asked Ulric. "To go left to escape or go right to Galigore. Why did you hesitate? Why did you begin to lead Calvin and Stone down the right corridor if he was supposed to be waiting behind the door?"

"I . . . I don't know. I guess I got mixed up."

"You do know where Galigore's followers are held captive, don't you?" said Ulric. "Right where you just came from . . . Erewhon. Did you enjoy your short stay?"

"Calvin, please," said Perry. "You've got to believe me." Perry tried to fight back his emotions.

Ulric nodded to Calvin and said, "Come with me."

Ulric led Calvin and Perry to the room where the Pool of Veracity was kept. He turned to Perry. "How certain are you of the facts you just shared with us?"

"I'm telling the truth," Perry said. "I promise."

"Perry, I want to believe you," Calvin said. "I do believe

you."

"We need to validate what you have said," Ulric said. "Do you want to take back anything?"

Perry shook his head, wiping a tear from the corner of his eye.

"Maybe change things slightly?" asked Ulric.

Another shake. Another tear.

"There are plenty of cold cells in Erewhon that would suit you well." Ulric looked over at Calvin. "Maybe we ought to just take him back now?"

"Look," said Perry. "While I was at Desolation, Galigore came to see me. He let me hold his staff and feel the power that could be mine. While I was holding it, something came over me and I suddenly wanted to be important . . . powerful." More tears leaked from Perry's eyes. "He promised me anything I wanted if I led Calvin back to him. He told me I could have his staff if I got him Calvin's sword. And I was tempted to do it. The desire for power was all I could think of. He told me how inadequate and worthless I was. How Calvin could cast spells without a wand and I couldn't. How Calvin anticipates things when I don't. And I believed him . . . that I was good for nothing. Then he took the staff away from me. As soon as he did, it left me feeling completely empty. I wanted what I had just felt. I made up my mind that I would turn you in." Perry looked up at Calvin, tears flowing from his eyes.

The transformation of the room had already begun. The stones had shifted. The walls had vanished and the iron rods were connecting the floor to the ceiling. The shimmering water was beginning to fill the vast stone ring. Perry hardly noticed the change and continued his plea of innocence.

"Then I saw you," Perry said to Calvin. "I looked into your eyes and something started to come over me. It wasn't powerful enough to make me turn away completely from Galigore's offer, but it made me unsure. By the time we reached the fork, I was thinking about holding the staff and how good it felt. It caused me to lead us to the right. But only a few steps into it, I knew deep down that the right thing to do was to avoid Galigore all together. I insisted we go back the other way. I felt good about the decision and was relieved that I didn't waver again. That's why I was so shocked to find Galigore waiting for us. I could have gotten us killed." Perry snorted. "I should have just followed you out—the way you came in."

"Lean forward over the pool of water, Perry," Ulric said in a gentle tone. "Look inside."

Perry looked in and saw his reflection staring back at him. Tears fell into the silvery water. Ripples distorted his reflection and then images of his experience came to life. Ulric and Calvin looked on and saw the story unfold exactly how Perry had recounted it. The wrestling match that Perry had in his own mind surfaced. Seeing the events from Perry's point of view, Calvin, and even Ulric, could sense the great struggle Perry had gone through.

"Understandably, Galigore tried to deceive you," concluded Ulric as the images upon the water erased. "He let you feel powerful for a moment, but that power would not last. Real, long-lasting power is earned. Worked for. There are no shortcuts in life, I'm afraid. Progress and growth require work. They require discipline. Until one can master his own self, he will not become powerful. Therein lies true power. Control over your own self. I commend you, Perry, for overcoming an extremely difficult mental struggle. You are stronger from having gone through it."

Smiles began to melt away the heavy air inside the empty room. "I owe you an apology, Perry," said Ulric. "I hope you can forgive me for being harsh on you. The Pool of Veracity only works with tears. I needed to stir up some emotion to get the sprinklers going, if you know what I mean."

30 • Pool of Lineage

Calvin felt relieved that Perry was back on their side. He couldn't imagine seeing his friend ally himself with the forces of evil. Amid all the hoopla over the past few days, Ulric decided it was too dangerous to have any of them stay anywhere other than the castle. Perry's parents were still away, helping out with the funeral. They would be gone for several days more. It gave Kristal some time to think about how to explain to Mrs. Goldwin that Perry needed to stay in the castle of Cambria—a place she knew nothing about. Magic was completely foreign to Perry's parents.

Ulric took care of Anna's situation. Anna's parents were impossible to get along with. She wasn't really sure how the whole conversation went, but when she heard that it had been worked out for her to stay, she was ecstatic. She suspected magic was involved. Perhaps it was a brainwashing charm? Or was it a memory twister? Either way, she was where she belonged.

Ulric explained the castle rules, indicating that they were mostly free to wander around as they pleased outside. One exception was Erewhon. Ulric described the nature of prisoners held within its walls. Calvin and Perry were fine with avoiding the prison altogether. They had been inside of it, and the atmosphere was dark and heavy. As for inside the castle, Ulric granted permission for them to wander the halls as they'd like. He pointed out only a few rooms that were off-limits.

Anna was assigned a small bedroom on the main floor. Perry insisted that he share a room with Calvin. He wasn't sure he could stay in a room by himself, considering the things he had just gone through. Calvin politely obliged.

Just atop the staircase leading to the second floor was a large loft made into a sitting room. A huge, stone fireplace spanned one of the walls entirely, while a large wooden railing overlooked a foyer below. On another wall, numerous books were contained in a rich mahogany bookcase. The long hallway leading to Calvin and Perry's room was through a single, arched doorway between the bookcase and the railing.

"What a crazy few days we've had," said Calvin, plopping down on the nearest chair in the loft.

"You're telling me," said Perry. "I'm exhausted." Perry stretched his body out over a long, leather sofa, his hands resting behind his head.

Anna rocked in a wooden chair enjoying the crackling sounds of wood burning in the fireplace.

"Where do you think Tobran went?" Calvin said, replaying the previous days in his mind.

"I don't know," Anna answered. "I thought he was pretty sincere when he swore his loyalty to you."

"I wonder if he was captured," Calvin said.

"Captured?" Anna said. "By who? I think Tobran can hold his own. . . I mean, he's huge."

A few chewing sounds resonated from Perry, followed by a couple of snorts, and a long exhaling moan. A deep inhale later and Perry was out like a log.

"And you have to sleep in the same room as him?" Anna jeered.

"Yeah, imagine that."

Calvin and Anna sat in silence for a moment.

"This castle is huge," Anna said as she stared at the open ceiling that stretched many floors above them.

"Yeah . . . I bet you can spend days wandering through this place." Calvin interlocked his fingers and brought his hands behind his head.

"That's pretty neat about your dad," Anna marveled. "After all this time, he was alive and no one knew it."

Calvin sighed as he thought about the unbelievable experience of unlocking his dad from that desolate dungeon cell.

"What is it?" asked Anna. "What are you thinking about?"

"Just what you said. About my dad being alive." Calvin continued to stare upward.

"You're lucky, Calvin. I never knew my real parents."

Calvin snapped out of his happy stupor and sat up immediately.

"What is it?" asked Anna, surprised.

"I . . . I can't believe I didn't think of this sooner. Hurry. Come with me."

Calvin led Anna quickly down the stairs toward Ulric's room. He remembered entering a door from the main corridor that led him to the Pool of Veracity. He knew there was another door that would lead them to the Pool of Lineage.

Calvin opened one door after another.

"What are you looking for?" whispered Anna.

Calvin opened another door and another.

"Calvin? Where are you taking me?"

Calvin opened a final door at the end of the hall. "This is it!" Calvin whispered excitedly. Looking both ways to see if anyone was nearby, Calvin grabbed Anna's hand and slipped through the door, dragging her with him.

"You aren't going to believe this," Calvin said.

"What is it?"

"This is the Pool of Lineage," answered Calvin.

"What are talking about? There is nothing in here."

"Yes, there is," Calvin said pointing. "Read that."

Anna read aloud. " 'With this pool, one might wish to follow his life sublime. Be it bright, or be it glum, this water will not lie. Place a hair into the pool and watch with real intent. But be aware that once submerged, the truth will sometimes hurt.' "

Anna thought for a second. "I still don't get it."

The room began to shake as vines emerged from the cracking walls. Trees sprouted high above, filling the room with thick vegetation. Headstones and graves took their places underneath the trees throughout the room. A gaping hole formed in the middle of the floor. Anna looked on, in disbelief, as an effervescent liquid filled the cavity.

"Do you think it works? Will it tell me about my family?"

"It worked for me."

Anna yanked a hair from her head and held it over the water. She looked over at Calvin, who was prodding her to drop it in. She separated her forefinger from her thumb and watched the hair fall, twirling through the air, and finally resting on the surface of the lustrous liquid. Faint ripples spread away from the

247

hair and on the surface of the water formed an image. It was of her. She looked as she did that day. The reflection vanished and a dark figure appeared—a Zarkon. He was locked up, behind bars, in a dark abyss. Glowing letters appeared, spelling out the word: EREWHON.

The image faded away and a new one appeared. Anna was sitting on her bed back in Wolf Creek. In an adjacent frame, however, she couldn't identify where she was. She appeared to be in a world where she was larger than what seemed normal.

Before she could make sense out of what she was seeing, the image faded and a new one materialized. She saw another scene of a man she imagined to be her dad. He was a Bordarian—a wizlum—fighting against the Zarkon, casting spells from his hands. She then saw him at the castle of Cambria, receiving medals of honor and bravery. The image changed again. She saw her dad holding a baby wrapped in a blanket and handing it to a young couple.

Anna continued looking into the pool as it revealed one image after another. Tombstones lined the hills. Anna's father knelt in front of her mother's grave with his head bowed. Anna peered deeper inside the water and read the gravestone.

Here lies Amelia Kane. Survived by her husband, Nikolas, and daughters, Annabelle and Alayna. God Bless. R.I.P.

Another scene showed a doctor holding up a baby girl. A nurse took the infant and wrapped her in a blanket. The doctor held up a second baby. Another girl. Anna continued watching as the moment intensified. Her mother screamed in pain. Her father dropped to his knees and wept as the scene changed again. As she looked on, her eyes also pooled up with emotion.

There was a young couple at a wedding. Her mom and dad were so happy—dancing and laughing.

A new image of her dad appeared. She saw her father look up as his facial features began to transform. His healthy skin became pale—then translucent. His cheekbones stuck out and his eyes became sunken. His smile drooped, changing to an expression of hopelessness. His countenance resembled perfectly the Zarkon she saw moments ago locked away in Erewhon.

Calvin became startled by a noise from the other room.

"Let's go," he whispered to Anna. The images in the pool disappeared. Within seconds, the room was back to its original form. "Ulric is in his room."

Calvin quickly led Anna out of the room and hurried back up to the sitting area where Perry was still asleep.

"I'm sorry, Anna," Calvin said, sadly. "I shouldn't have taken you there."

Anna cried quietly to herself.

"I guess some things are better off left unknown," Calvin thought aloud.

Anna sniffed, fighting to gain her composure. "I'm glad I saw it. I've always wondered what happened. What they looked like. What their names were. Every day I have asked myself why my mother didn't want me. And to think . . . I have a twin sister? This brings closure to my curiosity." Anna wiped the corner of her eye with the backside of her finger. "Don't feel bad. I would have done the same for you...Thank you."

Perry's sudden, loud snore lightened the mood in the room. Calvin and Anna looked over at him. He had shifted positions on the couch. He was face down, with one leg firmly wedged into the cushions and his other dangling over the edge and onto the floor. Drool puddled around his face.

"Good luck trying to sleep tonight," giggled Anna.

"No, kidding. Do you know any deafening charms you could try on me?"

* * * *

Anna lay awake that night. She tried to fall asleep, but her thoughts wouldn't let her. The scenes from the Pool of Lineage replayed through her mind—over and over again. She had a twin sister? But where was she? Could it be true—her father, who had become a Zarkon, was still alive? And he was just a few minutes away? Sleep had fled from her completely.

Anna climbed the staircase back up to the sitting room. She browsed the bookcase, curious as to what kind of books would be available in the castle. Row by row, she read the titles. Several piqued her interest, including *Spells for the Advanced*, *How to Increase Your Sense of Intuition*, and *A Bible for the Potion Master*. But no book made her pull it off the shelf until she came to *Erewhon:*

The Making of an Impenetrable Prison.

Flipping through its pages, Anna read about the secure prison that was guarded by a squad of Cambrian dwarves. Known for their powerful magical skills and their love for treasure, skilled dwarves were employed to look after the prisoners in Erewhon. The prison was a hollowed-out hole that burrowed deep into the earth. The entrance was cave-like—a passage carved into the side of a hill.

The book explained how the different levels worked. Each was classified with a number from one to three. Anna learned that the prisoners who committed less-severe crimes were kept on the first level of the prison. Those who were most wicked were locked up in a place referred to as "The Hole," located three levels beneath the prison entrance. Anna was certain her father was securely held in "The Hole."

As she continued reading, she became more and more certain of something else, too: she was going to find her father and her sister, no matter what it took.

About the Author

Rusty Anderson discovered his passion for writing in the fourth grade when he was given an assignment to write, illustrate, and bind a book. He enjoyed it so much, he wrote not one, but five. One of his first books, *Smoug's First Creation*, received recognition at a school district writing competition. Rusty enjoys spending time with his wife, Jayne, and their six children. He credits his children for keeping his imagination alive as they have routinely asked for bedtime stories over the years. Some of those stories are now being shared as *The Adventures of Jazzle Divine*. His debut book, *Calvin Sparks and the Crossing to Cambria*, is the first book in the Calvin Sparks series. Rusty lives with his family in the beautiful mountain valley of Heber City, Utah.

Made in the USA
Middletown, DE
05 December 2020

26425160R00156